LA&
WITN

ALSO BY CHRIS MERRITT

Bring Her Back

CHRIS
MERRITT
LAST
WITNESS

Bookouture

Published by Bookouture in 2018

An imprint of StoryFire Ltd.

Carmelite House
50 Victoria Embankment
London EC4Y 0DZ

www.bookouture.com

ISBN: 978-1-78681-511-8
eBook ISBN: 978-1-78681-510-1

To AK, friend and mentor — you are missed.

PROLOGUE

I didn't know people had so much blood inside them.

Hidden in the pantry, I watch through narrow slats, holding my breath. I'm so scared, I can't move – not even a millimetre. I don't think anyone has seen me, but I can see them. I saw what they did. And those pictures are playing over and over like a video tape in my brain.

Something terrible has happened upstairs. But I don't know what, exactly. There were screams that sounded like my mum. Then some loud bangs.

A man comes downstairs and whispers quickly to his friend. I catch the word 'dead'. And I feel sick now, because I think I know who they're talking about: the two people I love most in the whole world. I want to burst out of here, run upstairs and see for myself. Shout their names and hear them greet me before I'm wrapped up in a big hug. Feel my hair stroked, my back rubbed. Be told that it's all OK.

But I can't move.

I can see a grown-up sitting down where the kitchen floor and wall meet. His head is bowed like he's sleeping. But I know he's not, because he's covered in blood. Thick, red blood, soaking his clothes, like when you stay out in the rain too long or you trip and fall in a puddle. They lean towards him like he's a zoo creature they've never seen before. One of them stretches out a shaky hand towards the man, fingertips getting closer, until—

His eyes open. The man's head lifts, and they move back, horrified. He stares at them – like he's looking through them, like he can see into them. Then he gives one long breath out, and his head drops again. He doesn't move any more.

A gun is wiped and placed into his hand. I see who does it, just like I saw who shot him.

Then they leave, and I'm alone.

But I still can't move.

CHAPTER ONE

Thursday, 30 November 2017

When it rains, it pours, his old man used to say. The guy grew up in Ghana, so he knew a thing or two about thunderstorms. His dad would've agreed that the deluge right now was more common in a West African wet season than South Croydon. It had burst out of a night sky just minutes ago and Detective Inspector Zachariah Boateng was already drenched. He'd had to walk from where the bus dropped him, after taking two trains. Technically, this was still London, but the place felt like countryside. Cold rainwater ran off his flat cap and down the back of his collar. Zac muttered something under his breath about bringing an umbrella next time. Maybe taking a cab, despite the cost. Or even driving – but that'd limit the booze, of course. And his host, Sergeant Troy McEwen, would never permit such half measures: his invitation had been for a Christmas drink. Troy was slightly early for the festive season, but his offer had been uncharacteristically late, the text message only arriving after work today. Zac might've made an excuse, but the words 'need to talk about back then' had caught his attention.

So, he'd reluctantly abandoned his plans to relax at home and accepted. It was the right thing to do. They'd had the occasional phone call and exchanged texts, but it'd been two years since he'd last visited his old friend, and Zac knew he shouldn't have left it so long. The effort he'd expended getting to this isolated tip of south London, not to mention the large bottle of Troy's favourite whisky tucked inside his overcoat, would go some way towards assuaging that guilt. Zac had a family, but Troy had no one. The least Zac could do was join his mate for a few drams. And see what exactly he wanted to say about 'back then'.

Zac reached Troy's small, detached house and jogged up the path to his front door. Sheltering under the porch, rain hammering on its roof, he rang the doorbell. Nothing. Rang it again. Cupped hands around his eyes and leaned against the frosted glass, but all he could make out was a low light inside. To his left and right – Troy's living room and dining room – curtains were drawn. Zac banged his palm on the door, then squatted and cracked the letterbox.

'Troy!' he bellowed through the gap. 'Open up, mate, I'm freezing my bollocks off out here.'

Zac listened: no response. Peered through but couldn't see any movement in the narrow hallway. What was Troy playing at? Probably several drinks down, headphones on, in the toilet, take your pick. Zac rang his mobile, but it went straight to voicemail. He pocketed the phone and, plunging back into the rain, tried the wooden side gate: locked.

'Troy, come on, man!' he yelled over the two-metre-high fence. 'It's pissing down, in case you hadn't noticed.' No reply. But Zac didn't give up. He hadn't come all this way just to admire the front garden. Perhaps he should take a quick look to make sure Troy was OK. After all, the guy lived on his own.

Cursing silently, he hauled himself up and over the side gate, barely keeping his balance. Such manoeuvres weren't as easy as they had been twenty years ago when he and Troy had joined the Met together. At least the neighbour's hedge was thick enough that no one could see him; he didn't want the embarrassment of explaining to his Croydon colleagues that their suspected burglar was in fact a police officer.

The back door was locked too, and after another failed attempt to rouse Troy, Zac scouted around the patio until he found a loose brick among the neglected flowerpots. True to form, his mate had a spare key lodged underneath it. Zac let himself into the utility room at the back of the house and stood on the doormat, dripping, eyes adjusting to the gloom. Took out the whisky.

'Hey, wake up, fella!' He reached for the door handle and yanked it open. 'I've got the Glenmorangie, it's your favour—'

Something was wrong.

Zac knew immediately: the stillness, the air, the faint odour. He marched through the kitchen, wet shoes sliding on tile, following his nose, quicker now, into the hallway, where he threw the living-room door open.

First thing he saw was the blood. Spattered thick across the white wall, chunks congealed in it, streaks running down. Even some on the ceiling. Zac's breaths became jagged, his stomach turning at the smell of raw meat and iron, the trace of gunpowder. He fought back the bile and stepped inside. Rounding the door, he froze. The bottle slipped from his hand, thudding on the carpet.

Only the familiar forearm tattoos confirmed that the disfigured man slumped in the armchair was Troy McEwen. A shotgun rested between his legs, its long steel barrel pointing up towards the head, or what was left of it. Tipped forward, the back half was gone, exposing a warped mass of pink, red and black in the open skull.

'Troy!' he blurted, stumbling across the room, half tripping over a table. 'Jesus, no.' Stepping closer, Zac reached out slowly, touched his friend's arm. It was still warm. 'No,' he repeated, quieter this time, his voice thickening, facial muscles tightening. 'What've you done?'

Zac knelt next to the body, sinking until his forehead rested on the arm of the chair, inches from Troy's limp hand. He stayed kneeling for a long time, eyes screwed shut, as if that was enough to block it out.

'You didn't do this, mate,' he whispered eventually, a rolling tear catching the corner of his mouth. 'I know it.'

Zac had worked with death long enough to understand that denial was a common immediate reaction in those close to the deceased. Despite that, he stood, wiped his face and began to examine the room. Troy's body, the weapon, the angles, the blood pattern, the lack of rigor mortis. His text, not even three hours ago: *Need to talk about back then.* Something wasn't right. Already, Zac's analytical mind was taking over, mastering the emotions, telling him he shouldn't disturb anything more.

Not if this was a murder scene.

*

'I'm so sorry, love.' Zac's wife, Etta, pulled her kitchen chair alongside his and wrapped an arm round his shoulder. He took a gulp of the Glenmorangie; not his first since discovering Troy's body.

'The two of you went way back,' she said.

Zac nodded. He and Troy had enrolled on the same basic training course at Hendon in '96, had their first jobs together on the beat. Back in the day, they were inseparable – partly through choice, partly because each knew the other was the only person he could really count on.

'I liked him a lot.' Etta's voice was soft. The shock of seeing a uniformed officer bring her husband home at 11 p.m., damp and shivering, seemed to have subsided now. Zac knew she wasn't just empathising; she'd be feeling the loss personally too. Before they'd had kids, Troy had crashed at their old place in Stockwell so often that Etta called the tiny spare room 'Troy's suite'. She squeezed his shoulder. 'I remember the last time he was here – what, three, four years ago?'

'Three and a half.'

'He came for dinner.' Etta reached across, helped herself to a sip of Zac's whisky.

He snorted a small laugh. 'Ate three platefuls of your jollof rice.'

She smiled. 'Then asked if he could take the rest home.' They sat in silence a moment before she spoke again. 'Did you have any idea he was—'

'Depressed? Yes. No.' Zac spun the glass in his fingers. 'I mean, Troy was always kind of up and down, I knew that from the start. After he shot that guy in '08 he had some post-traumatic stress disorder, but he did the assessment, the treatment, he got over it. Right as rain. Enough for the doctor to sign off on his shotgun licence in 2011, he told me. But I hadn't seen the man in two years, so I don't know…' His tone hardened. 'I should've been there for him.'

Etta stroked the back of his head. 'You're not responsible for his suicide, Zac.'

'I know.'

'OK, good.'

'I don't think it was suicide.'

She didn't respond; just stared at him.

Zac broke eye contact, tried to push away the image of Troy's body in the armchair, that raw-meat smell coming right back to him. He took a big pull of whisky, swallowed. 'I know it looks that way. The guy's alone at home, with his own shotgun, barrel pointing at—' He stopped himself, didn't want to traumatise his wife any further. 'Wounds consistent with suicide. Add a history of mental health problems and that's case closed for any coroner.'

'But?'

'About a third of people who take their own lives leave a note, thinking about who'll find them, who'll miss them, things they're sorry for. Or just raging against those who've wronged them. But there was no note, no warning.'

'So he's in the two-thirds that don't give an explanation.'

'No sign he'd been drinking, either. And he'd texted me less than three hours earlier, saying he needed to talk. Needed, not wanted. He hadn't invited me round to reminisce. He had something to tell me. Why would he do that if he was going to kill himself half an hour later?'

'No idea.' She frowned. 'What do you think he needed to talk about?'

'Don't know,' he mumbled.

'Is it possible he wanted you to find his body?' suggested Etta. 'You were probably the closest thing he had to family.'

Zac fought back a fresh pang of guilt and shook his head. 'Doesn't make sense. I just don't believe it was suicide.'

She took the glass, poured some more whisky. 'Sorry. You haven't convinced me, love.'

'Says the lawyer.'

Etta sighed. 'You and I work with hard evidence. This sounds more like a feeling to me. Maybe you're still in shock? We both knew him so well, it's hard to accept that he could've—'

'No.' He cut her off.

'An accident then? He's cleaning the shotgun and—'

'No way. The guy had been firearms trained in the Met. He knew what he was doing.'

'Look, if you're saying he didn't kill himself, you realise what that means?'

'Yes.' Zac reached for the glass. 'He was murdered.'

Three drinks later and with Etta already upstairs, Zac trudged up to bed, trying to make the pieces slot together. Trying to think of anything that might give a clue about what the hell had happened to Troy. If the text message had some bearing on his death, what did that mean for Zac and the others involved 'back then'? If Troy had been murdered, was anyone else in danger? But the alcohol was slowing him down. When he tried to think, all he could see was the image of that living room. A stair creaked under his weight, and a rustling came from behind the half-open door on the landing, followed by a small voice.

'Dad?'

Zac paused. Knew he'd drunk too much; wondered if he should let his ten-year-old see him like this. But that thought was quickly overtaken by a powerful urge to be close to his family. Troy's death had brought back memories of his daughter, Amelia, also killed by a gunshot, five years ago. It made Zac want to be near his son, to hold him. He stepped across and eased the door open. Kofi's bedroom was all long shadows in the glow of a night light. The boy was sitting up, clutching the duvet around his waist, his rangy legs and little feet outlined beneath it. He wore Spider-Man pyjamas and his big brown eyes were half closed.

'Alright, son?' Zac perched on the bed. 'What're you doing awake at this time?'

'I saw the police car outside. Were you fighting the bad guys? Did you have to arrest anybody?'

'No, I—' Zac realised he had no idea what to say. Kofi had known Troy too, albeit more distantly in recent years. This wasn't the time to break it to him. 'I had to go out to see someone.'

'Who?'

'A friend.'

'Why did you go in a police car if it was a friend?'

The kid was on the ball. Zac hesitated. 'He's a friend in the police.'

'Oh, OK.' That seemed to satisfy Kofi's curiosity. He knew that when his dad worked at night, it often meant something exciting, and he'd always probe for stories of action. Fortunately, the questions stopped there for now.

Zac leaned in for a hug. 'You OK?'

'Yeah. Your breath smells.'

'I had some whisky.'

Kofi wrinkled his nose. 'Gross.'

'Come on, let's get you back to sleep, mate.' He tucked the boy in as he wriggled down, kissed the top of his head, the tight curls of hair soft on his lips. 'Got school tomorrow, need to get some rest so your brain's sharp.'

'Like yours and Mum's.'

'Mainly your mum's. I'm not too sharp right now. Good night, Ko.'

Zac stood and watched Kofi shift and curl up under the duvet. How precious his life was; how quickly it could be erased. He'd do almost anything to protect it. After a minute or two, Kofi's breathing began to slow into a sleep rhythm. He envied his son. Zac didn't expect to get much rest tonight. He knew exactly what he'd be seeing in his dreams. Maybe staying awake was preferable to being back in that living room.

The uniformed police officers sent to Troy's house after Zac had called it in were confident it was suicide. At the very least an accident, they said, once they'd recovered their composure, maybe death by misadventure. When Zac had suggested another possible cause of death, they'd looked at him like he was crazy. Told him he was probably just feeling a bit emotional – anyone would be, under the circumstances. One PC had been more interested in how Zac got into Troy's house. He hadn't pushed it. Etta was right, he had no firm evidence. Not yet.

Zac didn't know if he was just deluding himself, based on the timing of a text message and a refusal to believe a friend would kill himself. But he trusted his instincts. If Troy had been murdered, then his killer was out there somewhere. Zac would have to find him, because no one else was going to be looking. And if 'back then' referred to what he thought it did, Zac had to be prepared for this killer finding him first.

CHAPTER TWO

Friday, 1 December 2017

No grapevine operates faster than the police. As Boateng picked his way through the open-plan office of Lewisham Major Investigation Team, just after 9 a.m., his colleagues stopped what they were doing. They would've heard from mates in Croydon about his discovery last night, and they'd known that he and Sergeant Troy McEwen were old pals. One or two young officers would be interested in the gossip and gore; they'd learn better, eventually. Others would use the story to highlight how stressful police work was these days, how the Met still wasn't doing enough on staff welfare, pushing everyone too hard, for too long. How suicide was the second most common cause of death in serving police officers after road accidents, the unnoticed 'epidemic'. Some would maintain an uncomfortable distance and avoid mentioning the word 'suicide', just letting Boateng deal with it in his own way. The decent ones would want to know how he was coping and what they could do to help. He exchanged nods with a couple of detectives standing by a whiteboard across the room, then hung his overcoat and flat cap on the stand by his desk.

'Morning, guys.' His greeting had none of the usual enthusiasm.

'Zac.' Detective Sergeant Kat Jones was the first to speak. 'We heard this morning about Sergeant McEwen. Just want to say we're all so sorry. If there's anything you need from us, then please – you know.'

'Thanks, Kat.'

'Aye, that Troy was a good lad,' offered DS Patrick Connelly. The Irishman kept his humour in check for once. He leaned back in his chair and ran both hands through his curly grey hair. 'Worked with him a few years back when we had that joint case with Bromley borough. Fine police officer, so he was. I'll raise a Guinness to him after work, if anyone wants to join me.'

'He'd appreciate that.'

'Boss.' Detective Constable Nasim Malik looked unsure how to follow the others. Like Jones, he hadn't known Troy. At twenty-five, he'd not encountered death too often either, though Boateng knew his refugee parents had told him enough stories of loss from their home country of Iraq. Malik scratched his neat beard awkwardly, and in the end, simply said, 'You alright?'

Boateng bit his lip, nodded. 'I'm OK. Cheers, Nas.' They were all looking at him. 'Listen, I know you probably think it's pretty soon for me to be back in, after what happened last night. But this is the best place to be, believe me. I can make sure you lot aren't skiving and take my mind off Troy for a bit. Reckon that's what he would've wanted. No let-up, right?' This seemed to ease the atmosphere. 'So, tell me what's going on.'

Jones gestured to the ops board that tabled MIT's active cases. Each one was handwritten in its own row, with specific actions filling the columns. 'We're still working on the murder of Mehmet Bardak, the Turkish restaurant owner, from a week ago. No leads except the five-pound note found near his body, which is at the lab for DNA testing. Last night there was a similar attack on Vikram Kumar, who runs a convenience store in Lewisham. He survived but we're treating it as attempted murder. Both victims were from minority ethnic backgrounds, and large blunt objects – probably baseball bats – were used in both incidents, so we're checking out any other links. The two cases have been brought under one investigation: Operation Spearhead. Possible hate crimes.'

'Or financial,' suggested Connelly. 'Each had cash stolen from commercial premises. I think it was about the money. The owners just happened to have been born overseas.'

'I'm with Kat,' said Malik.

'You wish you were,' replied Connelly with a wink.

'Piss off.'

Boateng held up a hand. 'We need to keep an open mind. Different motives give us different lines of inquiry. Close one down too early, we might miss something. Maybe it's both. Everyone's got actions for today, then?' They all nodded. 'Alright, get to it. I'm off to speak to the boss.'

Down the corridor, Boateng heard Detective Chief Inspector Siân Krebs issuing orders well before he reached her open door. He knocked and, glancing up, she discreetly ended the call and stood, walking round her desk to greet him. Though she was about six foot two in her heels, a few inches above Boateng, the imposing presence was offset by her gentle tone. 'My deepest sympathies, Zac.' Krebs was usually politician first, police officer second, but the words seemed genuine. She offered a firm handshake, placing her other hand on Boateng's arm. 'I didn't know Sergeant McEwen personally, but I gather the two of you were very close.'

'We were.' He didn't elaborate on the lapsed contact, or his guilt about it.

'Suicide is such a tragic end to a person's life. You can't help but think there must have been some hope, possibly a way out, if they'd been able to speak to someone at the right time. In our line of work, it's too common, unfortunately.' Krebs's gaze became unfocused and she seemed lost in some memory for a moment. 'Will you be taking compassionate leave?'

'No.' He cleared his throat. 'Actually, I wanted to offer my help to Croydon with investigating his death. I hoped you could square it with—'

'Investigating?' She narrowed her eyes. 'What do you mean? The coroner will examine the body and present his or her findings at the inquest, obviously. Given the circumstances, I wouldn't expect any ruling other than suicide or accident. Possibly an open verdict. I know you cared about him, Zac, but you won't be involved in that process.'

'Ma'am, I don't believe that Sergeant McEwen killed himself. I think he was murdered.'

She folded her arms. 'That's quite a claim. I've heard nothing to that effect from Croydon. What gives you that idea?'

'He'd invited me over for a drink last night, probably only about half an hour before he died. Said he needed to talk. And there was no note.' Boateng realised he was on shaky ground. 'I just don't reckon he'd end his own life. I knew the bloke twenty-one years; he wouldn't do that.'

Krebs pursed her lips. She did that when she was choosing her words carefully. 'Zac, I know some of what you must be going through at the moment, and I understand your disbelief. But there's nothing in what you've said that remotely indicates murder, or even unlawful killing. A confused state of mind, perhaps. No outside involvement, though.'

His jaw set. Before he could counter, she spoke again.

'Losing somebody who's dear to you is very tough.'

'I know,' he growled.

'Goodness, I'm sorry, Zac. Of course you do.' Her expression softened. 'All I'm saying is that denial is very normal in these situations, and rather than setting hares running on no greater basis than a hunch – apologies for putting it so bluntly – wouldn't it be better to talk to someone about those feelings?'

Boateng said nothing.

'You know we have access to a counsellor who's working across several boroughs now? Tom Summers. Apparently he's very good. We can set you up with a session, if you like?'

'No, thanks.'

'Up to you. At least think about it. Take the rest of the day off, Zac. Get some rest and come back in on Monday morning. We've got you covered here.' She returned to her desk.

'Thank you, ma'am. I'd prefer to stay.'

Frustrated as he was with Krebs, Boateng felt that the day's work had been useful. They'd made some progress on Op Spearhead, submitting a request for a comparison of clothing fibres taken at both scenes. Now they were trying to identify any common suspects for the two attacks, which was proving a lot harder. Jones and Malik had gone to interview the store owner's family, while Connelly combed CCTV footage and Boateng looked at criminals with form for similar violence. The flow of their investigation had distracted him a bit. At 6 p.m., the four of them, plus a couple of other detectives, were ready to head into nearby Blackheath in search of a pub. Boateng felt drained but said he'd join them for one drink. Then he wanted to go home and just be with Etta and Kofi.

As they began walking away from the bustle of the High Street, Boateng heard quick footsteps behind him.

'DI Boateng?'

He spun round and saw a woman approaching. She was early thirties, tall and trim, with a lean, angular face and long hair, dyed bright red. 'Can I help you?' he replied cautiously.

'I'd like an interview.' She gave a wide, attractive smile.

'You're a journalist?'

'Yeah.'

He wasn't in the mood for this. 'Whatever it is, speak to the press office, OK?' He turned back and resumed walking with the others.

'It's about Troy McEwen's suicide.'

Boateng stopped. How could she have known about his connection to Troy? The death hadn't even been made public yet – Croydon police were still locating next of kin. He thought for a second before glancing at his colleagues. 'Go ahead, I'll catch you guys up in a minute.' As they set off, he stepped closer.

'What do you know about Troy?' he demanded of the redhead.

'You found his body, didn't you?' she replied. 'Last night. Can you describe the scene to me? Or maybe you took a photo?' Her lips bent into a smirk. 'I'd pay for that.'

Boateng snorted. 'You're not paying for anything, because I'm not telling you anything. And you should learn some respect for the dead.'

'So, he is dead. Thanks for confirming it.'

Boateng felt pissed off: she'd caught him out. 'Who are you?'

'Faye Rix.'

'Who d'you work for?'

'Myself. I'm freelance.'

'Listen to me, Faye Rix.' His tone was hard. 'You need to tell me right now where you got this information, do you understand?'

She grinned and Boateng became aware of a figure approaching from the shadows behind her. A tall guy, muscular build, in a leather jacket. He was square-jawed and shaven-headed, with hands like shovels. He held a German Shepherd tightly on its leash. Rix looked over her shoulder. 'It's OK,' she told the man. He said nothing, but his stare was fixed on Boateng, who began to wish he hadn't sent the others away.

'You used to work with Troy McEwen, didn't you?' said Rix.

Boateng felt his frustration growing. The emotion was still raw. 'I'm not having this conversation with you. You can either tell me how you know this, or we can chat inside the station with you under arrest.'

'For what?' Rix laughed. 'Check your media law, Detective. I don't have to disclose my sources to you. Where's the greater public interest?'

Boateng knew that so long as Troy's death was considered an accident or suicide, she was right. And that irritated him even more. Perhaps she was bluffing, and didn't have any sources. She'd probably just hoovered up some loose chat in a local café; journalists occasionally did that around big cases when they got desperate. Maybe she was paying someone inside the station for snippets; that'd happened before as well. Whatever her source, he didn't need this right now. He turned and began walking away.

'At the time of his death, Sergeant McEwen was involved with Dez Hayworth. Would you care to comment on that, DI Boateng?'

Where was she getting this stuff from? Hayworth was one of south London's most notorious career criminals. He'd served time, but the Met had never managed to pin anything big on him; he always kept himself too far removed. The suggestion Troy was 'involved' with him was ludicrous. Boateng's old pal had his flaws, but working with criminals was not among them. He felt the anger rising. 'What the hell are you talking about? You need to watch what you're saying.'

Rix laughed again and the big guy behind her took another step towards them. He was within striking distance now. The dog emitted a low growl, straining towards Boateng. His pulse quickened with the stab of adrenalin, hands balling into fists. The two men glared at each other before Rix put a hand on the guy's arm. 'Leave it, Adam. You know I can look after myself.' Then, to Boateng: 'All the major channels are gonna want this story.

The big papers, too. I can see the headlines now: suicide, murder and police corruption, going back years. You'll talk to me then.'

Boateng stood alone on the pavement, staring after Rix and the huge man as they strode away together, the dog alongside them.

•

Etta tipped a half-kilo of king prawns into the bubbling okra stew, added a dash more palm oil and stirred the pan. She had her mum to thank for the classic Nigerian recipe. Zac had been through it the last twenty-four hours and she wanted to take care of him. She went into the living room and found her two boys side by side, Zac showing a photo album to Kofi. She leaned against the door frame, watching them.

'Check this one, Ko. That's me and Troy in '96, when we graduated from our training course. Got the full uniforms on and everything. Eleven years before you were born, that was.'

'Look how skinny you are, Dad.'

'Oi!'

Etta knocked on the open door and they both looked up. 'Five minutes till dinner for big boys, five minutes till bedtime for small boys.'

Kofi groaned. 'I want to stay with dad.'

'I know. But you'll see him tomorrow. He's taking you to football in the morning. Aren't you, Zac?'

'Yeah.' Her husband looked a bit distracted. He was staring at the photographs.

'Come on then. Up you go and clean your teeth.'

'Can I have a story?'

She and Zac exchanged a glance, knew they couldn't say no. 'Go on, do your teeth and we'll be up in a minute.'

Kofi ran off and she plonked herself down next to Zac. 'Stew will keep for ten minutes.' She tapped the graduation photo. 'Get you two, best mates from the word go.'

'Wasn't easy back then. I took stick off everyone: colleagues, suspects, public – white and black. Troy was in the majority, as far as the outside world was concerned, but he reckoned some of the lads in the station knew. I used to tell him, don't act tough, like there's something to make up for, just be yourself. Guess you could say we looked out for each other. I owed him.' He closed the album, and she noticed he was trembling slightly. His eyes were wet.

'Zac, love. You stuck at it, you and Troy. You came through those challenges, and you'll come through this now.' She hesitated, unsure if this was the right moment. 'You know, when we lost Amelia, I got those sessions through the GP. Bereavement counselling. You found your own way then, I appreciate that, but what about some therapy now? It helped me so much to just talk through it all. Could help you too.'

'Damn.' He slapped the album down on the coffee table. 'First my boss and now you. I don't need therapy. What I need is to find out who killed Troy.'

Etta placed a hand over his. 'Don't do this, please.' She'd seen Zac drive himself half-crazy over their daughter's death. Her husband's stubbornness was vital in his professional work; in his personal life, it could be disastrous.

Zac stood. 'Can you pick Kofi up from football tomorrow?' he asked her.

'Why?'

'There's someone I have to see.'

CHAPTER THREE

Saturday, 2 December 2017

The only mistakes you make are the opportunities you don't react to. That's what they said in jazz, anyway, where no one ever knows what's coming next. Boateng wasn't improvising on his sax this time, though. He was driving south towards Sydenham, trying to formulate a plan for the impending encounter. Truth was, he only had one question to ask Dez Hayworth. For the rest, he'd just have to react.

Boateng parked his Audi at the edge of the waste ground and entered on foot. No way he was taking his car into this place. Passing through corrugated iron gates, he entered a graveyard of metal. Washing machines, microwaves, radiators and pipes were heaped high as buildings on both sides of the path; decaying appliances, scavenged from across south London. Most of it taken with the owners' permission, but not all. Moving deeper inside the yard, Boateng found himself walled in by old vehicles. They were stripped and crushed, piled on top of one another. A giant hydraulic loading machine lowered its arm, grabbed a car by the roof and hoisted it over his head, buckling the metal before smashing it on top of a stack. Rounding a corner, Boateng saw a young, heavyset guy swing an axe over his head and bring it down on a bicycle. The frame cleaved in two and he took another huge swing, splitting the metal once more. He seemed to be enjoying his work.

'Is Dez here?' Boateng had hands in his pockets, hoping he looked more relaxed than he felt.

Axe-man stopped mid swing and glanced at him. 'You a scrapper?'

'What?'

'Got any metal?' The guy straightened up and leaned on his axe handle.

'Not on me.' He didn't want to give too much away. 'I'm an old mate of Dez.'

Axe stared at him. 'From where?'

'Football.' He grinned, hoping that was suitably non-threatening. 'Back in the day. Came to see how he's doing. I might have a car for him too. Where is he?'

Apparently satisfied, the guy jerked a thumb over his shoulder. 'In the cabin.'

'Cheers.' As Boateng walked past, the guy watched him closely, both hands on the axe. It occurred to Boateng that not only did no one know he was here, but he hadn't seen a single security camera since he'd arrived. He knocked on the Portakabin door.

'Speak to the lad in the yard.' The familiar voice from within was low, rasping. It made Boateng's skin crawl, just as it had years ago.

He pushed the door open and walked in. 'I already did. You should do something about the customer service.' Hayworth was seated behind a desk, his feet up on it, upper body obscured by a *Daily Star*. As Boateng approached, Hayworth tossed the newspaper to one side. The face was rounder and more jowly, the head balder, and a belly had sprouted since the last time Boateng had seen him in the flesh, nearly twenty years ago. He'd also acquired a gold Rolex, though he wore the same chunky silver cross around his neck that he always had. Boateng removed his flat cap and Hayworth's expression shifted from surprise to confusion, before settling on smugness.

'Fuck me. Constable Boateng.'

'Inspector, now.'

Hayworth grunted. 'Moving up in the world.'

'Likewise.' Boateng nodded to the yard. 'This is a step up from burglary and GBH.' He glanced around the small office, then wandered over to a ledger on the side and flicked through some pages. It contained handwritten records of who had deposited what: weights, makes and models, metal types, car number plates, even serial numbers for the larger white goods. 'Looks like business is going well since you got out, Dez. Rag-and-bone trade's not too bad these days.'

Hayworth took his feet off the table and stood. 'I turn over about four million quid's worth of metal every year. Five per cent profit. That's a lot more than I ever made when I was nicking stuff.'

'Or tying people up at home, torturing them into giving you the family silver.'

'That too.' Hayworth sounded unrepentant. He pointed through the window. 'Quarter of a mil in scrap out there right now.'

'Not very well protected, is it? I can't see any CCTV.'

Hayworth emitted a noise somewhere between a growl and a chuckle. 'Sellers don't really like it. Buyers don't either. So, I ain't got none. Look after my own security – you seen the lad outside – and most people know who I am. Anyway, the stuff doesn't stick around long. Matter of fact, some geezer's coming to take a lorry-load off me later today. I'll ship it out to China, India, any of you lot that'll buy it.'

'Sorry, *us* lot?'

'You know what I mean.'

'Don't think I do.' Boateng fixed him with a stare, and it was Hayworth that blinked first.

'The public.' He smirked. 'My buyers. So, what d'you want then?'

'Troy McEwen.'

Hayworth frowned. 'Jesus, I ain't heard that name in a long time. What about him?'

The reaction seemed genuine. 'You two in touch?'

'In touch?' His voice had the high pitch of incredulity. 'The bastard arrested me. You were there, remember? It was nineteen years ago, but my memory of that day is pretty fucking clear. The only touch I'd want to give him is a smack in the mouth, and that's putting it politely. But since he ain't scrapping metal, our paths don't cross that much.'

'You haven't seen him, then?'

'He's your mate. You should know what he's up to. Speak to him.'

Time to improvise. 'I did. Recently. He mentioned you.'

Hayworth paused, his eyes darting up in search of a hit. 'Did he now? Nice to hear I'm still talked about by the Old Bill. What's he saying about me, then?'

'That there was contact between the two of you.'

'I don't think so. He's confusing me with some other bloke.' Hayworth tilted his head. 'Give my warmest regards to Constable McEwen when you see him, Inspector. Now, if you don't mind, I've got some stuff to do.'

Boateng studied his face, then nodded to the newspaper, open at the picture of a topless blonde. 'Don't let me keep you from an honest day's work.' He pulled his flat cap on and stepped out of the office. Navigating the spaces between blocks and piles of old metal, Boateng glanced back, but Hayworth and his cabin had already disappeared among the junk. The young guy stopped again as Boateng passed, then swung the axe over his head and let fly an almighty blow that took the leg clean off a table. Boateng shivered; kept walking.

As he drove back to Lewisham, he replayed the conversation. If Hayworth was lying, he was a damn good actor. His surprise was consistent with the unexpected mention of Troy's name, and all his references to Troy had been in the present tense. People often slipped up on that; it took a lot of brain-work to pretend that someone was alive when you knew they were dead. Hayworth didn't seem bright enough to keep that up, but perhaps Boateng wasn't giving him enough credit. After all, he'd got away with several crimes he'd committed. Was the journalist mistaken, or her source misinformed? He needed more data before he could be sure.

At his computer in the MIT office, Boateng opened the Police National Computer database and tapped in 'Dennis Hayworth'. A string of offences was returned, going back thirty years: assault, robbery, burglary, possession of illegal weapons, handling stolen goods, trespass and extortion. Hayworth had been in prison six times, including a five-year stretch for the incident that had brought him so violently into contact with Boateng – and Troy, of course. His last conviction was five years ago and he'd served eighteen months before being released. Finished his parole time and opened the scrapyard, apparently now a successful small business owner. A perfect story of redemption. But Boateng didn't buy it. He liked to believe people were capable of change for the better, but experience had taught him otherwise. There had to be something more. He checked the Met's own Crimint database next, scrolling through the hits. The most recent note on the file, from a year ago, caught his eye. *Named as suspected member of National Right.* There were no further details. Named? That suggested an intelligence lead, but who would have access to—'

'Sneaky overtime, Zac?'

He whipped round to see Kat Jones standing there, flushed and sweating, head to toe in gym gear, mopping her hair with a towel. She must've come up the stairs from the basement and through the fire exit behind him. The big door closed so silently on its smooth mechanism that a running MIT joke was that your murder suspect could walk right in and you wouldn't hear them.

'What're you doing here?' he asked her. A good attack was the best defence for an ambush.

'Been in the gym.'

'It's Saturday.'

'Best time to use it; there's no one else here. What's that?'

Too late for him to shut down the screen. He'd have to style it out. 'I was just, um…' He pointed to Hayworth's record. 'Looking for people who might have form for racially motivated violence. This guy's got convictions for GBH, and he's a possible member of National Right.'

'The neo-Nazi gang?' She leaned over the desk. 'So, you think I'm on to something with Op Spearhead? About the hate crimes, I mean.'

'Probably.'

Jones smiled. Boateng knew there was some unspoken competition between her and Connelly. It was only natural – Connelly the old veteran, with no more qualifications than a school leaver's certificate to his name, taking exception to the bright young graduate fast-tracked to his rank in just five years. Boateng was aware he needed to balance Jones's ambition and Connelly's ego.

He nodded at the screen. 'We'll compile a full list on Monday.'

'OK.' She reached into her desk drawer, pulled out a sports drink. 'So, you just got the urge to work on this now?'

He forced a laugh. 'My wife's taking Kofi to football today, for once. Didn't feel like playing my sax, so here I am.'

'Yeah, of course.' Jones was obviously interpreting his words through the lens of Thursday night. 'How're you feeling?'

'OK.' In truth, Boateng was doing better today than he had been yesterday. Perhaps it was just an illusion created by the sense of activity – visiting Hayworth, searching the files. Did it add up to anything? He was beginning to doubt his instincts about Troy's death already, and he'd barely started looking into it. Now he was uneasy about holding back the truth from Jones; had he not already learned he could trust her? The problem was that to explain why he was so interested in Hayworth, he'd need to disclose what had really happened back in '98. And those were some lies he didn't want to unravel. 'Cheers for asking.'

Jones nodded, paused. 'Need any help?'

'Nah, I'll be OK.'

'Alright then.' She swigged her drink. 'I'm going for a shower. See you Monday?'

'Sure.'

Jones departed through the fire door, leaving Boateng staring at the computer screen.

*

Kat Jones made one of those affirmative noises, the sort you can throw into any conversation at any point. It's meant to show you're paying attention, but Kat used it precisely because she wasn't listening. The guy she was on a date with, Jeremy, had lost her about twenty minutes ago, which was impressive, considering the date had only been going for thirty minutes. It had started badly when he turned out to be significantly less hot than his Tinder picture, and at least three inches shorter than his profile claimed. He frowned when she ordered a beer, as if that was the sort of thing a woman shouldn't drink, and then offered her wine, in case she'd made a mistake, to which she replied no, she'd have a beer, thanks. Things had worsened quickly when, discovering her profession, he proceeded to monologue on how crime was essentially the work of bad people from bad neighbourhoods. He'd ignored her attempts to introduce caveats to that theory, drawing out the huge range of reasons why crimes are committed. Now, he was mansplaining the flaws of the prison system based on some documentary he'd seen. She couldn't drink the beer fast enough. On the plus side, the bar was nice. Intimate, with great old-school music and cool decor. Walking distance from her flat in New Cross. Just a shame about the company. Her thoughts wandered to Nas, and how she'd rather be sharing a drink with him. If Nas were here, he'd be listening, not talking over the top of her. Didn't hurt that he was fit – most of the girls at work thought so – with a nice body too. The problem was dating someone you worked with, who sat opposite you all day; what if it went wrong?

'Kat! Hello, Kat, did you hear me?'

'Mm. Sorry, what?'

Jeremy leaned closer than she was comfortable with. 'I said, what made you join the police?'

'Oh, I…' She wasn't sure how much to say, given that she planned never to see Jeremy again. Should she tell him about her father, her hero, the police sergeant who, in pursuit of some guys who'd held up a post office, was hit by a car and killed in the line of duty, when she was only ten years old? Should she mention the oath she'd sworn on her dad's grave when she was fourteen, to continue what he'd done, against her mum's advice and the pleas of her university tutors to stay on at UCL for a postgraduate degree? Should she let him know that, despite being one of the youngest sergeants in the Met, with some decent cases under her belt already, she'd trade all that to have her dad back? In the end, she decided to go with the simple conversation killer: 'My dad was a copper.'

Jeremy frowned. He did that a lot. 'Was? Is he retired?'

'No, he's dead.' She downed the beer and slapped the bottle down on the bar. 'Lovely to meet you, Jeremy, but I've got to go see my mates for dinner. Thanks for the drink.' Making her way out, she saw a guy sitting on his own at an outside table. Kat thought she recognised him, maybe even from work, but she couldn't be sure. He gave her a creepy look, up and down, expressionless. Enough dickheads for one night. She turned and walked quickly towards the train station. It'd been a mistake to arrange a first date on a Saturday evening. But there was still plenty of time to go join her mates up in Dalston and have a proper night out.

●

It's begun. For years I tried to fight that anger, hold it back, make it go away. Then I met someone from back then and it changed the way I saw things. Made my anger worse. Made me realise that it wouldn't go away until I got some justice for what happened. And there was no way that was coming from the police, so I had to act.

There are five people who need to pay for what they've done. One of them is dead now. I thought I'd feel more as he died, but after the initial shock, I was just kind of empty. Numb. Maybe the reaction's been buried somewhere in my subconscious. Wouldn't be the first time.

Boateng is investigating. I'm going to enjoy observing him work, because – like the others – he doesn't know that I'm already in his world. He doesn't realise yet that it's about him. It may even be too early for him to work out what's going to happen to him. He'll get that soon enough, though. Then I'll watch him try to hide it from everyone. He's good at hiding things.

CHAPTER FOUR

Sunday, 3 December 2017

Returning to the scene of a trauma can be a positive thing, Boateng had read in his psychology textbooks. In theory, it helped the brain to process bad memories. But so far, all that'd happened was a technicolour flashback to Thursday night, triggered by entering Troy's street. A normal reaction, he told himself. It'll pass. Boateng parked up and stood for a moment outside the house, hands jammed in coat pockets against the cold.

It looked so different in the morning sunlight, he found it hard to believe this was the place where horror had unfolded just three days ago. The body had been taken away for examination by a coroner, and the living room cleaned by professionals with strong stomachs, recommended by the police. A cousin had been found in Kent who, in the absence of any living parents, siblings, children or recognised partner, was Troy's next of kin. Carol Peterson, forty-six years old, hairdresser. Boateng had never met her, but Croydon police had put them in touch. A phone call last night had resulted in him offering to meet at Troy's house to help her sort through his things. What to keep, what to throw away, what to give to charity. The artefacts of a person's life – each a small reflection of who they were – categorised, parcelled up and shipped out. Before long, there'd be new occupants in the house. But Boateng was determined not to forget so quickly. He told

Troy's cousin that helping was the least he could do for his old friend's family. In fact, his motives were somewhat less altruistic. He figured that access to Troy's house would give him the chance to gather clues about the man's life in the weeks and months leading up to his death. And that could give him something to work with. Renewed hope was probably responsible for the strange euphoria he felt that morning. But he had to play it cool; he hadn't shared his murder theory with Troy's cousin. No need to raise the alarm too soon.

Carol Peterson was in the dining room, packing crockery. She had short hair with elaborate blond highlighting, wore a chunky sweater and leggings and navigated the room with quick, efficient movements. 'Thank you so much for coming to help. You must've known Troy very well. He used to talk about you – Zac this and Zac that.' Her Scottish accent was less pronounced than Troy's had been.

'He was a great guy,' replied Boateng, wishing again he'd made more effort to see his old mate. 'Always stood up for what he believed in. Not enough people do that; it takes courage.'

Carol wrapped some plates in tissue paper and placed them in a cardboard box. 'He was brave, that's for sure.'

'When was the last time you spoke to him?'

'About a month ago. He came to my little one's birthday party down in Kent. Uncle Troy, they called him.' She managed a smile. 'One day he's there, next thing he's not.' She gripped the box as if steadying herself. 'I still can't believe he'd do this.'

'Me neither.' Boateng didn't reveal why he shared her view.

'What do I tell my girls?'

'Kids have a way of dealing with death.' He spoke from personal experience. 'Below about ten, all they really know is that the person's not around any more. Most often, they're scared that someone else might be taken away too. You can tell them it's OK to talk about their feelings, though.'

She nodded; wiped her nose with the back of her hand.

Boateng knew the timing wasn't ideal, but he had to ask her. 'Carol, I'm sorry to bring this up, but was there anything that Troy mentioned to you when you last saw him? You know, about stuff going on in his life.'

'No.' She gave a tiny shake of the head. 'Not that I can think of. Just normal work stress.'

'Work stress?'

'Yeah. Targets, budget cuts, pay freeze, pension changes. I expect it's the same for you too.'

'That's the whole Met right now. Anything more personal?'

'Not really.' She stared into the cardboard box for several seconds. 'Except, he did have an argument with that man at the station.'

'Who?'

'Some guy called Evans. I'd never met him – I didn't know Troy's colleagues. He mostly kept the Met out of his private life.'

'What did he say about Evans?'

Carol exhaled hard. 'Can't remember, exactly. Not nice words. There was a bust-up in Bromley station; Evans and Troy had a fight. Not a fight, but, you know, a scuffle. I think he called Troy a poof or something in front of the others and Troy, well—'

'Stood up to the bully.'

'Yeah.' She raised her head. 'Oh my God. Do you think that pushed him—?'

'No, no. Troy had dealt with much worse before. He was thick-skinned. That wouldn't have made him do this.' *Because he didn't do it*, came the thought immediately. Boateng placed a hand on her shoulder before delivering a line he knew was hypocritical even before he'd said it. 'We can't go searching for reasons, tempting as it is. Humans are programmed to want closure. But sometimes, it's not there to be found.'

She nodded and then, surprisingly, leaned into him for a hug. Boateng had experienced this before: people affected by loss seeking human contact, even with strangers. Members of the public, victims of crime, relatives of the dead. And the only thing he could do in those moments was hug them back. Holding her, he felt a pang of shame at the ulterior motive for his visit. He was doing this for Troy, he reassured himself. But did that make it right?

Eventually, Carol let go. He cleared his throat. 'Shall I take a look upstairs, then?'

'Be my guest. There's boxes and tape in the hallway.'

Boateng climbed the stairs and spotted a framed photo of him and Troy on the landing wall – the same one he had in the photo album at home. Hendon graduation, '96. He paused, placed his fingertips on the glass. There was no room for emotion here; it would only cloud his judgement. He needed to look for anything out of place, any clue to Troy's activities that might be relevant to his death.

The bedroom was the obvious place to start. Boateng searched the wardrobe, chest of drawers and bedside table. Nothing unusual. He moved across to the small bookcase on the far wall. One shelf down, on top of a row of paperbacks, he found a diary, '2017' embossed on the cover. Troy was old school like that; he wrote stuff down. Boateng flicked through the pages. Troy had marked some things in for the rest of December: a couple of Christmas work events, a show in the West End one night, a Boxing Day football match. Not necessarily the plans of a man who'd lost all hope in life. He turned the pages back, saw Troy's routine laid out. Work, gym, clay pigeon shooting in Surrey on the weekends. He'd been active, physically and socially.

Scrutinising the handwriting, Boateng picked out a name appearing every Wednesday morning: Summers. Regular, like appointments, starting about three months ago. Was this the same guy Krebs had suggested Boateng see for counselling? Perhaps Troy was getting some treatment. If so, then not only did it decrease the possibility of suicide, but it also meant Summers might know what Troy had been doing in the final weeks of his life. Maybe it was worth arranging a session with him, after all. Only one other entry stood out. Under 9 November, a Thursday, Troy had scribbled an address: Unit 3, Holbeach Road, SE6. Apart from being a Catford postcode, it meant nothing to Boateng. He noted it on his phone and finished checking the room.

Boateng moved into the bathroom and checked the cabinets. A box of condoms, some missing, suggested Troy was perhaps dating. Maybe he even had a boyfriend. Boateng had no idea. In the last drawer, he found a packet of citalopram. Boateng checked the prescription date on the printed label against the dose and number of antidepressant pills left. Everything was as it should be. This was a man managing his mental health; a man with plans. Suicide was looking less and less likely. Boateng found nothing else upstairs and realised he should probably make some effort to help Carol sort Troy's things.

Heading downstairs for a cardboard box, he stopped outside the living room. A flashback hit again. Troy's body slumped in its chair. The odour of gunpowder, raw meat. His heart jolted, bile rising in his throat. He swallowed, breathed and opened the door.

This time it was the smell of bleach he noticed first. The wall and ceiling were washed clean, the carpet pulled up, the armchair gone. It was as if the whole thing had never happened. Almost. Stepping across to the window, he noticed a fine, dark spray on the curtain hem. Boateng tried to assess the room with fresh eyes, see if there was anything he might've missed. His gaze travelled over the familiar sofa, side table and mantelpiece, alighting on a low wooden unit against the wall. Its doors were shut, a small plastic internet router perched on top. Boateng opened the unit and found the interior humming, a mass of cables and winking lights. On the centre shelf was a much larger plastic box with several antennae protruding. He couldn't identify it, but he snapped a picture with his phone. He looked again at the internet router on top. Then he realised: if there was Wi-Fi, where was the device that used it?

Two hours later, he'd cleared out most of Troy's books and clothes and was ready to leave. Boateng said goodbye to Carol, who gave him the spare key to come back another day, if he had time. She didn't know anything about a computer, and hadn't found a laptop, tablet or phone in the clear-up, and that bothered him. But at least he had some leads now, even if none of them related to Dez Hayworth or the journalist, Faye Rix. Boateng threw some blues on the car stereo and set out for home in Brockley. Etta hadn't said so, but Boateng knew she was pissed off at his absences today and yesterday. He hoped to make amends by agreeing to Etta's suggestion of a date tonight. With her parents. And Kofi. Plus another three hundred members of their church congregation. If that didn't achieve forgiveness, he didn't know what would.

●

'"I have set before you life and death",' boomed the Nigerian preacher. '"Therefore choose life, so that you and your children may live!" That's what God says, my friends. The book of Deuteronomy.' Etta thought about those words. For her, choosing life so that you *and* your children could live meant accepting the loss of their daughter, and being able to move on with life, not dwell on death. She and her husband had both felt paralysed since Amelia had been killed five years ago, but she was determined to live. She wanted Zac to choose life too, even if his job often put him alongside death at its most violent. Etta glanced sideways at her husband, his brow tight with concentration, arm around Kofi.

As the service ended, they stood and she began waving greetings to friends across the hall, the murmur of conversation rising. Etta's parents were fussing over Kofi, straightening his little red tie. She was about to start the social rounds when she noticed that Zac hadn't moved from his seat. She placed a hand on his arm.

'You OK, love?' she asked gently.

Zac pressed his lips together before answering. 'I'll be alright.'

'Course you will. That's my man.' She hesitated before continuing. 'Have you thought any more about those counselling sessions?'

'Matter of fact, I have,' he replied with a nod. 'I'm gonna see the guy at work, try and make an appointment with him next week.'

Etta narrowed her eyes, lips wavering into a smile. 'You've changed your tune.'

'Ah, you know me, I'm an adaptable guy.' That wasn't strictly true. Well, as far as problem-solving went, yes. But her husband was one of the most single-minded people she'd ever met. Zac's flexibility was in finding new ways to achieve his aim, not finding new aims. He didn't give up, and that tenacity was one of the reasons she loved him. She knew that Zac's obsessions were usually motivated by his humanity. Ironically, that often made him selfish and tough to live with. She took his hand and squeezed it, then pulled him into a hug, as if that might stop him slipping into his own world.

Jim watched his target exit the African church amid a mass of men in suits and women in colourful dresses, wrappers and geles. Zachariah Boateng was holding hands with a curvaceous black woman and a kid with a bright red tie. Presumably his wife and son. They'd been in the building for ninety minutes. Service plus some chatting, he reckoned. They walked over to an Audi and climbed in. He waited for them to pull away and into traffic, then set out in his own vehicle, keeping a few cars behind. Earlier that day, he'd followed Boateng from his home to Croydon, to the house of the dead man. Boateng had gone inside and come out later with a few cardboard boxes – not clear what was in them. Wasn't clear either what he'd done in Troy McEwen's house, or why he'd even gone there. Jim wasn't worried, though; if you watched long enough, you normally found out. You just had to pay attention to the details.

Watching had always been Jim's thing. He'd been doing it for the last twenty years. Occasionally a 'special job' came his way: those assignments that required executive action. Usually with a bullet, and usually because of the threat they posed. This was one of those jobs.

Before beginning this gig, Jim had read up on his target: Zachariah Boateng, forty-three years old, detective inspector in the Met. Specialised in homicide investigation. Some impressive work under his belt. Today he had put a body to the name. Five foot ten, he'd guess, well built, although letting himself go a bit around the middle. Skin tone consistent with the Ghanaian heritage suggested by his surname. When he took off that flat cap he'd worn all day, the hair was short, neat and flecked with grey. Boateng had shaved off his stubble before going to church, and put on a suit and tie. He looked pretty calm for a man who'd found his friend dead from a shotgun blast on Thursday night. Jim needed to know what Boateng was up to. Then they could take the appropriate action. Two things were for sure, though. One, he'd need to keep watching. Two, the boss would want to hear about the visit to Troy McEwen's house.

As Boateng's car turned into their home street, Jim killed his lights and waited till they'd gone inside. Once he was satisfied that Boateng was done for the night, he removed the 9 mm pistol from his shoulder holster and locked the weapon in his glove compartment. It wouldn't be used tonight. The time would come soon enough.

CHAPTER FIVE

Monday, 4 December 2017

The smell of decent coffee wafted across the MIT office, heightening Jones's anticipation of the mid-morning briefing. Grabbing a notebook, she pulled her chair up to where Boateng and Malik were already assembled, catching the end of their exchange.

'Whoever it was, he's either the hardest or the stupidest guy in Lewisham,' said Boateng, plunging the cafetière and pouring out three mugs. 'Don't quote me on that, OK? I don't want to get my face punched in.'

'Yeah, right.' Malik laughed and helped himself to a coffee.

'Cheers, Zac.' Jones took one of the mugs. 'Who's that?'

'A new constable,' replied Malik, spooning three sugars into his drink. 'He's been here a couple of weeks. Sarah!' he called across the room. 'What's that PC's name again?'

'Evans,' came the reply.

'Evans. Right. He took down a drug dealer after foot pursuit in Ladywell last night. Wasn't even on duty!' Malik spoke quickly, his excitement visible. 'Evans corners him, right, so the guy takes out a hunting knife, tells him to back off and walk away. Then Evans just goes for him, proper rugby tackle, pins the knife under his left arm and drops the right elbow into the guy's face – boom!' He smacked a fist into his palm. 'Out cold. Evans found three rocks of crack in his pocket. Legend.'

Jones wasn't entertained by the story: it didn't sound like reasonable force, and this Evans could've easily ended up with a serious injury for what was a very small amount of drugs. There were too many macho guys in the Met, endlessly discussing their bench press stats and firearms training scores, or one-upping each other on how fast they'd driven that week. It was a shame that Malik found all that impressive. 'He should've waited for backup,' she said, trying to take the buzz down a notch.

'The others were too slow!' cried Malik. 'He had to do something, or the geezer would've got away.'

'Better that than bleeding to death from a stab wound.' Jones looked to Boateng for agreement, but her boss had zoned out and was staring into the middle distance.

'Whatevs.' Malik shook his head, stirring the coffee. 'Evans is nails, mate.'

'Evans?' Connelly wheeled his chair over to the whiteboard, clutching a mug of tea as thick and dark as Thames water. 'As in Constable Mike Evans? Used to be in Bromley?'

'Yeah, that's the one. You know him?'

'Not personally, thank God. Fella's a grade-A bastard by all accounts.'

'Serious?' Malik frowned. 'Come on, Pat. Did you hear about his collar last night?'

'Nope. I'm telling you though, he's unhinged.' Connelly slurped his tea. 'Ex-military, left the paras early last year. Mate of mine that worked with him down in Bromley said the fella got into a scrap with another officer. Not his first little bust-up on the job. No formal complaints filed, but he was encouraged to move on. He'd only been there a year and he'd managed to rub most of station the wrong way. Not even out of his probation period yet. Now he's our problem.' He raised his tea in a mock 'cheers'. 'Just don't push in front of him in the cafeteria – you'll be picking up your own teeth with a broken arm.'

'Who'd he get in a fight with at Bromley?' asked Boateng. Jones registered more caution than curiosity in the way he spoke.

'Dunno.' Connelly shrugged. 'Two or three different lads, I think.'

Boateng nodded silently, then took a slow sip of coffee. Jones wondered if he was still distracted by his friend's death. She'd not personally known any officers who'd died – yet – either in the line of duty or by accident, let alone suicide. But she was only five years into her career; the stats said it was just a matter of time. She guessed the deaths of people you knew were part of the Job.

'Zac,' she said gently, 'are you going to share the news?'

He started. 'Yeah, thanks, Kat. We've got a lead on Op Spearhead. Remember the five-pound note found at the scene of Mehmet Bardak's murder, round the back of the restaurant? Well, lab got DNA off it matching a guy with two convictions for violent crime. Kat, do you want to tell them what you found?'

She glanced at her notes. 'DNA belonged to Dale Rogers. His older brother, Liam, is listed on our records as a member of National Right.'

'They sound like…' Malik broke off.

'Exactly. A neo-Nazi gang,' said Boateng. 'Been around a few years, but they keep a low profile. Haven't been banned yet, but I think the Home Office is working up a case.'

Kat stuck a couple of mugshots on their whiteboard: two men in their thirties, each with the same jutting lower jaw, fleshy face and ruddy cheeks, both offset with severe buzzcut hairstyles. 'This is Dale on the left, Liam on the right.'

'You'd never guess they were related.' Connelly smirked and swigged his tea.

'Liam spent two years in Wormwood Scrubs for arson. Lit a petrol fire in an industrial bin next to a Hindu temple. Damaged the building but no one was harmed. At his hearing, he said he'd do it again if he got the chance, so the magistrate gave him a custodial sentence. And he served his time in the same prison as a guy called Dez Hayworth.' She pinned a third mugshot to the board with magnets. 'Zac trawled our systems for attackers in the area known to use baseball bats, and came up with Hayworth.'

'Among several other candidates,' added Boateng.

'But only Hayworth is listed as a member of National Right. Maybe he joined the group after meeting Liam in prison.' Kat tapped the photo. She was pleased at the clarity with which she'd explained the relationships. 'I reckon these are our guys for the Spearhead attacks.'

Connelly raised both palms, his thick eyebrows knitted together. 'Back up a minute. So, this guy's DNA is on a fiver near the murder, and on that basis we're also targeting these fellas? One's related to him and the other was in the same prison as his relative? It's not exactly a slam dunk, is it?'

'But they're linked,' protested Jones. She was still standing in front of the team and felt suddenly exposed. 'They've got form, motive and one of them has a DNA connection to the crime scene.'

Connelly snorted. 'But no witnesses, and no proof that the fiver was dropped at the time of the murder. Do we target everyone who's come out of Wormwood Scrubs after Liam Rogers arrived there? I don't want to piss on your parade, Kat. I'm just thinking about what the Crown Prosecution Service would say. Insufficient evidence.'

'With what we've got, Pat's right,' said Boateng. 'Sorry, Kat.'

Jones was annoyed. She'd thought her team would be pleased at her finding some suspects. Especially Boateng; he'd come up with Hayworth. She sat down heavily.

'Hey, it's a start.' Boateng put a hand on the arm of her chair. 'Listen, these guys aren't saints, and believe me, I want to nail anyone who's into hate crime. But our evidence is circumstantial, at best.' He turned his chair to face the others. 'Any suggestions as to how we proceed?'

'Follow the money,' replied Connelly, in a poor American accent. 'Couple of thousand quid was stolen at each place. We look for any evidence of laundering, bigger cash transfers, get handlers to ask their sources about it. Check with the victims to see if they had marked notes at all, that kind of thing.'

'Well volunteered, Pat. Don't give up on the CCTV, either.'

'Aye aye.'

'Anything else?'

'Speak to Hayworth,' offered Malik, one fist clenched. 'See what he knows about the Rogers brothers, check if he's got alibis for the days of both attacks.'

'Good, Nas.' Boateng scratched his chin. Jones watched him hesitate, considering something, before raising a finger. 'But I think you're a step ahead. We need to build up an intelligence picture on Hayworth. His supposed membership of National Right was from source reporting. That means there could be sensitivities; the asset informing on him could be from another operation. We don't want to jeopardise anything else or put someone in danger. So, let's try to work out which source is close to him. Check with whoever filed the report that's quoted on Crimint database. We need to know what Hayworth's into, now he's out of prison. How can we do that?'

There was a brief silence while they thought. Jones was still smarting from the challenge to her suspect list, and she needed to offer something—

'Hack his email.' The flat, nasal voice from behind made them turn. A couple of desks back, a man sat at a computer, head bowed. Though his hands were obscured, the clatter of keystrokes from behind the low screen indicated he was typing at furious pace. 'I can do it for you,' he added matter-of-factly. 'Piece of piss.'

The team exchanged smirks and raised eyebrows. Boateng gave a mock frown.

Connelly couldn't resist. 'Commissioner *Dick*, is that you behind the computer?' He stressed the surname, and despite her earlier irritation at him, Jones couldn't help but chuckle silently.

'No, my name's Jason Leather.'

'I didn't know we had a new detective in the MIT,' said Boateng.

'I'm not a detective,' he said, as if speaking to children. 'I'm a network engineer.' Finally, he stopped typing and raised his head. His black T-shirt was emblazoned with the gory image and jagged logo of a metal band. Jones took in his narrow face and straggly goatee beard. Though he wore a pair of thin-rimmed circular glasses and his long brown hair was pulled back into a ponytail this time, there was no doubt about it. He was the guy who had been sitting alone outside the bar on Saturday night, watching her. As his eyes locked on to her again, she felt her skin crawl.

·

One advantage of working in Europe's largest police station was that you had time to think: the long corridors, interminable staircases and different wings meant you could always find some privacy as you walked from A to B in Lewisham station. As Boateng marched towards an office at the far end of the building, he reflected on what he wasn't sharing with his team. Jones had caught him looking up Hayworth's file on Saturday, and Hayworth had become a person of interest in their current investigation. Given the links to National Right, it was inevitable that Hayworth would come across the team's radar after Dale Rogers's DNA turned up at the Bardak murder scene. But now Boateng was in a difficult position. If they followed the Hayworth lead, sooner or later it'd emerge that Boateng had paid a visit to him at the scrapyard. He'd then have to explain why he'd done that outside any official remit: because a random journalist had told him that Troy was 'involved' with Hayworth. Why was that information of interest to Boateng? Because he didn't think Troy killed himself.

But to explain that theory, Boateng might need to reach back to the incident in '98. People had died then who shouldn't have, and it'd been on his conscience ever since. Surely it was no coincidence that Troy had mentioned 'back then' in his text message, sent moments before his death? If that was the reason he'd been murdered, it meant there might be others in danger.

Problem was, no one believed Troy had been murdered. For people to pay any attention to his theory, Boateng would need to tell them what had happened that day. It could cost him his job – or more. But if he didn't do anything, then other victims might follow Troy, including – he acknowledged with a flash of panic – himself. Boateng tried to resist the adrenalin that surged through him following that thought. He paused to steady himself, not allowing the fear to take hold. Took a breath and continued walking.

All he could do was keep ploughing his own furrow, as discreetly as possible, and hope something would turn up that he could bring to light without compromising the house of cards stacked up in '98. On top of that, there was Troy's altercation with this guy Evans; might that have any link to his death? Boateng suspected he'd find out more before long. Right now, though, he was pursuing another line of personal inquiry. Checking the room number, he put an ear to the door and, hearing nothing, knocked politely.

'Yes? Do come in; it's open.' The voice from within was educated, calm.

Boateng stepped into a small, cosy space. The feeling of warmth was created by the replacement of garish Met-standard strip lighting with two tall lamps in opposite corners. A pair of comfortable chairs was positioned on one side of the room. At a desk on the other side sat a youngish man of around thirty, with the slim, athletic build of a distance runner. Boateng could see from the computer screen that he was on the Met's personnel database. The young guy looked up from the monitor, removed a pair of tortoiseshell spectacles and met Boateng's gaze. His face was symmetrically handsome, almost pretty, with green eyes and high cheekbones that caught the soft light. His dark hair was swept across his forehead. It was rare to see someone this good-looking in Lewisham police station.

'Who're you after?' said the younger man, switching the screen off and rotating his chair towards the visitor.

'Dr Summers?'

'That's me. Oh, but I'm not a doctor. Not yet.' He smiled. 'Please, call me Tom. Come in.'

'DI Zac Boateng.' He offered a hand, which Summers shook. 'I've, er...' Now he was here, Boateng wasn't quite sure what to say. 'I lost someone, recently. An old friend.'

Summers directed him to a chair and, before he knew it, they were facing one another, the counsellor listening intently. Boateng haltingly explained what was on his mind, how he wanted to talk to someone. He could almost feel Summers's attention physically; it was forceful, and yet something about the setting put him at ease. He didn't feel any judgement towards him, neither pull-yourself-together stoicism nor emasculating sympathy. Just listening.

When Boateng had finished speaking, Summers simply nodded and asked when he'd like to start the counselling.

'When are you free?' said Boateng. 'Sooner the better, to be honest.'

Summers consulted a diary and tapped the page. 'Could do first thing tomorrow morning, if that's any good for you? Eight thirty a.m., here?'

'Sure.'

'If you could just get your boss to sign off the form, that'd be great. Thanks.'

'OK.' Boateng stood to leave. Maybe it would help him feel better, being able to speak to someone outside his network. Then he remembered the original reason for his visit. 'I think you were having some sessions with my friend, the one who died? Troy McEwen.'

Summers reddened slightly, momentarily off guard. 'I can't discuss anyone else, I'm afraid. As you'll appreciate, my sessions are completely confidential. You'd want that privacy for yourself, I'm sure.'

'Of course.' Boateng smiled. 'See you tomorrow, then. Eight thirty.' Closing the door behind him, he felt confident. The guy had to say that about confidentiality, but Boateng reckoned he could still use the sessions to his advantage. Twenty-one years in the Met; he should be able to get something out of Summers. Beginning the long walk back to his office, he felt the buzz of excitement that kept him addicted to investigative work. He was a step closer to finding out what had happened to Troy.

Boateng had passed on lunch with his team. He waited for them to head to the cafeteria and, with the open-plan MIT office virtually empty except for a couple of civilian analysts across the room, he took his chance. Now at a different desk, Jason Leather was leaning back in his chair, furiously working a spring-loaded grip strengthener in one hand while the other tapped occasional commands on a keyboard, the black screen in front reeling off lines of white code. Boateng strolled over and stood next to him, close enough to catch a faint whiff of body odour from Leather's T-shirt. But the engineer didn't move, just kept working his hand grip, chewing gum, touching keys. There was white scar tissue on his right wrist and hand, like he'd been cut sometime in the past. Was it an accident, an attack, or self-harm? Boateng cleared his throat.

'Alright, Jason? You in training, then?'

'What?'

'The hand grip.'

Leather swivelled his head to face Boateng, then back again to the monitor, expressionless throughout. 'Jeet kune do.'

'The martial art?'

Leather sighed. 'It's not a conventional martial art. It's a system, a philosophy.'

At least Boateng had him talking. 'Developed by Bruce Lee, right?'

'The one and only.' Leather gave a single laugh. 'He was ahead of his time. It was basically the first mixed martial art. It's not my only fighting style, obviously.'

'So, what are you working on here?'

'Firewalls, network security. Trying to stop you lot getting done over by ransomware, spyware, scareware or any other kind of malware. You can thank me later.'

Boateng put his hands in his pockets; tried to look casual. His right hand was on his own smartphone, which he'd prepared moments ago. 'Been in Lewisham long?'

'Twenty-three days.' Leather didn't expand.

'Right, nice one. Listen, Jason – can I call you Jason?'

'That's my name, so, yeah.' He switched the hand grip to his right palm while the left took over at the keyboard.

'OK. Can you tell me what this is?' He produced his phone and rotated the screen to Leather. On it was the photo he'd taken in Troy's house of the machinery inside the small unit. 'My wife sent me the pic, but I'm not much good with technical stuff, so…'

Leather glanced at it for a fraction of a second. 'It's a Netgear Nighthawk X10.'

Boateng let the silence hang; that was usually a good way to get someone to say more.

'VPN router,' added Leather. 'High spec.'

'And what would you use it for?'

Leather sniggered. 'Do you mean, what would I use it for? Or what would a mortal human being use it for?'

'Either.' Boateng had dealt with a lot of technical people in his time. He had to appeal to Leather's specialist knowledge, play to his ego. Then they might get somewhere.

'Well.' Leather stopped flexing the grip and rotated his chair to Boateng. 'Mainly, you use it for disguising your IP address and generating point-to-point encryption.'

'OK. Because you want to…'

'Access something you shouldn't be able to get online, like a TV programme that's only available in a foreign country.'

'Anything else?'

'Basically, to hide what you're doing. Fool anyone that's looking for you into thinking you're somewhere else in the country, or another part of the world.'

'Who does that?'

Leather blew out his cheeks. 'Shitloads of people. Criminals, terrorists, hackers, government agents, or just someone who wants to watch BBC iPlayer without a TV licence.'

'Could you work out what they were hiding?'

'Depends. Theoretically, yeah.'

Boateng pocketed the phone. 'Thanks, Jason. I'll let you get back to it.'

Without a word, Leather spun towards the screen, picked up his grip and resumed the rapid squeezes. Boateng finally relaxed, relieved to get away. But one phrase stuck in his mind, in the network engineer's monotone: *to hide what you're doing.*

CHAPTER SIX

Jim knocked on the door; no response. He waited. That was normal; he knew his boss had a lot of irons in the fire. This particular job was full-time for Jim, but it would be just one of several for the big man. He didn't envy that responsibility. Better to stay in the background. Some people liked high-stakes games, but the power of life and death? That was too much. Jim was content to leave those decisions to others, like the boss.

'Come.'

Jim opened the door and stepped into the large office. Despite its size, the furnishings were minimalist, almost spartan; the decor of a person too busy to care about rugs, cushions or comfort. No one had stopped to consider how to fill the space. Room size was proportional to authority, whether or not the space was needed. His boss probably regarded the seven seconds needed to cross between door and desk as wasted time. The heating was off and Jim felt goosebumps lift on his arms and neck as he walked over to the empty chair.

'Sit down.'

The boss was in his high-backed leather chair, behind the usual mass of paperwork, files and folders. Jim examined the top of his bowed head as he signed and dated some document. He noticed the scalp was flaking slightly beneath the thin, grey hair. His boss's suit was tailored, and the fine, dark wool looked expensive, but the shirt, tie and pocket square were mismatched. He knew the big man had taste, which suggested the outfit had been thrown together while his mind was on other matters.

'Troy McEwen,' said the boss, slapping a heavy fountain pen on the blotter in front of him. 'What the fuck's going on?'

Jim coughed into his fist. 'Detective Inspector Zac Boateng, he's the guy who found—'

'I know who he is.'

'He went back to McEwen's house yesterday.'

'Why?'

'I don't know, sir.'

The boss drummed his fingers on the desk. 'What did he do there?'

'I'm not sure, I couldn't see anything. He was inside for almost three hours, then came out with a couple of cardboard boxes. Couldn't tell what was in them, but they looked heavy.'

He knew the big man was irritated at the lack of detail. The boss stared at him, not making eye contact but instead scrutinising Jim's cleft lip, his eyes making tiny movements as they followed the scar from mouth to septum and back down. He was used to that. People stared at his lip a lot.

'And you're tracking his phone?' said the boss, eventually.

Jim nodded. 'What do you want me to do?'

'Stay on Boateng. He knows something, and it's not in my interests for it to become public knowledge.'

'I understand.'

'And it may become necessary to remove him.' The big man wafted a hand. 'If he gets too close. You carrying?'

'9 mm pistol, sir. In the car.'

'Good. You might need it soon.' The boss picked up his fountain pen and took another document off the pile. 'That's all for now. Keep watching.'

Jim could do that. It was what he did best.

●

This could be the break they'd been waiting for. Jones hustled downstairs towards the custody suite, Malik and Connelly with her. A call had come up to the MIT office ten minutes earlier, from the custody sergeant, to say that a man named Antony Webb, arrested that afternoon for a public order offence, claimed to have information on the murder of a Turkish man. But he refused to leave the holding cell, saying he wasn't safe outside. Boateng was in a briefing session with DCI Krebs, so Jones decided to take the initiative and follow up immediately, hoping Boateng would be impressed by her judgement call. She pictured herself interviewing the guy, winning his trust, coaxing out the details on Mehmet Bardak's death and blowing Op Spearhead wide open. She couldn't get down there fast enough.

'Which room?' she asked the custody sergeant, imperious behind his high counter.

'Cell 18. Far end on the left.' He pointed along the corridor. 'If he's got proper evidence, young lady, he'll have to give it on record.'

'Sure.' She resisted the temptation to remind him that she was the one who'd passed detective's exams. 'Let's just see what he has to say first. What's he in for?'

'Threatening violence. He was wandering around by Lewisham clock tower. Unarmed, but said he'd kill anyone who came near him. Boys had one hell of a job arresting him – he's a big lad. The constable will show you where he is.'

Jones turned to see a huge uniformed officer standing behind them. He was over six foot, and his biceps, chest and shoulders seemed close to bursting out of his shirt. She guessed he was only a few years older than her, perhaps thirty, but he was almost completely bald and had shaved off what little hair remained. His cheeks were pocked with acne scars. Jones zeroed in on the name badge: Constable Evans. She glanced at the others: Malik had a look of awe on his face; Connelly, suspicion. Evans pushed between them, jangling a big set of keys. 'Follow me,' he said, in a surprisingly well-spoken baritone. They walked through a door and under a security camera, passing cells on their left and right, a couple of prisoners muttering to themselves behind the walls. It was rare for a detective to be down here; the place was effectively a jail, with many of the cells used as overspill from London's crowded prisons.

Pausing outside Cell 18, Evans turned to them. 'You realise this bloke is a nutter.'

'We'll judge that for ourselves,' she told him.

'Don't say I didn't warn you.' He hammered on the cell door and slid the tiny window up, glancing inside. Then, without another word, he unlocked the door and swung it open.

Webb was sitting on the bed. He was massive, overweight, all beard and hair, dressed shabbily in tracksuit trousers and a woolly jumper. He smelled as if he hadn't showered in days, and Jones wondered if he'd been sleeping rough.

'Hello, Mr Webb,' she began, stepping slowly into the room. 'I'm Detective Sergeant Kat Jones. We heard you'd like to talk to us.'

Webb pushed straggly hair from his eyes. 'Will you let me out?'

'Well, I can't do that, but I can promise to try and help you, if you help us.'

He glanced nervously from her to Malik to Connelly. 'I'll only talk to you.' He pointed at her. She nodded to the others, who stepped out of the cell, standing discreetly to the left and right of the open door.

'What can you tell us about the Turkish man who was murdered?' she asked.

'Mehmet.'

'That's right, that's his name.'

'Read it in the paper.'

'OK.' Jones hoped this was going to be worth the trip downstairs from their office. 'What do you know about his death?'

'They killed 'im.'

'Who did?'

Webb's gaze darted around the cell. 'The government.'

'Right. What do you mean?'

'You don't believe me, do ya?' Webb thrust an accusatory finger at her. In the corner of her eye, she noticed Connelly moving into the doorway.

'Hey, it's OK.' She held up both palms. 'I didn't say that. I'd just like to know more about it, please.'

Webb shook his head, hands trembling slightly. He seemed about to say something else, but stopped. Then, with surprising speed, he stood and threw himself at the open doorway, forcing his way past Connelly and into the corridor. She heard Malik shouting and emerged to see Webb locked in a struggle with Evans, the two powerfully built men grappling and breathing hard. Evans was trying to block his escape, but Webb was taller and bulkier. He knocked Evans off balance, sending him stumbling backwards, then advanced towards him, arms out, fists ready. Evans drew his baton and extended it with a crack, then swung it at Webb, but missed. Webb lunged forward and grabbed his arm, the baton now held fast between them as they lurched together towards the main door. Evans threw a kidney punch with his left hand but it had no effect on Webb. Connelly and Malik stood close by, poised to intervene but unable to get closer as the two giants wheeled round, neither man in control. The custody sergeant had appeared in the main doorway with his baton ready. Detainees began hammering on their cell doors in support of the ruckus.

'You won't kill me!' bellowed Webb. Evans's baton flailed up and back, smashing the security camera just above the door. Webb twisted to look, planting his feet for balance. Before he could react, Evans rammed a knee into his groin and the prisoner dropped, gasping for air between screams, slapping the floor in pain. Connelly and Malik raced across as Evans pulled his arm back, ready to strike. Connelly caught his baton mid-air and Malik hooked his other arm.

'Fucking scum!' yelled Evans, straining forward. 'You want some more?'

Connelly was struggling to stop him swinging the weapon. 'Easy, lad!' he cried. 'He's not going anywhere now.'

'Get off me,' snarled Evans, shaking Malik and Connelly away and rounding on the Irishman, who had assumed a boxing stance, ready to defend himself. Evans had the baton half raised, spit trailing from his mouth, eyes wild.

'That's enough!' Jones stepped forward, arms out. She pulled Connelly back and moved in front of him, placing herself between Evans and the others. Her heart was pounding against her ribs and she could feel her top lip quivering, but she stood firm. Evans glared down at her, his chest heaving, but the baton began to lower.

The custody sergeant was kneeling on Webb's back, cuffing his hands.

'You see?' shouted Evans, pointing his baton at Webb. 'Told you he was a nutter. He could've killed you in that cell.'

'But he didn't, did he?' Jones tried to keep her voice even. 'He wanted to get out because he was scared.'

'Well, now he should be scared.' Evans smirked. 'Of me.'

'Alright, Constable Evans, put the baton away.' The custody sergeant eased himself off Webb, who had stopped struggling. 'Let's get this fella back into his cell.' Then, to Jones: 'Don't worry, young lady. We'll have a forensic medical examiner come down and check him over. If the counsellor's free, he could drop in for one of his nice chats, too.'

Jones ignored his passive sexism; she was used to it. She suspected that a call to local mental health services would confirm that Antony Webb was known to them. If they were lucky, they could persuade a liaison psychiatrist or psychiatric nurse to visit the station, or for Webb to be taken down the road to Lewisham hospital for assessment. Chances were that he needed some medication, then perhaps they could speak again. Maybe he was deluded, a bit paranoid, but she didn't want to dismiss his words out of hand. That's what Boateng would do: treat every lead as serious until proven otherwise. She hoped she wasn't clutching at straws.

'Come on, guys.' Jones steered Malik and Connelly out of the corridor. 'We'll talk to Mr Webb again later, once he's seen a doctor.' She shot a glance at Evans. 'And when there's a different officer on duty.'

Etta had never thrown a punch in her life. In fact, she'd go as far as saying she hated violence. Yet, as she had stepped through the doors of Double Jab Boxing Club in New Cross, something felt right. Women of all ages, shapes and sizes were training: some hitting the bags, others skipping, a few on the fitness equipment in the other room. Before coming here, Etta wasn't sure if boxing would be her thing; she didn't have an aggressive bone in her body. But maybe she was missing the point.

Her friend Jennie swore by the place, especially these female-only sessions. She'd said it wasn't just about fitness; it was discipline, self-development, confidence. Using your body in a new way – a change from spinning, yoga or Zumba. Now, Etta could see what she meant.

Two younger women were sparring in the elevated ring, their faces barely recognisable behind headgear and gumshields. They traded punches, ducking and weaving, staying on their toes. There was a self-defence element to it, but practical uses aside, this looked like fun. She realised she was smiling.

The coach started her off with some basic shadow-boxing, getting the feel of a jab. Pretty soon, her shoulders were burning, arms heavy with lactic acid. Her calf muscles ached with the up-and-down movement, back and forth, over and over. But it was a good tiredness, one she'd worked for. This was exactly what she wanted after the stress of the past few days.

She became aware of a rhythmic slap and grunt from across the gym. When the coach signalled her to stop and take a break, Etta grabbed her water bottle and turned to see where the noises were coming from. A woman, tall and athletically built, with well-defined thighs and shoulders and a full-sleeve tattoo on one arm, was working on a heavy bag. Her long, red hair was pulled back tightly into a ponytail, exposing a close-shaved undercut. But it wasn't just her physical appearance that was arresting. It was the power with which she was striking the bag. Etta stood, mesmerised, as the woman rained punch after punch with increasing force. Even the huge man holding the bag for her was struggling with the bigger hits, though he didn't say a word. There seemed to be something driving her fists, a fury from within, palpable in every grimace and snort. Etta imagined some terrible pain had given rise to this rage.

The coach called Etta back for another round of shadow-boxing, and she returned to her station invigorated. She resumed the jab combinations, concentrating her mind and body, trying to hit like the red-haired woman.

*

The second one will die tonight. Someone who has never properly been punished for their crimes. There should be a satisfaction in killing them; a catharsis. But maybe it'll be the same as the first: blank, the absence of feeling. Just a job, something that should have been done a long time ago. That numbness is probably a good thing for the moment; I don't want emotions getting in the way. Not when there are three more to deal with after tonight; a lot more work to do.

When it's finished, perhaps I can enjoy it. Watch them scratch their heads, trying to make sense of it. Trying to piece together things that don't fit. Trying to find an answer. There isn't much hope of them working it out, though, because the information they need to understand this is known only to a few people, all of whom are going to die before they share their secret. And one of them is Zac Boateng.

CHAPTER SEVEN

Tuesday, 5 December 2017

Stepping into Summers's office was like stepping out of Lewisham police station. Almost as soon as Boateng had assumed his position in the comfortable chair opposite the young therapist, with the low lighting, the quiet intensity of Summers's attention focused on him, he'd begun to relax. Summers had set the boundary of fifty minutes together, then asked him how he'd like to use the time.

Boateng hesitated. 'Well.' He coughed. He wasn't used to this. 'Like I mentioned yesterday, I lost an old mate last week.'

Summers nodded. 'And how are you feeling about it now?'

'Pissed off. No, I mean, that sounds selfish. Sad, I guess. But more… angry, if I'm honest.'

'That's quite common with a recent bereavement. What about it would you say is making you feel that way?'

Boateng was silent. He glanced down, brushed a speck of fluff from his suit trousers.

Summers cocked his head. 'It's a safe space here, Zac.'

'I know, it's just…' What the hell, he was here now, and this was confidential. Counsellors were bound by oaths about stuff like that, he was sure. He took a deep breath. 'I think Troy was murdered. That's why I'm angry, because I believe someone killed him and no one else agrees with me. Not even my wife,' he added.

Summers shifted his position; Boateng guessed he was trying not to make his shock too apparent. 'Feeling anger is normal when a death is unexpected,' began Summers, slowly. 'All the more so if a person was murdered. But...' He looked unsure how to voice the obvious response. 'I understood that Troy had killed himself. What makes you say he was murdered?'

Troy. Summers had used his first name. That suggested he had known him: a confirmation of Troy's diary entry, despite Summers's professional refusal to comment yesterday. Boateng couldn't open up to him about the incident in '98, about the possibility that someone might have wanted revenge on Troy after all these years and may yet be seeking revenge on others – him included. Reminded of the danger he was facing, he felt that tremor of fear return, spreading quickly through him. But perhaps Etta and Krebs were right and he was seeing shadows where there were none. 'Instinct' wasn't a good enough answer to Summers's question. He imagined himself saying it; the word sounded weak. He was aware that nearly thirty seconds had passed in silence since the therapist's question. 'I don't know,' he said feebly.

'That's OK.' Summers gave a gentle smile. 'You know, high levels of emotion can make it hard to think, and they can lead us to judgements that we otherwise wouldn't reach. If there's something more, we can talk about it when you feel ready. But I should remind you that my confidentiality can be broken if what you say makes me think you or someone else might be in danger.'

'Sure.' Then it hit Boateng: maybe this was the way to access Summers's knowledge of Troy. He just needed to present the counsellor with evidence that Troy was involved in something that could have serious implications for others, then he'd be obliged to talk. Would it be courtesy of Dez Hayworth at his scrapyard, or the red-haired journalist Faye Rix and her source? Was the answer in Troy's house, with his specialised computer kit? At the moment, all Boateng seemed to be facing were dead ends. But he'd been in this position with investigations before, and if nothing else, he was tenacious. A stubborn bastard, some might say. The trick was knowing when stubbornness became self-destructive. And in forty-three years, he hadn't mastered that yet.

Jones looked up from her desk as Boateng crossed the open-plan office towards her. There was a lightness and purpose in his step that hadn't been there the previous afternoon. It was nearly 10 a.m. and she hadn't seen her boss yet today, though she knew he was in because his Chesterfield overcoat and flat cap were on the stand by their desks.

'Sorry I've not been around, guys,' he said, hands spread in apology. Malik and Connelly glanced up too. 'Had a medical appointment this morning.'

She put her pen down. 'You OK?' He nodded. She didn't want to pry any further. 'We've had some good news – well, news, at least.' She wasn't sure if anything about a murder investigation could be described as 'good', unless it was the judge's sentencing at the end of it. And even that was all too rare.

Boateng helped himself to coffee and sat down, grimacing as he sipped and registered that it was cold. 'Go on.'

'Lab came back with a positive fibre match for the samples found at Mehmet Bardak's murder and at the store where Vikram Kumar was attacked, which we're treating as attempted murder. So, they're officially linked now, with at least one common suspect.' Jones grinned. She knew that occasionally such reactions to police work might seem inappropriate, but she'd already learned that if you didn't celebrate the small victories – those incremental steps towards breaking a case – then you'd lose all motivation for the Job.

'What do we know about the fibres?' asked Boateng.

Jones consulted the forensic report on her screen. 'Black wool, with identical colour profile, cross section and age. There's a 99.9% probability that both samples originated from the same garment.'

Boateng scratched his neck. 'Probably a balaclava or gloves, maybe a scarf. Something you take on and off a lot, which would loosen the fibres. Good result, Kat. Now, we just need to find the owner of that item of clothing, and maybe he'll have the original to match it to. Easier said than done. Any DNA on the samples?'

Jones shook her head.

Connelly rocked back in his chair, eyebrows arched. 'I'd imagine half of south London owns something made out of black wool.'

'It's a step forward, Pat,' said Boateng evenly. 'What about suspects?'

Connelly jerked a thumb at the mobile whiteboard, which had around a dozen mugshots stuck on it now; all white men between twenty and fifty years old. 'These are the likely lads who've been associated with National Right, according to our databases. Since there's still no leads from the money or CCTV, looking into this lot is probably our best chance of success.' He pressed his lips together. Jones knew he thought the attacks were not racially motivated, that they were barking up the wrong tree by following National Right. Something told her that he was keen for her theory to flop, to see her wings clipped. She didn't have Connelly marked as one of those old guard who took an instant dislike to anyone under thirty, with a university degree, who'd been promoted beyond constable. Some of those guys just seemed to be marking time until their retirement. Maybe he was more like them than she'd previously imagined.

'I've run traces on the new names,' offered Malik, his tone more optimistic. He glanced at her for approval. 'Quite a few convictions racked up between them. I haven't located the source that named Hayworth as part of the group, though.'

Boateng surveyed the board. 'So, these are our Spearhead targets? Anything connecting any of them to either crime scene, apart from Rogers's DNA on the fiver?'

They were all silent, Jones included. She'd briefed him on their abortive interview with Antony Webb yesterday, and her hope to speak to him again, albeit with the slim possibility of aiding their hunt for the murderer. Apparently, the in-house counsellor had visited the cells, made a quick assessment of Webb and referred him on to a liaison psychiatrist at the hospital. That was good, but she was pissed off with herself for getting so carried away with it at the time.

'OK.' Boateng leaned forward, elbows on his knees. 'We need to remember that this is a murder inquiry, not an operation to counter extremism. Everything we do needs to focus on who killed Bardak and who attacked Kumar. If there are two incidents that are linked, then we should be prepared for a third.'

The idea came to her in a flash. 'What if it was one of them – say, Dale Rogers – but we could prove that the others knew about it? That's joint enterprise. We could go for the lot of them. Even though the law's tighter now, we might get manslaughter.'

Boateng nodded. 'I like it, Kat. Great idea.' She felt herself redden slightly at the praise. It meant a lot. 'Let's take what we've got on the two attacks, plus these new names, and run it all through HOLMES. See if that gives us any new ideas. Geographical links, maybe?' He turned back to the board.

Jones knew the HOLMES system stopped loose ends creeping into investigations and reduced the chance of missing obvious leads. But it was clunky and often only as good as the human querying it or interpreting its output. 'We'll check it out,' she said. 'Do you want us—'

'What's this?' Boateng leapt to his feet. He was pointing at one of several names listed on the periphery. *Faye Rix.* 'How did she get on here?'

Malik squinted across at the network they'd sketched out. 'Faye Rix. She's listed as living at the same address as Liam Rogers, brother of our DNA-fiver suspect. I checked the electoral register. Could be his partner? You told us to build up an intelligence picture,' he added, catching Boateng's confused expression.

'D'you know her, boss?' asked Connelly.

Boateng hesitated before responding. 'You all saw her on Friday night. She was the journalist who doorstepped me outside the station.'

'The red-headed lass? I'd remember her anywhere.' A broad smile spread across Connelly's face.

'But… Rix wanted to know about Troy McEwen, right?' Jones was struggling to comprehend the connection. It was quite a coincidence.

'Yeah,' replied Boateng. 'And I didn't tell her anything.'

She waited for him to elaborate, but he said no more. Perhaps he was still sensitive about discussing his friend's death; it had only been five days. Just as she was wondering how to follow up, Jones had the uncomfortable sensation of eyes on her. She turned sideways to see Jason Leather behind a computer, staring across at her, expressionless. He immediately dropped his gaze and carried on typing. She scanned the office. There was so much sensitive material on display here, and Leather had access to it all: photographs, crime scene reports, suspect lists, op names, even their conversations. His intervention at their briefing yesterday showed that his hearing was obviously sharp. Still, if he was here, it meant he had the proper security clearances. OK, so he was a bit weird, but he wasn't the only creep in Lewisham police station. And she had more important things to worry about right now. Like how to make some progress in this investigation before anyone else got attacked and killed.

Boateng filled a plastic cup from the water cooler and stood alone in the narrow office kitchen, staring at the wall. He took a sip and felt a cold sensation flowing down and into his stomach, much as when he'd seen Faye Rix's name on their target board. What was going on here? Now that Malik had turned up a link between the journalist and Liam Rogers – an associate of Hayworth's – it suggested that Troy was somehow connected to these Spearhead targets. If Rix and Rogers shared a flat, then he was probably her source on the 'involvement' between Hayworth and Troy. But why would he give her that information, knowing she was a journalist? Even if they were a couple, it didn't make any sense. Boateng felt like tipping the rest of the water over his head on the off-chance it would stimulate his brain. Before he followed that thought, a chime in his pocket announced the arrival of a personal email, and he automatically reached for the phone. Probably just an update on his five-a-side football practice. Nonetheless, like everyone else these days, he was programmed to read messages instantly. He flipped the cover and tapped his PIN—

'Zac.'

He spun round, like a schoolboy busted smoking, to face Krebs. Realised his heart was thumping. That wasn't normal; it was the reaction of a person on edge. A person with something to hide.

'Ma'am.'

She dipped her head. 'How are you doing?'

'Fine, thanks.' He took a deep breath.

Krebs continued to regard him, concern etched on her face. She obviously needed a bit more evidence.

'I've had a counselling session with Tom Summers, like you suggested.'

'Wonderful.' She beamed and folded her arms with satisfaction. 'People say he's excellent. All voluntary, as well. He's doing it for some advanced training course.'

'Seems like a good bloke.' Even as he said it, Boateng knew his judgement of Summers rested not on his therapeutic skills, but on how much the younger man would reveal about Troy.

'And Spearhead?'

He filled her in on the fibre match, the mapping of National Right's network, the use of HOLMES. He omitted the part about Troy being somehow associated with it, for now.

'I assume you'll be making a public appeal?' Her query sounded more like a statement.

Boateng usually liked to exhaust other options before going public; appeals were generally a sign that they were getting nowhere, and often produced more chaff than wheat. 'Yes, we're considering it.'

'I'll expect something prepared by the end of the day, then. I'm happy to be involved in any press briefings.'

'Ma'am.' He knew Krebs wouldn't miss a chance to get in front of a camera or be quoted in a paper. That was all fuel for her journey up to superintendent. More often than not, she had his back, but Krebs was definitely quicker to associate herself with his successes. As she walked away, Boateng entered the PIN for his phone and opened the email app.

The rest of the room seemed to blur as he focused on the sender: *McEwen, Troy.* Boateng's palms prickled with sweat. No mistake; it had arrived two minutes ago. He glanced up, as if expecting someone to reveal the prank, but the rest of Lewisham MIT were about their business. He tapped the email and the message appeared. It had been forwarded from Troy's usual address. The original sender was Dez Hayworth.

Troy – you have been a naughty boy, havent you son? You thought you could get away with it, taking us all for a bunch of mugs. If its money your after, you can fuck right off. This is going to cost you big time. Don't forget, my memory goes WAY back. People love to get the truth behind LIES – everyone wants to read about that, don't they?

Boateng pocketed the phone and wiped clammy hands on his trousers. If Hayworth was blackmailing Troy – or counter-blackmailing him – did that make it more likely that Troy was murdered? It had to relate to '98. He began to walk slowly back to his desk. Boateng knew that the technical data of the email could offer leads, including where it was sent from, but he was hesitant to submit it for analysis under Spearhead: Hayworth was only a marginal target and there was nothing to link Troy to the two attacks. He'd definitely need to pay Hayworth another visit, that much was clear. Maybe Leather could take a look at the message, unofficially…

As Boateng crossed towards the desk where Leather was working, half hidden behind a fan of monitors, Malik raced over and intercepted him.

'Boss! We need to go. Local units have found a body. Murder victim.'

'They're sure it's a murder?'

Malik swallowed, nodded.

CHAPTER EIGHT

Boateng hadn't expected to return to the scrapyard in Sydenham so soon. He retraced his footsteps through the iron gates and across the yard piled high with dead appliances, Jones alongside him. Scene of crime officers were already at work in their hooded white suits and face masks, photographing, marking and sampling. The activity intensified as they entered the rear section, where claustrophobic alleyways formed between the walls of crushed cars. He and the others from the MIT had already donned their own basic protective kit, enough to reduce unnecessary contamination of the scene. Standard procedure whenever a body was found. They flashed warrant cards and one SOCO pointed them past another corner, simply shaking her head. He and Jones exchanged a glance and stepped around.

Even after years of murder inquiries, Boateng was not prepared for the nightmarish scene on the other side. Seated on a metal chair, between two stacks of old vehicles, one rubber tyre round the waist, another round the neck, was a body. It was smaller and thinner than he'd expected. The exposed skin of head and hands was charred black and blistered. Soot lay over ragged, burned clothes. The arms were bent at the elbow, fingers and hands curled inwards. The legs had flexed at the knees, drawing the feet under the chair. Boateng had seen this once before, in a house fire: they called it the pugilist stance. Extreme heat caused the large muscles to shrink, pulling the body into the defensive pose of a boxer. As they approached, he caught a waft of sweet petrol fumes and felt something lurch in his guts.

'DI Boateng,' said one of the white suits, turning to him. He took a moment to register who it was, the only clue her sharp blue eyes, watery in the cold air. Among London's forensic pathologists, he trusted Dr Mary Volz the most. Her observations and deductions had proved pivotal on his cases in the past. There was no pomp, no ego and no chit-chat with her. Given most of their interactions were over dead bodies, that suited Boateng fine.

'What've you got so far?' he asked.

Her mask flared out slightly as she exhaled. 'Not much to identify this chap, but the young man who discovered him earlier is convinced it's Dennis Hayworth, the owner of this place.' Boateng had deliberately dispatched Connelly and Malik to interview the guy off-site; he suspected it would be the axe-wielding assistant he'd encountered before and wanted to avoid any possibility of being recognised from his previous visit.

He took a step closer and inspected the body. The corpse had a thick watch on the left wrist, much like Hayworth had been wearing a few days ago, chinks of gold visible beneath the soot. Peering into the neck tyre, he noticed the same chunky silver cross at the victim's collarbone. He thought back to the fleshy figure he'd confronted in the Portakabin on Saturday. 'These look like Hayworth's watch and chain,' he ventured. 'But I knew him, and he was a lot bigger than this person.'

'Prolonged fire exposure will do that,' said Volz. 'Several hours of burning can cause a body to lose more than half its weight. Once he's at the mortuary, we can check the teeth against Hayworth's dental records and confirm his identity.'

Boateng nodded. 'What about time of death?'

'Fire does make that more difficult to estimate accurately, but we have some clues. Looks like heat damage stopped his watch just before eleven, so the fire was alight then. Given that the tyres were cold when we arrived, we're talking eleven last night, not this morning. That's consistent with the dryness of the skin here,' she added, pointing at the hands. 'So, I'd guess he was killed between around 8 p.m. and midnight.'

'OK.' Boateng studied the body position. 'No restraints other than the tyre, and the chair hasn't been tipped over.'

'There doesn't seem to have been much of a struggle.' Volz continued his line of thinking. 'You're wondering what made the victim accept his fate so meekly?'

'Right. Even if you were coerced into that chair at gunpoint, you'd move once the fire started,' he said. 'Try to hit the ground, roll around, put it out.'

'Maybe he was already dead when he was set alight?' offered Jones. 'Or knocked out, at least.' She was holding it together pretty well. Boateng briefly wondered if she'd ever seen a body in this state before.

'That's possible,' said Volz. 'But there are no signs of blunt force trauma; no stab or bullet wounds. So, if he was unconscious, he was probably drugged. Toxicology report should tell us, assuming we can salvage anything from inside him.' She gestured to the larger tyre at the corpse's waist. 'His abdomen has split open beneath the rubber. That can happen when sustained heat causes internal gases to expand. I just hope he wasn't alive when it occurred.'

They contemplated this in silence for a moment before Boateng spoke. 'Anything else you can tell us for now?'

'Only this.' Volz stooped to indicate the forearms and lower legs. 'Can you see how the burns are more extensive at the extremities? It looks like they were lit first, and the trunk and head burned later.'

'Torture?'

'That's quite likely. The tyres were probably used afterwards to keep the body alight. If the victim wasn't already dead by then,

' that would have finished him off. And it may have been a way for the killer to erase any traces of their DNA.'

Boateng and Jones stepped back to allow the SOCOs to continue.

'The killer didn't take his jewellery,' stated Jones. 'So I doubt it was a robbery gone wrong. Just ruling out the obvious.'

'I agree.'

'Do you think it's linked to Spearhead?' she asked. 'I know Hayworth wasn't directly connected to it, but it's one hell of a coincidence, right? We put him on our ops board and he's murdered less than a day later.'

'Maybe,' he replied, vaguely.

'What is it?' Jones cocked her head. 'You OK, Zac?'

'There's something not right,' he replied. 'In the method. This is an execution. Tyres around the neck, burning – it's an extreme form of punishment used across the world – Africa, Asia, Latin America. Normally reserved for people who've broken the rules, big time. It's vengeance.'

'Do you think it might've been payback for the Spearhead attacks, by Bardak's or Kumar's family?'

'No, I…' Boateng frowned. 'What I mean is, why would you drug someone senseless – even unconscious – in order to execute them, then spend time torturing them?'

Jones shook her head. 'Maybe the murderer enjoyed it? Some psychopaths get a kick out of hurting people.'

'True. But if the victim could feel that pain, he'd struggle. That's human instinct. Hayworth – if that's who this is – wasn't the type to go without a fight. And he didn't move. He wasn't even tied to the chair.'

'Then I don't get it.' She shrugged, glancing back towards the body.

'Me neither.'

Right now, the only thought that came clearly to Boateng was that this represented a second data point, another victim connected to the incident in '98. Two dead; two still alive. And him. Boateng turned away, peeling off his gloves. His hands were trembling.

.

Jones hadn't eaten since she saw the corpse. Anytime she thought of food, her stomach acids churned and the image of scorched, broken flesh returned. She was almost getting used to the sour taste in her mouth. It was the gore that had shocked her, though she tried to hide it from Boateng and the others. She'd hoped that it would get easier with each murder victim she saw, but her reaction to this one was the strongest yet. Was it the drawn-out death by burning alive, which she kept imagining? Or just a simple biological response: the body trying to protect itself, her disgust system on overdrive? Either way, it was now nine hours since she'd last eaten. Despite the hollow pangs of hunger, she took one look at the chocolate muffins that Connelly offered – their dark surfaces cracked and mottled white – and waved the bag on. That was just too close.

An hour ago, dental records had confirmed that the victim was Dennis Hayworth. Krebs assigned the case to Boateng's team, since they'd already been looking at him in connection with Spearhead. They'd been working to generate leads since then. The scrapyard assistant who'd found the body hadn't been much help. He was obviously traumatised, but seemed wary of talking about his employer, monosyllabic to the point that they wondered what he might be hiding. Maybe he didn't want to get drawn into whatever Hayworth was doing that had led to his murder. In any case, the guy's alibis were rock solid: independent witnesses confirmed that he'd been at the gym in Lewisham until 10 p.m. before returning home to a shared house in Catford. The near silence could just be his way of coping.

There was an estranged daughter somewhere that the Family Liaison Officer had identified and was contacting to break the news; Jones wondered if it would be greeted with sadness, joy or indifference. She thought briefly about her own father. She had never seen his body after the car accident; her final memory of him would forever be of a strong, capable man in uniform on his way out to work that day. Maybe that was best. Life in the MIT was starting to teach her that violent death sucked any power and dignity from a human body, made it appear brittle and weak, almost pathetic. She didn't want to remember her dad like that.

Jones caught herself: God, she was getting seriously morbid. Was that part of the Job too? Enough. The full post-mortem, scheduled for tomorrow, might offer more clues. But for now, they needed to answer the question Boateng had posed: who would've wanted Hayworth dead?

'A hell of a lot of people.' Malik tapped his biro on the notepad. 'The guy had six convictions. Two for assault, both GBH and ABH. Aggravated burglary back in '98 – that one was bad.'

Jones noticed Boateng shifting in his seat.

'Another count of burglary,' continued Malik, 'one firearms possession offence and some extortion to round it off. He'd spent more than half of his life in prison, and that was with early release on parole in each case. If he'd served his full sentences, then he would've been inside' – he checked the notes, frowning – 'longer than he'd been out.'

Connelly bit into a muffin. 'Maybe they should bury the fella in prison, just to be on the safe side.'

Boateng seemed to snap out of a trance. 'Thanks, Nas.' He took a deep breath. 'So, he was a man with a lot of enemies. There's the victims of those offences, as well as any crimes he wasn't caught and punished for, plus anyone inside the criminal world who might've wanted him dead. A rival, or someone he screwed over, maybe.'

Jones studied him. Boateng was normally razor-sharp, but something about his delivery today suggested his mind was elsewhere.

'What about the source on his link to National Right?' she asked.

'Dead end,' replied Malik, giving her an apologetic smile. 'There's no record of that intel being recorded on the Crimint system. Could be a technical problem. Or a filing error. Sorry.'

'Maybe it was a jilted lover that set him on fire?' offered Connelly, his eyebrows arched. 'Hell hath no fury…' He glanced at Jones. She didn't laugh. 'Come on,' he urged. 'I'm just trying to lighten the mood a bit. Let's face facts. This guy was a bastard and nobody's going to miss him now he's up in smoke.'

She wasn't interested in Connelly's jokes today. 'Hayworth was murdered,' she stated. 'He deserves justice, whoever did it. Doesn't matter if he was a bad guy killed for good reasons. It might've been the relatives of the Spearhead victims, for all we know. Even then, you can't just dish out a death sentence to someone. That's why we have laws.' She surprised herself with the force of her words.

'Alright, Your Honour.' He threw his hands up in mock surrender. 'Anyway, there's no proof yet that Hayworth was involved in the Spearhead attacks. That's your guesswork.'

'Oi, Pat.' Malik was scowling at the Irishman. Jones wished he wouldn't jump to her defence like this. It came from a good place, but she needed to argue for herself.

Connelly pointed at the younger man. 'Be fair now, lad. You can't just side with her all the time cos she's pretty.'

She flushed. 'What's that got to do with—'

'Hey, take it easy, everyone.' Boateng held up a palm. 'What actionable leads do we have for the moment?'

'The logbook thing in Hayworth's office,' replied Malik. 'That was a great find, boss.'

Boateng didn't acknowledge the praise. 'What's the latest entry in it?'

'A car, brought in at 8 p.m. last night. Peugeot 306, registration recorded. It wasn't in the yard – the other cars listed in the logbook were.'

'Might be our man. Or woman.' Connelly gave her a wink. He could be a real prick sometimes.

'So, maybe the killer comes in with a cover story about scrapping a car, and Hayworth makes a few notes,' continued Malik. 'Killer then strikes and uses the vehicle to get away, but doesn't realise that Hayworth has kindly written down the number plate for us to trace.'

'Not a bad theory, Nas,' said Boateng. 'You put it through the system?'

'Yeah. PNC says it belongs to Justin Edwards, with an address in London, SW16 – that's Streatham. Car's not reported stolen, and the guy doesn't have a criminal record.'

Jones shrugged. 'Could just be his last customer.'

'Maybe you're right, Kat.' Boateng inclined his head; he seemed to be considering something. 'Try to get hold of Mr Edwards anyway. Nas, can you run the car through DVLA as well? See if anyone else is insured on it.'

'No worries. It'll take a day, probably.'

'I hope we've got that long.' Boateng's jaw set.

'What do you mean?' asked Jones.

'Nothing.' Boateng clapped his hands, once. 'Let's get to it.'

•

Etta sat on Kofi's bed, an arm round her son. His bedside lamp cast a glow across the Anansi storybook. Kofi loved the old Ghanaian folk tales – almost as much as Zac, whose own father had told him the same fables from memory. Each generation passed them on to the next, and Zac kept up that tradition. Often, he would read to their son, but tonight he just sat quietly beside them.

He had told her about today's new murder investigation. On top of Troy's death last week, she could tell the pressure was piling up on him, visible in his distracted manner, his skittering attention. She knew he'd had the first counselling session that morning; they hadn't spoken about it yet, but she hoped it'd been OK and that he planned to go back for more.

'Boom!' Kofi slapped the page in delight. 'The lion fainted. Anansi played a trick on him with the magic rock and then stole his food!'

This was the problem with trying to teach a moral lesson through stories: kids often thought the bad acts were the best bits.

'Yes, he did,' she said carefully. 'He fooled all the animals with that magic rock and took their food for himself. But what happened next?' She tapped his fingers to signal that he should continue.

Kofi knew the story back to front. He flipped several pages at once. 'The little deer tricked him back!'

'Right!' Etta was pleased that her son had remembered Anansi's comeuppance after his campaign of deception. 'The small and shy deer waits patiently for Anansi to trip himself up with the magic rock. Then' – she pointed to the picture of the upturned, unconscious spider – 'the deer takes back everything that Anansi stole from the other animals.'

'But,' protested Kofi, showing her the last page of the story, 'Anansi didn't stop his tricks.'

Etta gave her son an admonishing smile. 'No, he didn't learn his lesson. What does the story tell us then?'

'That if you tell lies, you get good things?' Kofi giggled. He knew the right answer but liked to pretend it was the naughty alternative.

'Er, no!' She widened her eyes. 'It's the opposite, isn't it? If you tell lies, eventually they come back and cause you trouble.' She prodded him gently in the ribs, and he laughed again.

'What if you had no choice?' Zac said suddenly.

'Sorry, love?'

'I mean, what if you had to lie?'

She studied his face. He looked concerned, almost fearful.

'Anansi didn't have to lie,' she said to Kofi. 'Did he? He could have been honest, but he chose to trick the others.'

'Maybe sometimes there's no choice,' said Zac.

She reached out and flicked his arm. 'Hey, come on, Mr Morals. What are you teaching our son here?'

'Sorry, yeah.' Zac forced a smile. 'Your mum's right, Ko. Don't tell lies.' He walked his fingertips up Kofi's arm like a spider, and the boy flinched, batting them away. 'Or they'll come and get you in the end.'

•

Zac was scared. His gut feeling from Thursday night had grown and taken hold. Troy had been murdered because of their intervention 'back then'. Too many links to ignore: Troy and Hayworth in contact, apparent blackmail between them, and now both men dead. It pointed to a single person responsible. If he brought Hayworth's email – assuming it was genuine – out into the open, maybe people would take his idea about Troy being murdered seriously. He'd resisted doing that so far, because he preferred to leave that memory locked away, to protect himself. His position now was grim: tell people and risk his own job; or stay silent and potentially let others die. He might be putting himself or even his family at risk. No way. He made his mind up: he had to tell people what happened that day. Two others knew about it. One was a fellow officer, Ana-Maria de Souza. She and Zac weren't close; he didn't even know where she worked these days. The only other person still alive was a guy called Vic Walker, another career criminal like Hayworth. Zac knew he had to get in touch with de Souza to make sure she was OK. To warn her. Maybe she knew something about all this. He fired up Facebook on his phone and began searching. After a few false starts, checking

the pages of people with the same name, he found someone he
thought was her. The photo wasn't clear, but there was a strong
similarity to the woman he remembered working with back in
Kennington. He clicked on 'Message' and stared at the blank
box, wondering how to express himself. He typed:

Hey, are you alright?

His thumb hovered over the keypad. Eventually he began
typing again. He couldn't think of any better way to get his point
across, so he just wrote:

Need to talk about back then.

CHAPTER NINE

Wednesday, 6 December 2017

Doublethink – holding two incompatible thoughts at the same time – was stressful enough, but when your mind wouldn't slow down and you'd barely slept, it was almost impossible. Boateng couldn't reconcile the MIT's official investigation into Hayworth's death, built on the premise that it was payback for some recent criminal activity gone wrong, with his own theory of what had happened. And despite his resolution, he hadn't yet told anyone what he thought was really going on. He was just grinding through the motions with his team while he tried to work out what the hell to do next.

'Heroin?' he asked Connelly, who was scrolling through a CHIS – Covert Human Intelligence Source – report.

'Aye, that's what he says.'

'That Hayworth was a heroin importer?'

'Well' – the Irishman cocked his head – 'he doesn't exactly call him a heroin importer, just says he was mixed up in the business, like.'

'And by implication a drugs gang killed him.' Boateng pushed out his lower lip, nodded.

'You don't sound convinced,' observed Jones, who was sitting alongside him.

'I'm not.' Boateng glanced at her. 'What gang is it, then?'

Connelly shook his head. 'He doesn't know. Just something he picked up. Probably a load of bollocks, but if others are saying the same thing too, we could be on the right track.'

'Just because others say the same thing, that doesn't make it true,' said Boateng. 'Could be circular reporting.'

'Ah, the good old rumour mill.' Connelly grinned. 'We're used to that. It's how police stations operate, isn't it?'

Boateng allowed himself a brief chuckle, but it died abruptly with the recognition that they were no further forward. They'd put the word out to CHIS handlers yesterday afternoon. It was nearly 11 a.m. and they'd only had one response so far, which was probably just hearsay or fabrication to please a handler and get some cash. If Hayworth's death had been an organised criminal job, the wires would be buzzing on the street, word getting around. Instead, there was near silence. Still, he hoped to get some forensic reports back from the scene today, and that might—

'Boss.' Malik's tone was urgent. 'DVLA have come back to us.'

He stood and walked round to Malik's desk.

'The Peugeot 306 logged in Hayworth's book is insured for one other driver – a woman called Ana-Maria de Souza, date of birth July third, 1975. Same address in Streatham. Most likely his partner.'

'What the fuck?' Boateng couldn't contain his disbelief. But there it was on the screen: the personal details and photograph of his old colleague from Kennington station in the late nineties. The same person he'd messaged last night, though she hadn't responded when he checked Facebook this morning.

Jones came over to join them. 'Why'd you say that, Zac? Do you know her?'

He inwardly berated himself for the reaction; no point trying to hide it after that. 'Um, yeah.' He pointed at the screen. 'She's Job. We used to work together.'

'Could she be involved?' asked Jones, alarmed. 'Did she know Hayworth?'

Boateng swallowed, the panic rising again. 'She might've.'
He tried to process the news. His first instinct was that de Souza
couldn't have done that to Hayworth. But if she didn't, why was
her car recorded at his yard just before his death? Did she know
who had murdered him? Or was someone trying to suggest her
involvement by listing her car? Had something happened to her?
He could feel an insistent throb building at his right temple.

'Perhaps Hayworth was the target of another operation?'
suggested Jones. 'I mean, he appeared in that anonymous source
report in connection with National Right. Maybe de Souza is in
some special unit. Undercover, even?'

'Don't get carried away, Kat. Check the Met Directory and
find out where she works now,' he told them. 'Then I'll give her
a call and figure out what's going on.' Boateng returned to his
desk, grabbed his mug and marched off before anyone could ask
any more questions. This was all wrong.

He slipped into the staffroom, which was quiet, as usual; people
didn't hang around here. Only three others were in the room:
two uniformed officers at the kettle making tea; and a huge guy
seated alone, bodybuilder's frame hunched over a book. Boateng
perched against a table scattered with newspapers, took out his
phone and opened Facebook again. One new message. He got a
stab of adrenalin as he registered it was from de Souza, but the
anticipation quickly turned to disappointment when he read it.

*Hey Zac, long time! Didn't know you were on here. Yeah,
all good. What's up?*

Had she missed the reference in his message? His gaze roamed
around the room as he wondered how to reply. That was when
he clocked the name badge of the big guy: Evans. Boateng gave
a sharp intake of breath. This was the bloke Troy had fought in
Bromley; the man who'd knocked out a knife-carrying drug dealer

on Sunday night and who'd wrestled with the possible Spearhead witness Antony Webb down in the custody suite. He needed to contact de Souza, but he couldn't let this opportunity pass. As the two officers took their tea out, Boateng walked over, refilled the kettle and flicked it on.

'Want a brew?' he asked Evans.

Evans looked up, and Boateng saw that his face was badly scarred, probably by acne, the skin of his cheeks rough and pitted. Boateng guessed he was about thirty, but his baldness made him look older. Evans stared at him for a moment, his expression unreadable. 'Yeah,' he said, eventually. 'White, one sugar.' The smooth voice didn't fit his appearance.

Boateng threw tea bags in a couple of mugs. 'Any good?' He gestured to the book.

Somewhat reluctantly, Evans held up the cover: *American Sniper*. 'It's alright, yeah.'

'About Chris Kyle, right?'

Evans smiled. 'Most lethal marksman in US military history. Patient, dedicated, single-minded. He's talking about how they ran the operations in Iraq, drew on intelligence sources, planned it all out carefully. Then whack!' He mimed a backhand slap and laughed. 'They fucked people up. Evil people who had it coming to them and got what they deserved.'

Boateng considered the reality of that conflict a lot more complicated, but this wasn't the time to pick an argument. He nodded. 'So, you new?'

'Yeah.' Evans sniffed. 'Transferred.' He didn't elaborate.

'I'm Zac Boateng,' he said, pouring out the water. 'I'm in the MIT.'

'I know,' replied Evans. It wasn't the response Boateng had been expecting.

He forced a small chuckle. 'Don't believe what anyone round here tells you.'

'I don't. I looked you up.'

Boateng wasn't sure what to make of this. 'OK,' he said, noncommittally. 'Teabag out?'

'In, cheers.'

Handing him the drink, Boateng nodded at his name badge. 'You're Evans, then. Someone said you were in the army.'

'Used to be.'

'Why'd you leave? Had enough?'

'It was time for a new mission.'

'Uh-huh.'

When Evans didn't say any more, and resumed reading, Boateng decided to cut his losses. Maybe he could pick up the contact again later, try to find out what this guy knew about Troy over a beer. For the time being, his priority was to get hold of de Souza and work out how she fitted into the events of the past few days. He raised his mug. 'Enjoy your tea.'

Evans grunted a reply without looking up.

※

Something strange was going on. As Jones queued downstairs for coffee, she tried to piece together the unusual sequence of events involving Boateng in the past week. First, he found his friend dead by suicide. Shortly after that, he was looking at the Crimint data on a guy who, just two days later, was burned alive. She shuddered again at the thought. Then, a car recorded at the murder scene turned out to be driven by Boateng's old colleague. He wasn't giving them the full picture. It felt almost like that time six months ago, when he'd been freelancing with his own private investigation. She wanted to help.

She was about to give her coffee order when the guy ahead of her fumbled one of his cups and sent its contents across the counter, swearing as he shook his scalded hand. Reflexively, she moved sharply backwards, away from the splash. Off balance, she felt her back and bum contact something solid behind, and a pair of strong hands caught her by the arms. Mortified, she spun round to see a man standing in front of her. He was about six foot, maybe slightly over, with a slim, chiselled face, framed by dark brown hair, styled just enough to look good. His green eyes shone in the sharp lighting, and for a moment all she could do was gaze into them, speechless.

'Sorry,' he said with a smile. 'I just, um – I didn't want you to fall over.'

'It's OK,' she said quickly. 'Thanks. I could've ended up on my arse there.'

'Lucky escape.'

How could she have missed this hottie, standing right behind her for the last five minutes? She'd obviously been deep in concentration; she blamed Boateng. Jones assessed the guy's outfit of collared shirt, dark chinos and suede loafers; not formal enough for a detective, not street enough for a plain-clothes unit. Civilian analyst? She'd never seen him before. He wasn't wearing a security pass, which was unusual. *Make a move*, she told herself. Months on Tinder meeting nothing but chumps, and now this gift! *Don't wimp out.*

'Let me get you a drink,' she said. 'For saving me from stacking it in front of this lot.'

'Oh, you don't have to, I—'

'It's cool. What're you having?'

'Well, er, filter coffee, please. Very kind.'

She ordered two and turned back to him. 'Where do you work, then?'

'Right on the other side,' he pointed vaguely over one shoulder. 'I do the counselling sessions.'

'Oh, cool.' That was the second time she'd said 'cool'. *Come on, Kat.* She wished she hadn't yanked her hair back into a ponytail this morning, but it'd look weird if she tried to change that now, zhoosh it up.

'How about you?' he asked.

'I'm a detective – upstairs in the MIT.'

His eyes widened and she felt a little glow of pride in her chest. The drinks were placed in front of her and she tapped her card on the machine.

'I'm Kat,' she said, handing him one of the cups and pushing her chest out slightly.

'Tom.' He offered a hand and she shook it, both giving a little laugh at the formality.

'Good to meet you,' she said, looking back up at those eyes.

'You too.' He grinned, his cheeks dimpling. 'Well, ah, I've got to get back for another session, but, um' – he ran a hand through his hair – 'see you. And thanks for the coffee.'

'Sure, see you around.' As Jones turned to leave, she noticed Jason Leather standing alone at the far wall. Her smile vanished. The computer geek was watching her, expressionless, a cardboard coffee cup held in front of his black T-shirt. She didn't know how long he'd been there.

●

In a far corner of the sprawling MIT office, Jason Leather was staring dead ahead at a monitor, his fingers click-clacking over the keyboard. As Boateng approached, he could detect the tinny hum of what sounded like thrash metal leaking from Leather's earphones. The network engineer's jaw was clenched and an empty coffee cup sat crushed viciously in front of him.

'Jason?' Boateng arced his approach so that he entered the younger man's field of vision. 'Jason? Jason!'

'What?' Leather pulled the earphones out. 'I'm on the clock here.'

'Sorry.' Boateng glanced around. 'I've got something I need your help with.'

This seemed to do the trick. Leather stopped typing and spun his chair towards Boateng. 'Shoot.'

'Well, it's—'

'Is it about the VPN?'

'What?'

'The router. Do you want to know more about the router?'

'No, it's something else. You know what you said the other day, about hacking email?'

'Yeah.'

'Kind of related to that. If I give you a message, can you tell me where it was sent from?'

Leather frowned. 'What's this for?'

'An investigation,' replied Boateng.

'Don't you have a team of people to do that for you?'

'Yeah.' Boateng leaned down conspiratorially, close enough to smell the stale sweat on Leather's T-shirt. 'But those guys are all tied up doing counterterrorism work. It'll take them two weeks to get round to this. Plus' – he lowered his voice – 'they're shit. But if you don't know how to do it, then that's OK, I'll—'

'Course I know how to do it. Piece of piss.' He scribbled an email address on a sticky note and held it up. 'Forward it to me here. The complete, original message. Do *not* copy and paste it, or you'll lose the metadata.'

Boateng took the note. 'Then you can tell me where it was sent from?'

'I'll tell you what the sender had for dinner.'

'Really?'

'No. But I can tell you where it was sent from.'

'Awesome. Cheers, Jason.'

Leather coughed. 'Is this… official?'

'Not yet. That OK?'

'I can do covert.' A broad grin spread across Leather's face as he replaced his earphones.

It was only when Boateng returned to his desk and prepared to send on Troy's email that he realised the IT expert hadn't asked him for anything in return. He knew technical staff liked a challenge, but he'd expected some quid pro quo request. Maybe that would come later. As he teed up the message, Boateng wondered if he was making the right call. He quickly rationalised it: if Leather found anything that was relevant to Hayworth's murder, Boateng would immediately submit the same request to the Met's computer forensics guys. He'd go on the record as soon as he knew what he was dealing with here. He'd already made that decision last night. It was just a question of when. Did that count as doublethink? He pressed send.

*

Jim hastily knotted a necktie as he walked down Piccadilly. Luckily, he always kept one in the glove compartment, alongside his 9 mm sidearm. In his line of work, you never knew when either one might come in handy. He pushed open the door to Wiltons restaurant and scanned the interior. Jim was relieved to see he'd made the right decision on the tie. Despite that, he felt out of place. For a start, he was about thirty years younger than everyone else inside. When you were forty, there weren't many places where that happened. Then there was his tie. It wasn't from the right school; in fact, it wasn't from any school. He didn't seem to have got the memo about wearing absurdly bright socks with his suit, either. And where were all the women? The only ones he could see were waitresses. Jim thought he spotted a geriatric ex-prime minister at a table to his left. Or was he a former home secretary?

As the maître d' glided up to him, a hint of concern on his face, Jim wordlessly indicated his boss, tucked in a booth to one side. The maître d' gave a deep nod of recognition, allowing him to pass. Jim discreetly checked that the big man wasn't with anyone else before sliding onto the green velvet banquette opposite him, the light even dimmer here than in the entrance. He glanced at the silver bucket of ice water next to the boss, the gold foil of a champagne bottle poking up. His employer was writing something in a little leather-bound notebook and didn't register Jim's interest in the bottle. If he had, Jim wouldn't have asked for a glass. And if the boss had offered a glass, Jim would've declined. That was how these things worked. When the boss summoned Jim, it wasn't to have lunch with him. It was to get an update, then tell him to bugger off before the real lunch guest arrived. Someone important enough to bring the big man here and make him order champagne in the middle of the day.

The boss snapped his diary shut and looked up suddenly. His gaze was unblinking, like that of a bird of prey. 'Go on.'

'There's been another death,' said Jim. 'Yesterday, early hours. It looks like Hayworth.'

'Looks like?'

'There wasn't much left of him.'

'I see.'

'They're probably confirming his ID now,' continued Jim. 'The full post-mortem is later today. I should be able to find out for sure after that.'

'And Boateng?'

'I'm pretty sure it wasn't him, sir. He was at home with the lights off when it happened, and his phone didn't go anywhere.'

The boss plucked a silver fork off the table and inspected its hallmark in the lamplight. 'That's two gone, then.'

'The '98 incident?'

He pointed the fork at Jim. 'Remind me: how many people died that day?'

'Four, sir.'

'And how many survived?'

'Six, though one of them passed away later.'

'Are we sure about that?'

Jim shrugged. 'Sure as we can be.'

'So, there were five. And now there are three.'

Jim didn't know if he was supposed to respond to that. He kept quiet.

'Is Boateng covering his tracks?' resumed the older man. 'You'd imagine a detective would know how to avoid leaving evidence. Is he working with someone else?'

'I don't know, sir.'

The boss stared at Jim's lip for several uncomfortable seconds. Jim wondered if that was just what he did when he was thinking. Nevertheless, he self-consciously ran his tongue over the scar on the inside.

'Will we need to do anything about Boateng?' said Jim, breaking the silence.

'I'm not sure yet.' The boss put down the fork and sighed. 'If '98 gets out, it'll be big news. And we'll be fucked.'

Jim swallowed, nodded.

'As it stands, things are not looking good,' said the boss gravely. 'Not for us. And certainly not for Zac Boateng.'

CHAPTER TEN

Registering Boateng's arrival, Dr Mary Volz glanced up from the charred body, laid on its side. The limbs were still bent in the pugilist stance, although lying on the cold mortuary table, the term seemed even less appropriate than it had at the murder scene. Far from resembling a fighter, the victim appeared submissive, almost foetal.

'Come in, Inspector.'

Boateng approached and studied the corpse. It struck him again how much pain this person must have felt, their forearms and lower legs set alight before the murderer eventually decided to engulf their whole body in flames, sustained by rubber tyres and petrol to eliminate any chance of survival. This was a pitiless killer, a person who wanted to take their time. It wasn't heat-of-the-moment stuff. Boateng suspected the act – or acts, if the same person had murdered Troy – had been a long while in the planning. And that scared him even more.

'Anything that might give us a lead?' he asked.

'Not much so far. But there is one thing.' Volz beckoned him round. 'You can see here that the burns are far less extensive around the top of his hamstring muscles, buttocks and lower back.'

'Because those areas were up against the chair?'

'Exactly. They weren't directly exposed to the fire in the way that much of the rest of his body was. If you examine the skin here' – she indicated the base of his spine – 'what can you see?'

Boateng peered at the lumbar region, catching a whiff of cooked flesh off the body that made him reel back. Resuming his inspection of the marbled surface, he noticed a distinct area of dark discolouration.

'There.' He pointed. 'Looks like bruising.'

'Indeed. Anything special about it?'

'It's circular.' He remembered what Volz had said at the scrapyard. 'You think he was injected?'

'That's a safe bet. Given what happened afterwards, he was almost certainly administered some kind of paralysing agent. Wouldn't be the first time a murder has been committed that way.'

'Could you identify what it was?'

'I can't guarantee anything, but I'm going to take samples from his internal organs and have his blood plasma checked.'

'The drug might still be in his bloodstream?'

'Unlikely, but its metabolites could be. Most drugs react and break down inside the body, and they leave distinctive products that last much longer than the original substance. Unfortunately, the metabolites are sometimes the same as naturally occurring compounds, which means you can't be sure if they originated with the drug.' Her gauze mask shifted in a half-smile. 'But I'll do my best.'

As Volz moved across to a side bench to prepare equipment, the seed of an idea took root in Boateng's mind. He pictured Troy's living room, the arrangement of the body. A paralysing agent would've been the perfect method to set him up for what appeared to be suicide. Boateng closed his eyes briefly at the thought of his friend's final moments. At what point had Troy realised what was happening to him? Had he been ambushed and injected in the back, like Hayworth? Could the killer have been someone he knew? Even someone he invited into his house? The paralysis theory suggested that the same person may have killed both Hayworth and Troy.

'Mary,' he began. 'Can I ask you something?'

She didn't turn around. 'Fire away.'

'Did you hear about the death last week of the sergeant in Bromley? They found the body in his home.'

Volz stopped working, a Petri dish held in mid-air. 'Troy McEwen. Shotgun suicide, wasn't it? What a terrible shame.' She let out a long sigh. 'I can't pretend to know what you officers have to cope with on the front line. There are things that stay with you.' She glanced over her shoulder at the body. 'I experience some of that, but it's an order of magnitude higher when you're dealing directly with victims, family members, perpetrators.' She put the Petri dish down and turned to face him. 'This new wellbeing drive of ours is far too late, if you ask me. Officers should have ways and means to talk about what they're going through, and get help long before they attempt suicide, whatever their reasons. Poor Sergeant McEwen.'

Boateng took a deep breath. 'What if I told you he didn't commit suicide?'

Volz's clear blue eyes widened. 'You're saying his death was unnatural, Inspector?'

He outlined the theory to her: his knowledge of Troy's character over twenty-one years, the invitation for a drink on the day of his death, the antidepressants which he appeared to have been taking. He described Troy's link to Hayworth in vague terms, holding back from telling Volz about the email until he knew more. After her initial surprise had passed, the pathologist listened intently, dropping her gaze to the floor and nodding as he spoke.

'Troy's going to be buried tomorrow,' said Boateng. 'If I could arrange it with his family, is there any way you could test his blood plasma too, maybe as part of the same lab request?'

Volz looked at him for a long moment, studying his features. It felt like she was analysing his thought process, as she might scrutinise a sample under the microscope. She tucked a strand of grey hair behind her ear. 'Inspector Boateng,' she began, 'I know Sergeant McEwen was your friend. I understand how upset you must feel about his death. I've lost—' She stopped herself. 'It's heartbreaking to lose someone close to you so young, and in such traumatic circumstances. But there's no investigation into his death, no reason to think he was murdered, beyond your' – she searched for the words – 'personal conviction. Even if you could get a sample of his blood before he was buried, which itself is not a given, how could I justify requesting a toxicology work-up on it?'

Boateng was halfway through preparing his counterargument when Volz spoke again.

'Unless there's something else that makes you think the two deaths are connected?'

He hesitated. The chance to find proof of foul play in Troy's death versus opening the old case again. Boateng reminded himself of his vow the previous night to be open about what had happened in '98, but something held him back. There had to be another way. Leather was analysing the email, and they still hadn't been able to get hold of de Souza. He had to exhaust all other options before he risked igniting the tinderbox. 'No, nothing else. Not yet.' He set his jaw.

'Not yet?' Volz arched her eyebrows. 'Be careful, Inspector. I've seen that determination before – investigators deciding on their end point and desperately trying to fill in the blanks to get there. As a scientist, I start with a hypothesis and then test whether or not the data support it. There's less risk of confirmation bias that way. You may want your theory about Sergeant McEwen's death to be true, but as much as you believe it, that doesn't *make* it true.'

Boateng knew she was right. He decided to let it go, for now. He confirmed the timeline for toxicology with Volz, thanked her and made his way out of the building, grateful at least for his lead.

It was almost dark outside, the winter afternoon even colder than the mortuary. Boateng pulled his flat cap down and his collar up to keep out the biting air and hurried back towards his car. As he fished the keys from his pocket, a movement registered at the edge of his vision. But there was no one in the street. Had he imagined it? Boateng crept to the end of the high brick wall surrounding the mortuary buildings and glanced down the side road. A figure in a long dark coat was walking purposefully away from him. He watched as it turned into the street that bordered the long edge of the mortuary. Boateng had been here enough times to know the layout of the site. He quickly doubled back on himself, cut through the second mortuary entrance and broke into a jog to cross the gravel courtyard. The opposite wall was lower. He pulled himself up and over, dropping into a narrow car park on the far side. As he landed, a woman screamed and he backed away instinctively, hands raised. It took him another second to recognise who it was.

'Faye Rix,' he stated. 'Do you want to tell me what you're doing here?'

Overcoming her shock, Rix quickly regained her composure and cracked a smile. 'It's Dez Hayworth's post-mortem today, isn't it? I guess that's where you were just now.'

'It's none of your damn business where I was.'

'But it is my business to follow the news, Inspector.'

'Were you following me too?'

Rix emitted a single laugh. 'Don't flatter yourself. I'm here for the post-mortem. Would you care to comment on it? I heard the death was particularly' – she sucked her teeth – 'grizzly.'

'No comment.' Boateng was furious. How did Rix know the post-mortem was today? Then he remembered her link to Hayworth via the Rogers brothers. 'Did the family tip you off?'

Rix pursed her lips. 'As I told you last time we met, I don't have to disclose my sources to you. Especially not when I'm following a story of significant public interest.'

Boateng held up a finger. 'You're on my radar now.'

'And you're on mine.'

Despite the encroaching darkness, a shadow fell across Boateng and he turned to see Rix's giant friend staring him down.

'No dog this time?' Boateng asked the guy. He didn't expect a reply, and he didn't get one.

'He's got some behavioural issues, so we have to medicate him every now and then. Give him some stuff to calm him down,' said Faye Rix. 'Means we can't always take him out.'

Boateng narrowed his eyes.

'The dog, not Adam here.' She chuckled. 'Though you can get very protective, can't you, darling?' Rix raised her eyebrows. The big guy still said nothing.

Boateng snorted. 'Is that some kind of threat?'

'A threat?' Rix laughed again. If she weren't so Machiavellian, Boateng would've said that life was one big joke to her. She laid a hand on her chest. 'I'm the one that feels threatened, Inspector. I was calmly walking to my car when a man lunged at me from over a wall.'

'That isn't what happened.'

'How about we stop playing games?' She took a step closer to him and Boateng could smell her perfume. There was a latent power in the way she held herself. 'Two men dead in the space of a week and you're the thing that connects them. What's going on, Inspector?'

Boateng was silent.

'Of course, we could do an interview, an exclusive.' She spread her hands to illustrate a headline. 'Met detective blows lid on cover-up.'

'What the hell are you talking about?' growled Boateng. He felt the man behind him take a step closer.

Rix cocked her head. 'You used to work with someone called Ana-Maria de Souza, didn't you?'

Damn. Rix had to have an insider in the Met – maybe more than one. He checked his temper and held her gaze. 'How did you get that name?'

She ignored his question. 'What happened between you all back in '98?'

The car park walls seemed to crowd in on Boateng. He steadied himself, kept his breathing even. 'What do you want?' he asked her.

'The truth.'

Boateng didn't respond.

Rix gestured her huge companion over and clicked a key fob to open her car doors. 'I'm coming for you, Inspector. Better keep your guard up.'

※

The second one is dead. While the first was spectacularly fast, this one took his time to go. I imagine them standing around the cold, blackened body yesterday morning. Observing all the hallmarks of a gang execution, probably picturing several attackers. Suggesting a vendetta as the motive. Well, they'd be right about the last part. They'll be looking for criminal connections, deals gone bad. They'll check their databases, conclude it was Hayworth up to his old tricks.

The only one who might see a connection between the two is Boateng. Of course, there's still some chance he'll think it's a coincidence, explain it away. That'd be easier for him. But tomorrow there'll be no question. He'll be forced to tell people *why* these deaths are connected. Because of a secret he's kept buried for many years. Now that secret is coming to bury him.

CHAPTER ELEVEN

Thursday, 7 December 2017

'So, Zac, how would you like to use our time together today?'

Boateng placed his hands on the armrests and allowed himself to sink slightly deeper into the comfortable chair. He wanted to gather useful information about Troy from Summers. But so much had happened recently that he welcomed the respite of the counselling room. The soft lighting, the escape from his immediate stresses, the quiet focus of Summers's attention; it was a good way to start what would be another long day. Etta might be right about the benefit of speaking to someone.

'I want to talk about Troy.'

'OK.' Summers inclined his head, in listening mode, his expression neutral.

'I've been thinking a lot,' began Boateng. 'In fact, it seems like I can't switch my brain off right now. I said some stuff last time about Troy being murdered, but I realised it's not just his death that's making me angry.'

Summers continued to gaze at him without speaking, and Boateng briefly wondered whether the younger man was using one of his own favoured interview techniques – silence – to elicit more information. Although it was good to open up, some part of him feared he would reveal too much in the process.

'Troy was forty-four,' continued Boateng. 'He had so many years to live, there were probably a ton of things he still wanted to do. But then life just, you know, left him. Before his time. It's not fair. Good guys like Troy die while scumbags like the person who killed him carry on living.'

'And where is that anger, Zac?'

Boateng thought for a moment. Was the ambiguous question another counselling technique? He needed to release a bit of control, otherwise the session would go nowhere. 'Well, obviously with whoever killed him. But also, I guess, with myself. I let our friendship drift. He supported me so much back then – the early years, I mean. If I'd been in touch with him more this past year or two, I might've known about the stuff he was getting into that led to his death.'

'So, anger at yourself?'

'Yeah.'

'And guilt, too?'

'Mm.'

'I can see you've got your fist pressed into your stomach there. Is that where you experience the anger, or perhaps the guilt?'

Boateng glanced down; he wasn't aware he'd made that movement. 'Maybe. It's here, too.' He flexed both hands, looking from the right one to the left. Something felt good about connecting the emotion to his body.

'That's normal, you know. Feeling those things when someone dies suddenly.'

'I've felt them before.' He thought about his daughter, Amelia, and about her murder. About the person using the nickname Kaiser who had been involved in her death and got away with it. Boateng couldn't let that go. Etta said she didn't blame him for Amelia's death, but she didn't need to; he blamed himself. He felt his face get hotter, the muscles in his limbs tightening as he gripped the armrests. 'That anger, it does things to me.' His voice was louder now. 'I can't think straight, it makes me want to hurt someone. Make them pay.' He slapped one armrest on the last word.

'OK, Zac, I understand—'

'I want justice,' he growled. 'For the bastards who pick on people weaker than themselves.'

Summers held out both palms. 'I know, I know.'

'Do you?'

'Believe it or not, yes.' Summers spoke gently. 'But we're not here to talk about me.'

'Sorry.' Boateng shook his head, blinking away the moisture in his eyes.

'No need to apologise.' Summers smiled. 'That's all part of what we're trying to do here. We want to link experiences and emotions, to help you process them.'

Boateng wiped both hands over his face, let his body relax. 'I just hope I can hold it together this afternoon. It's Troy's funeral. I'm giving the eulogy.'

'I'll be there.' Summers looked slightly embarrassed. Proof at last that their relationship was close enough for Summers to attend his funeral. Boateng studied the younger man's face, noticing again how handsome he was, in a smooth-skinned, androgynous way. Was it possible that he and Troy had been seeing one another? Troy's diary entries had read 'Summers', like an appointment. But who was to say what might have gone on between them. He had to keep all lines of investigation open.

'You know what I said last time about Troy being murdered?'

Summers nodded.

'I have reason to believe that others could be in danger.'

'But Troy took his own life.'

Boateng shook his head. 'I don't think so. He was connected to a persistent offender called Hayworth, who was murdered three nights ago. I reckon their deaths are linked, and I'd like to know if anything Troy said to you gave you some idea he might be in danger.'

'You're asking me to break confidentiality?'

'Yes.'

Summers straightened his back. 'Is this still a counselling session? Or are we in an interview now?'

'We could do this in an interview, if you'd prefer?' Boateng hoped Summers wouldn't call his bluff. He hadn't released the email evidence connecting Troy and Hayworth into the official murder inquiry yet, which meant there was no legitimate basis to probe Summers. But he was banking on the counsellor not knowing that.

Summers bit his lip, breaking eye contact. He was silent for a moment. 'You said other people might be in danger?'

'Yes. And you can help them, Tom.'

The younger man tapped one foot on the carpet and drummed his fingers on the armrests. He let out a long breath through his nose. Then he seemed to make a decision, and lifted his head to meet Boateng's level gaze. 'In the last few weeks, Troy seemed... mixed up.' Summers paused; now it was Boateng's turn to use silence. 'He talked about being unsure what to believe, you know, in terms of his personal values.'

'OK.'

'He mentioned a group that he wanted to join. He never named them, but they sounded pretty hardcore, politically. He was using phrases like "It's time for action" and "The need to protect our society". I asked him more about what he meant, but he wasn't making sense. He said they had to do the work that the government couldn't do. No, *wouldn't* do, that was it.'

'Wouldn't do?'

'Yeah. He said there were people in our country who shouldn't be here, who needed to get out.'

Boateng couldn't make sense of this either. 'What do you reckon he meant?'

'He wouldn't say, exactly. But it gave me the impression that' – Summers hesitated, shaking his head slightly – 'he was in some kind of extreme right-wing group. You know, anti-immigration, all that stuff. He mentioned a guy called Liam.'

'Liam Rogers?'

'I don't know, sorry. I didn't think anyone was in danger, otherwise I'd have…' Summers trailed off into silence.

Boateng was stunned. The far right? That didn't sound like Troy at all. But for the last couple of years, they'd barely been in touch. People's beliefs could change, of course. Dramatic conversions frequently occurred in politics, religion and in social groups. The truth was, he didn't know what Troy had been through recently, because he hadn't been there for him. But what Summers was saying suggested a connection for Troy that Boateng had never imagined: National Right. Perhaps he'd been viewing it the wrong way around. Maybe it was Troy who'd been distancing himself from him?

The thought made Boateng feel sick.

॰

'What did she say, then?'

'Huh?' Jones snapped out of her daydream. She'd been thinking about Tom Summers, drifting involuntarily into a fantasy which was just getting started. She needed sex; that much was clear. But what excited her about Summers was that there could be depths beneath the surface. He was hot and probably emotionally literate. A rare combination. It made Jones want to talk to him – and then shag him…

'De Souza?' enquired Malik. 'You got hold of her, finally. What did she say about the car in Hayworth's logbook?'

'Oh.' Jones sat up straight. 'She didn't know anything about it. She was at home in Streatham all of Monday night with her partner, and their car was parked outside the whole time.'

'Weird. Does it check out?'

Jones shrugged. 'Dunno. She said they had food delivered around 8.30 p.m. I haven't looked into it yet. She thought it was probably a mistake by Hayworth.' Even as she said the words, Jones knew how unlikely that was. Boateng's old colleague linked to the murder of someone he'd been looking up on their system – no coincidence, surely.

Connelly glanced up from his computer. 'Or someone wanted to point the finger at her.'

The thought had occurred to Jones. When she'd called it through to Boateng, he'd been vague. She wasn't sure if he was just distracted; it was Troy's funeral today. She resolved to look into the background a bit more, see what she could dig up.

A deep voice resonated through the air. 'Is Boateng here?'

They turned to see Evans filling the MIT office door. He strode towards them, brandishing a copy of the *Metro*.

'He's out,' she replied coldly. He had some balls, marching into their space like this after the incident with Webb on Monday.

'Where is he?'

'What do you want?' she asked.

A smirk spread across Evans's face as he unfolded the paper and slapped it down on the desk between Malik and Connelly. 'I thought he'd probably want to see this.' Jones stood and read the headline upside down: SUICIDE COP AND MURDER VICTIM CONNECTED. There were two photographs below the headline. She recognised one of them as Sydenham scrapyard; the other depicted a house on a quiet street. She leaned closer to check the writer's name: Faye Rix. Liam Rogers's flatmate. The woman who'd been waiting for Boateng outside the station the day after Troy's death. It was hard to chase down every lead in a big case, but she made a mental note to speak to the journalist.

Jones came around the desks and Evans stepped back to allow her to see. She skimmed the piece, which was alleging some kind of police cover-up of the connection between the deaths. Two thirds in, it mentioned a Lewisham detective named Zachariah Boateng, who, according to 'Met sources', was investigating Hayworth's murder and had previously worked with Troy McEwen. The writing was sensationalist, but she noticed that Rix was careful not to accuse anyone directly of anything. And Jones had to admit that she was thinking along the same lines as Rix. OK, maybe not a cover-up, but there was something Boateng wasn't telling them. She wondered if he'd already seen the article. He was under enough stress as it was, and Krebs would surely add to it when she saw this negative publicity.

As Jones began rereading the piece, she registered that Evans was no longer looming over them. She glanced up and saw that he was standing in front of their ops boards, examining the networks of Spearhead and Hayworth's murder. He traced the line from Hayworth to de Souza with his finger and tapped her name, mumbling something to himself.

'What are you doing?' she barked. 'That's confidential material.'

Evans grinned. 'Shouldn't be up there for everyone to see then, should it? When I worked with intel in the army, we kept this kind of stuff secret. Let your leads get out and people end up dying.'

'Thanks for your help, fella,' said Connelly. 'But we'll take care of our own investigations.'

'You looking at the families of these two, then?' Evans pointed to the Spearhead victims named on the board: Bardak and Kumar. 'Obvious motive for revenge against Hayworth, isn't it? If these National Wing boys did the original attacks.'

Jones put her hands on her hips. She was a step away from telling him to piss off.

'It's National *Right*.' The nasal voice came from behind them. Jason Leather glanced at her as he approached the ops board. He was wearing another black T-shirt, this one with a flaming, horned skull with bloodied swords crossed underneath. The T-shirt was as creepy as its wearer.

Evans chuckled. 'Sorry, what?'

'You got it wrong,' said Leather. 'It's not National Wing. It's National Right.'

For a moment, Jones watched as both men stood their ground. Evans was six inches taller and a hell of a lot bigger than Leather, but something in the way the IT engineer held himself suggested physical strength. He didn't seem intimidated by Evans's size; maybe he was tougher than she gave him credit for, although all this macho posing was so lame. Evans reached down to the baton clipped into his belt and curled his fingers around it. Leather appeared poised to react. Half expecting another fight to break out, Jones felt her palms getting clammy. Then something changed in Evans's posture and he let go, smiling again.

'I'm going for lunch. Let geek-boy help with your investigation.' Evans strolled out, his shoulders barely fitting through the doorway. By the time Jones looked back, Leather had taken up a seat across the room and was logging on to a terminal.

Connelly shook his head. 'What an odd guy.'

'Which one?' whispered Jones.

Malik leaned in. 'You know, word is that Evans has killed people. Up close. Proper, like, Taliban and stuff in Afghanistan. Phil from Domestic Crimes told me.'

Again, Jones wasn't impressed. 'Doesn't make him a better police officer. If anything, it's the wrong background altogether.'

'He probably only got through the personality tests to join the Met because "Beat the shite out of 'em" wasn't an option for every question.' Connelly laughed at his own joke, but Jones didn't join him. She suspected Evans wasn't as blunt an instrument as everyone was making out. There was something bothering her about the guy, and it wasn't his obvious hair-trigger temper. It was his new interest in Boateng.

❀

Boateng pulled up alongside Troy's house and took out the keys that Troy's cousin Carol had given him. He'd called her on his way down to Croydon to check if she'd be there. As he'd hoped, she was already at Nunhead Cemetery. The funeral started at 2 p.m., which gave Boateng half an hour. Krebs had willingly signed him off for the afternoon on compassionate leave, though Summers's revelation that morning about Troy's possible involvement with National Right changed the shape of things. He needed further data. He had to remember how Troy had stood up for him over the years. He owed him for that, regardless of what had happened since.

Locking his car and walking up the path to Troy's front door, the rain-soaked night of a week ago appeared once again. But the nascent panic of his flashback was pierced by a movement of air, a whisper that brought him back. Someone was there, watching. Scanning the street, taking in the parked cars and trees, he saw nothing. If he hadn't caught Rix outside the mortuary yesterday, he might've thought he was losing his grip on reality. Stress and lack of sleep could do that, no question. But it wasn't impossible that he was being followed. He waited a moment longer, but nothing stirred in the grey winter light, so he slid the key into the door and let himself in.

The house was cold and silent. Boateng eased open the living room door, trying to focus on what he'd come for. He couldn't stop himself from seeing Troy's disfigured body, but he tried to lower his rising heart rate by contrasting the memory with the room today: clean, sterile, disinfected. The carpet and chairs had been removed, but the curtains remained. That was where he hoped the key to Troy's death would lie.

Boateng took out a pair of nitrile gloves from an inside pocket of his suit jacket. He snapped them on, then withdrew a miniature sampling kit from his other pocket and began to inspect the curtain fabric. It had been cleaned, but the thick weave and folds of cloth made the job more difficult than a smooth surface. Working his way carefully down, he was frustrated to see that none of the small, faded bloodstains seemed deep enough for his purposes. Finally, at the edge of the hem, he found it: a congealed blob, wedged between stitches, dark red. He extracted the swabbing stick from its cylinder and reached out towards the mark, fingers trembling slightly at—

The shift of air made him freeze. There was no sound, but the movement was unmistakable: a current, like a breeze or a breath. He remained still, crouched by the curtains, just below the window frame. He could feel his own pulse pounding at his temple. Was another person in the house? If he went out to check and found someone, he might lose this chance. He made a rapid decision: pressing the swab hard to the bloodstain, he quickly returned it to the cylinder and packaged it up in the sterile bag. He stuffed it back inside his jacket and ripped off the gloves, jamming them into a trouser pocket. Getting to his feet, he approached the open living-room door and peered back into the hallway. Empty. He glanced into the kitchen before heading upstairs, cursing himself for not checking the rest of the house when he arrived. He pushed open each door in turn: nothing. Back on the landing, he stood still and listened. The only sound he could hear was his own breathing. Then it came from outside: *tap, tap, tap*. Like footsteps, receding on the pavement. Heart thumping, he burst into the front bedroom and yanked up the blinds, but the street was empty. The tapping had ceased, replaced now with quiet birdsong. Maybe he was starting to imagine things.

Boateng rubbed his eyes. He needed to go.

CHAPTER TWELVE

Jones found herself as close to being alone in the MIT office as you could get during a day shift. There were a couple of detectives working away at their terminals down the other end of the huge open-plan room, and Leather's ponytail was visible ahead of her to the left. He seemed absorbed in screens of code: she was grateful he wasn't sitting behind her. She'd started to feel his eyes on her regularly and had come close to calling him on it, though she wasn't sure exactly what she'd say; an accusation of 'staring' was pretty deniable. If it got any worse, she'd speak to Boateng. She missed his reassuring presence in the office. Without him there, she noticed the opportunities to learn were fewer. She had nothing against Connelly and Malik, but they didn't have Boateng's spark, his intuition, his experience.

However, his absence did afford her the chance to do some digging. She'd deliberately passed on the offer to join Malik and Connelly in calling in on Hayworth's known associates. She guessed that whatever connected Boateng, Troy, Hayworth and de Souza was probably something from back in the day. She'd been working through Hayworth's criminal record – itself large enough to warrant a separate database – in search of links. And she'd found something.

In 1998, Hayworth had been arrested as part of a very serious crime that had taken place in Cleaver Square, Kennington. Jones knew the address: a super-wealthy pocket of luxury Georgian townhouses facing each other across a little park lined with grand old trees. She'd been to a 'summer fete' there once. It was like stepping into *Country Life*, despite being ten minutes from Brixton. The square was home to bankers, barristers, MPs and the occasional oligarch who was bored of Chelsea. Its beauty could not have contrasted more sharply with the events that had occurred there nineteen years ago.

Parts seemed to be missing, so Jones couldn't fully make sense of the report. But in essence, some officers from Kennington station had responded to a silent 999 call originating at 17 Cleaver Square, during the afternoon of Friday, 15 May. Hayworth and three other men had been discovered in the middle of a home invasion burglary. The PCs who attended weren't armed; the burglars were. After police entered the premises, firearms were discharged. But it was two of the criminals who were shot, and the husband and wife, tied up in their bedroom. Three of those shot died at the scene; the wife was taken to south London's trauma centre at King's College Hospital, but didn't make it. The other two attackers were detained in the house; one of them was Hayworth. The second was a man called Victor Walker; Jones made a note of the name. The report listed three arresting officers: Troy McEwen, Ana-Maria de Souza and Zachariah Boateng. A twelve-year-old kid was found in the house, too. But he refused to say a single word.

Jones thought back to the Saturday afternoon when she'd come up from the gym and found Boateng reading Hayworth's file on the PNC system. It clicked: he wasn't looking at Hayworth for Op Spearhead. He was looking at him in connection with the death of Troy McEwen.

●

Rain had started to blanket south London; a fine mist that swirled with the whims of the wind so that it came at you from every angle, even below. Etta could feel her tights getting damp and cold below the hem of her skirt. She cracked open a large black umbrella and held it almost sideways, sheltering under the ancient stonework of the chapel in Nunhead Cemetery. She and Zac had been walking here a couple of times, years ago, before they had kids and the parks they visited needed to have play areas.

Life had been precarious for Londoners a hundred and fifty years ago, when the Victorians built this place; accidents, childbirth, cholera and TB were common causes of its premature end, and life expectancy was around forty years. Today, the death of someone in their early forties was so rare that the circumstances were usually exceptional, the news impossibly tragic. The murder of their daughter, Amelia, had brought death into their lives, but despite this, Etta rarely thought about her own mortality. She was thirty-nine and still felt pretty invincible. At forty-three, Zac was probably much the same. Perhaps that was why Troy's death had seemed to affect him so much; its shock producing his denial of the suicide.

At the sound of footsteps, she raised the umbrella and saw her husband marching up the broad gravel path to the chapel. Etta checked her watch. It was 1.58 p.m. 'Where have you been?' she hissed as he reached her.

He shook his head. 'Sorry, love. Got caught up with something.'

'Everyone's here.'

Zac placed his hand on her arm and leaned in, kissing her on the cheek. 'Come on, let's go inside,' he said gently. The simple gesture made her regret her hard tone.

The chapel's interior was cold and dark, although the lack of light at least hid the fact that not many people had come to say goodbye. 'Everyone' had been an exaggeration. There was a woman slightly older than her with two children in the first row; she guessed these were Troy's cousins. A smattering of people who looked like police officers were there too; most hadn't taken off their jackets. As she and Zac walked to the front, she noticed a young man sitting next to a small, dark-haired woman. Her husband glanced at the woman, then exchanged a nod with the man.

'My counsellor,' Zac whispered to her. 'He knew Troy too.'

Before she could ask how, the Anglican priest called them to begin. He read a passage from the Bible, intoning, 'The Lord is my shepherd, I shall not want.' Etta recognised it as Psalm 23 and felt goosebumps prickle her arms at the words: 'Though I walk through the valley of the shadow of death, I will fear no evil, for Thou art with me.' The words always made her think of Amelia. Next, they sang the hymn 'Amazing Grace', but with so few voices, the beautiful words echoed and sounded hollow, deepening her feeling of sadness. One thing they said about dying young was that at least lots of people would come to your funeral. But Troy hadn't achieved that and Etta found herself moved by the loneliness, biting her lip to keep control. As the hymn ended, Zac stood to give his eulogy. He unfolded a small piece of paper and cleared his throat, looking around the scattered attendees. She was close enough to see the edges of the paper trembling in his hand.

'Good afternoon, friends. My name is Zachariah Boateng, and I'm an old pal of Troy's. We were colleagues for twenty-one years and at one point I even shared an office with him, for my sins.' There were a few brief chuckles from the pews. 'But I don't want to talk about Troy's police work today. Those of you who served with him' – he nodded at some of the group she'd pegged as officers – 'know how good he was at his job. He *was* Job, through and through. We don't need to hear any more about that. Instead, I'm going to tell you about the man I knew. A man who stood up for what he believed in.' She heard his voice catch slightly at these words. 'A man who wasn't scared to be different.' Zac blinked and took a breath. 'A man who knew pain, but didn't give up. A fighter, sometimes with his hands, when necessary, but most often with his words and his spirit. A spirit which was an example to us all.'

She watched as Zac bowed his head a moment, and wondered if he'd be able to finish. He stood still, the chapel's silence punctured only by the occasional cough or sniff. Then he raised his head again, eyes wet, and glanced at his notes. He read lines by the Scottish poet Robert Burns, from a poem entitled 'Epitaph on my own friend', and told a couple of stories about Troy. One of these received some laughs when he accused Troy of being a bad Scot, neglecting to fulfil his national stereotypes of thrift, hard work and bagpipe-playing, though his loyalty to Scotland's under-performing football team never wavered. The other was a simple tale of compassion: Troy had taken in a stray dog and nurtured her into a thriving beast, full of life.

'Somebody once said,' he continued, 'that if you don't stand up for something, you'll fall for anything. Well, Troy was a person who stood up tall. Even in his dark times, he didn't lie down. He refused to be beaten. He may be gone now, but I will do my best to carry his courage with me for the rest of my life.' Zac pinched his eyes and turned to Troy's casket, laid alongside him. 'I'll never forget you, my friend. Maybe I won't be able to repay my debt to you, but I hope you can forgive me all the same.' He folded the paper and walked slowly back to sit next to her. Etta wasn't sure what he'd meant by the last line, but she was proud of him for pushing through. She laid her hand on his and gave it a small squeeze.

As the ceremony concluded and they filed out after the coffin bearers, umbrellas opening, she and Zac fell into step with the handsome young man Zac had pointed out as his counsellor.

'Tom Summers.' He offered Etta a hand and she shook it, introducing herself. 'Did you know Troy well?'

'As long as I've known this one.' She inclined her head towards Zac. 'He used to visit us all the time. I mean, years back.'

'Sorry.'

'What about you?' asked Etta.

'Troy and I were getting to know each other,' he replied, gazing out over the gravestones. 'Zac. Um, I know this may not be the best time, but have you seen the piece in the *Metro* today?'

'No. What piece?'

'It's about Troy's suicide and the murder of someone called Hayworth, and it mentions you by name. I thought you'd like to know.'

Zac stopped walking. 'What?'

'Forewarned is forearmed and all that. In case, you know, there are any journalists prowling around.'

'Thanks, Tom.'

'I have to get back to the office for a session, I'm afraid,' said the young man. 'See you soon, Zac. Etta, it was lovely to meet you. I'm just sorry it couldn't have been in better circumstances.'

They both shook hands with him again and he jogged down the gravel towards the gate, trying to escape the rain.

'He seems nice,' said Etta. 'And he's helping you?'

'Yeah, he's a great listener.'

'Sometimes that's all you need.'

Zac took her hand. 'And other times, it's not enough.'

●

'And your concern is what, exactly?'

'Well, ma'am, it's DI Boateng. I'm worried that…' Jones trailed off. Now that she was standing in front of DCI Krebs, trying to voice her belief in some connection between the deaths of McEwen and Hayworth, she didn't quite know how to express herself. 'He's under a lot of stress, and—'

'DI Boateng is an experienced officer. He'll cope. He just needs some time to process the suicide of his friend.'

'But he and Sergeant McEwen were the arresting officers for the Cleaver Square home invasion burglary, where four people were killed. Then McEwen and Hayworth both die in the space of one week, and another of our investigative leads points to a former colleague from that incident back in '98.'

Krebs gave her a sympathetic smile, as you might give a child exposing his or her naiveté at the world. 'Boateng and McEwen have policed in south London for over twenty years. Dennis Hayworth was a career criminal operating on the same patch. It isn't surprising that their paths crossed. The links today are circumstantial, and unless I'm mistaken, there's no doubt that Sergeant McEwen's tragic death was suicide prompted by a bout of depression, which was something he'd struggled with for years. Is there any physical evidence to suggest otherwise?'

Jones sighed. 'No, ma'am. Not that I'm aware of.'

'Right, then. So, carry on investigating Hayworth's death, and if there's a connection to Op Spearhead, bottom it out. But make sure that the links you're drawing are based on solid proof.'

'Ma'am.'

Krebs gave a curt nod and turned to her computer screen, indicating that the conversation was over. Jones knew when it was time to quit; she felt a pang of sympathy for Boateng in his weekly battles with Krebs, shielding his team from her scepticism and PR obsession.

As she stepped out of Krebs's office, she almost collided with someone coming the other way. She caught a scent of body odour and pulled up to see Jason Leather in front of her. He was holding one of those funny little spring-loaded grip things like it was a weapon. He gave her a lopsided grin and looked her up and down.

'You know,' he said, pushing his glasses up his nose. 'If you ever get any shit from Evans, you come to me. I'll sort it out.'

'Will you?'

'Yeah.' Leather flexed the spring-loaded grip. 'I'm a martial artist.'

Jones studied the hand holding the grip. 'I'll keep that in mind, thanks.'

'Welcome.' Leather turned around and went on his way. So, he was that kind of guy. The type who turned a potentially chivalrous gesture into a reinforcement of his own hard-man credentials. As well as being a creep. As Leather walked off, flexing the hand grip and holding his shoulders stiffly, Jones realised that he was returning the way he'd come. Either he'd forgotten where he was going, or he wasn't going anywhere at all. Had he followed her? She could hear Krebs on the telephone through the thin walls, and wondered how much of their conversation Leather had overheard.

●

Boateng ordered a pint of strong dark ale and drank the first third in one go. He needed to steady his nerves; something about seeing Troy's coffin placed in the ground had hit home, sending dread through his guts. The realisation that it could've been him being buried there; that it could still be him. He took another big gulp of ale.

The Met contingent were already two drinks down, and they'd only been in here half an hour. Etta was alongside him, chatting to Troy's cousin Carol. He scanned the faces in the pub where they'd opted to hold the wake. He recognised many of those who'd attended the funeral. Then he noticed a burst of red among the black and white. It was Faye Rix, standing at the back, sipping a glass of wine. Without thinking, he went straight over to her.

'What the hell are you doing here?' he growled.

'It's a pub.' She smiled pleasantly. 'As in, a public house.'

'You've been writing about me.'

'I told you yesterday at the mortuary, I'm following a story.'

'You're being damned disrespectful.' Boateng took a large swig from his pint.

'Just doing my job.'

He raised a finger. 'Why don't you piss off and get your gossip somewhere else?'

'Zac, love, what's the matter?' Etta was standing alongside him, cupping his elbow, concern on her face.

'This so-called reporter is trying to dig for dirt on Troy by coming to his wake. It's not right.'

'I've seen you before,' said Etta, extending a hand to the journalist. 'At the boxing gym. Double Jab. I've just started going to the women's session there.'

Rix gripped her hand and beamed. 'Welcome to the sisterhood. If you ever want to train or spar, let me know.' She produced a card from her jacket and handed it to Etta.

Great, thought Boateng, *now they're mates*. That was classic Etta: she'd make friends with everyone, disarm the bullies. This didn't look like politics on her part, though. Despite the alcohol going to Zac's head on an empty stomach, he could tell that his wife was impressed with Rix, for some reason. He was determined not to lose his momentum.

'How about you stay away from grieving people, and give us a chance to—'

He was interrupted by his own phone ringing. Snatching it from his pocket, he read the screen: *Private number*. Boateng snorted his irritation. 'I should take this. But I want you to know, Rix, you're not welcome here.'

As he walked to the pub door, he heard Etta apologising on his behalf and glanced over his shoulder to see the pair of them chatting, all smiles and nice body language. Damn.

He swiped up to answer. 'Yes?'

'Zac? It's Jason Leather.'

'Oh, hi.'

Leather didn't enquire if this was a convenient time or not. 'I've found something about your email.'

Boateng's pulse quickened. 'Yes?'

'The IP address it originated from corresponds to a street in Croydon. Pretty isolated place.' He paused a moment, perhaps checking some notes. 'It was sent from a Wi-Fi network called TroysNet.'

'Thanks.' Boateng swallowed. 'Anything else?'

'Nope.' Leather paused. 'That's all.'

'OK. Cheers, Jason.' He closed the phone and stood staring into the street. Hayworth's email to Troy had been forwarded to him from Troy's email address, after Troy's death. That was weird enough. Now it turned out to have been sent using Troy's Wi-Fi. Boateng hadn't found a laptop in Troy's flat. If the killer had taken it, was he now using it to communicate with him? As Boateng recalled his three trips to the house, something dawned on him. If the messages were sent from Troy's Wi-Fi, it meant the killer had been back there, too.

CHAPTER THIRTEEN

Finally, Boateng spotted his opportunity. Ana-Maria de Souza peeled off from the group of Met officers in the pub, heading to the bar. He intercepted her and, gripping her arm firmly enough to show he was serious, steered her away to a quiet alcove.

'We've got to talk,' he whispered, aware that the beer was already loosening his speech.

'Sure, Zac,' she said gently. 'How are you coping? You were always closer to Troy than I was.'

Boateng let go and studied her. De Souza was a diminutive woman whose Portuguese parentage was visible in her olive skin tone, dark eyes and hair. She was one of those people who never seemed to age; he suspected her jet-black hair colour was partly from a bottle these days, but the rest was almost exactly as he remembered her twenty years ago, when they worked together at Kennington station. Her expression appeared genuinely concerned, the flat smile and furrowed brow giving no indication that she might be hiding something.

'I'm alright,' he lied. 'It's Dez Hayworth I wanted to ask you about.'

'Oh.' Her eyebrows lifted as her mouth formed a circle of surprise.

'Come on, what's the deal? Your car was the last thing logged in his book before someone burned him to death.'

She shook her head. 'I already told the young woman in your team, I haven't got a clue why that happened. I was at home all night with my partner and the car was outside the house. You know me, Zac. Do you seriously think I was involved in

Hayworth's murder?' She was speaking more quickly now. 'If you believe that, then you're an idiot. Check my phone's location history, look at the ANPR system for plates, check the takeaway delivery, speak to our neighbours if you have to. My partner and I weren't anywhere near that scrapyard.'

'Alright.' Boateng held up a hand. 'Don't blame DS Jones; it's her job to follow up on this stuff. Why do *you* think your car was in the logbook?'

'No idea.'

He leaned closer. 'Did you have any contact with Hayworth recently?'

'No!' she took a half step back, insulted.

'Did he threaten you?'

'No.'

'Has anyone else threatened you?'

'No.' She let out a weary breath through her nostrils. 'Look, Zac, I appreciate you're investigating Hayworth's murder, but believe me, I had nothing to do with it. I don't think I've even met the guy since—'

' '98?'

'Right.' She broke eye contact, swallowed.

'OK. So why the hell were your car's details in his logbook?'

'I told you,' she said slowly, deliberately. 'I – don't – fucking – know.'

Boateng relented slightly. She didn't seem to be lying, though he knew each person had their own signals for deception, and there was no automatic or reliable way of detecting it. 'Fine. I believe you.' He took a large swig of ale. 'So, let's imagine we're working this case together. Why would your car appear in the logbook?'

Her gaze darted about. 'Someone trying to set me up, make it look like I was involved.'

'And what's the only thing that links you to Hayworth?'

'Cleaver Square,' she replied quietly.

'So, it's about that. The killer's sending a message. Troy dies a week ago, and I get an email showing that he and Hayworth have been in contact.'

'What?'

'Then Hayworth dies, and your name comes up.' He leaned in closer. 'You could be in danger, Ana.'

'But Troy killed himself.'

'That's what it looked like, I know. But I'm sure he was murdered, by the same person who killed Hayworth. I can't prove it yet, but I'm working on it.'

'What do you mean, he—'

'Listen, the only other survivors from Cleaver Square now are you, me and Vic Walker. It's got to be about revenge. We've got to watch out for ourselves.'

'Hang on.' De Souza held up both palms. 'There's no proof that Troy was murdered?'

He winced. 'Not exactly, I mean, there's an email, he texted me, and it didn't seem like—'

'Are you sure you're OK, Zac?' It was her turn to place a hand on his arm. 'I admit, my car registration in Hayworth's logbook is odd. But it's one hell of a leap from that to a campaign of murder, including the suicide of our friend.'

'We need to tell people what really happened at Cleaver Square.'

She fixed him with a stare. 'I don't think that's a good idea. The official inquiry was closed years ago; it's water under the bridge. Why open that up again?'

Boateng stared at her a moment, then downed the rest of his pint and turned towards the bar. 'I need another drink,' he said to no one in particular.

●

Even as Jones walked briskly down the long corridor in Lewisham police station, she wasn't quite sure what she was doing. She'd located Tom Summers's office using the intranet, then waited till the end of the day. Late enough that he probably wouldn't have an appointment, hopefully not so late that he'd have gone home. Her reason for seeking him out was spurious, but she just wanted to start chatting. OK, she didn't *just* want that. She wanted a date. Oh God, was she asking him on a date? Her heart was beating quickly by the time she arrived outside his office, and she tried to calm herself. She leaned close to the door but couldn't hear any voices – just the tapping of computer keys. She almost found an excuse to run away. But she knocked before she could stop herself.

'Hello? I mean, come in.'

She prised open the door to see him working at his desk. He looked great in his designer glasses, shirtsleeves rolled up to display sinewy, strong forearms. The low lighting gave a sense of intimacy to the room as she stepped in and closed the door behind her.

'Hey,' she said, tucking a lock of hair behind her ear.

'Hi,' he beamed. 'Kat, right? How are you?'

'Great,' she said, a little too enthusiastically. *Take it easy*, she told herself. *Don't be too keen.*

Summers spun his chair to her, still smiling. 'What can I do for you?'

'Um.' She paused, trying to remember the rehearsed story as her pulse raced; he was so fit, it was distracting. 'I'm working a murder case at the moment.' Was she really using this as a chat-up line? 'I can't say too much about it, but the victim was burned to death.'

Tom's eyes widened in horror, his lips drawn back in disgust. 'Burned?'

'Yeah.'

'Wow.' He looked stunned, like he didn't know what else to say. Jones wondered if she'd shocked him too much with the bluntness of her opening gambit. Sometimes she forgot that most of the population didn't deal with this stuff.

'I wanted to ask you about the psychology of it. The choice of burning as a method of murder.'

He blinked. 'Aren't there people in the National Crime Agency that you're supposed to bring in for profiling?'

'Yes, but it takes days for the request to go through and another week for someone to actually turn up. I thought I'd keep it, er, in-house, so to speak.' She smiled.

He returned her expression but shook his head. 'Forensic psychology isn't really my area. I wouldn't want to have my random thoughts logged in an official file for some lawyer to take apart down the line.'

'OK.' She cocked her head. 'But if you had to take a guess, off the record. Just to give me somewhere to start. Why would you *burn* someone to death?'

Tom blew out his cheeks. 'Well, off-record – and this is just a personal opinion – fire is…' He searched for the words. 'It's dramatic; it's about anger. Flames consume, they erase. It's almost biblical, like a punishment. Behaviourally speaking, fire-setting in juveniles is a symptom of conduct disorder, which can develop into antisocial personality disorder in adulthood. So, we're talking about people on the psychopathic spectrum. It's a rejection of social norms, and demonstration of a refusal to be bound by rules. In terms of murder, I wouldn't know where to begin, but I'd say your perpetrator is someone with a lot of rage inside them. It might be someone who couldn't always vent that rage – historically, maybe – and the fire was one way for them to do that. But to be honest, I don't really know.' He flashed a little grin of embarrassment. 'Is that any use?'

'Yeah, that's amazing. Thanks.' Jones nodded vigorously. 'I'll read up some more on it, but that'll really help with our suspect identification.' She didn't want to tell him that it was obvious to her that a murderer would probably be full of rage and reject social norms.

'OK.' He smiled pleasantly and a brief silence hung between them. 'Anything else?'

'Actually, yes. I'm in your debt twice now – the café and the profiling. Maybe I could buy you a drink sometime to say thanks?' She shrugged, trying to make the offer seem more casual.

Tom's whole posture shifted, as if he was relaxing. 'Sure. When were you thinking?'

'Don't know. Sometime this weekend?'

'Great.'

'Saturday evening?' Was it a mistake to do another Saturday night date? She'd panicked at his acceptance and it was the first day that came to mind.

'Yeah.'

They remained smiling at one another for a moment, before she suggested exchanging numbers. Stepping out of the room and walking back to her office, Jones couldn't suppress a grin. She wondered if she'd been too forward, but then thought, no: Tom had said yes straightaway, and she fancied him, so why wait? Worst-case scenario was one rubbish date. And if that happened, then at least she didn't have to sit opposite him all day.

●

Etta watched her husband finish another pint of beer and order a follow-up. Zac normally held it together pretty well with alcohol, but the red flag was when he started ordering solo drinks without moving away from the bar. She was right next to him and he hadn't even asked if she wanted another glass of wine. His balance was going; he was using his arms as much as his legs to support himself. She was unsure how wise it'd be to intervene; maybe it was good for him to release some stress this way. When Zac got drunk, it was normally for decent reason. The past week qualified. She saw him lock on, through half-closed eyes, to a shorter woman, who had appeared alongside him at the bar. Etta recognised her from the church.

'I'll tell you what, Ana, this is my fault,' he slurred.

'Don't be stupid, Zac,' she replied over the noise. 'It's no one's fault.'

'It is!' he insisted. 'It's my bloody responsibility. All of it.' He took a huge gulp of beer and belched, wiping his mouth with the back of his hand.

'Come on,' said Ana. 'There was nothing any of us could've done.'

'Bollocks.' He drank some more.

Etta laid a hand over his, which was gripping the pint glass. 'Hey, love, just slow down a bit, you don't want to—'

'He's right,' came the voice from behind. The three of them turned, Zac slowest, to see the red-headed journalist. In her heels, she was taller than Zac. 'You both know the truth.' She jabbed a finger at Ana and Zac in turn. 'You're covering up, and I'm going to make sure you get what you deserve.'

'What're you on about?' demanded Ana.

'You know damned well.'

Ana put her drink down and glared up at Faye Rix. 'Come on, then. Why don't you tell us, eh?'

'Your sin will find you out.' Rix grinned and tossed her long red hair over one shoulder. 'It must be scary, knowing that things are about to come tumbling down. It's already started.'

'Fuck off,' spat Ana.

'Don't test me.' Rix rose even taller, turning her body slightly sideways in what Etta now recognised was part of a boxing stance.

Zac clumsily raised his arms. 'Oi! Let's all calm down, yeah?' He straightened up, but the pint glass slipped out of his hand, smashing on the floor. Etta felt the beer splash against her ankle. When she looked up again, a massive, shaven-headed man in a leather jacket was towering over all of them, his hand clamped on Zac's shoulder. The guy didn't say a word. It took her a moment to register that it was the bloke from the boxing gym who held the bag for Rix.

'Sorry,' blurted Etta. 'Zac, I think we should leave now.'

'No!' he roared. 'I'm fine, I'm not going anywhere. Take your fucking hand off me.' He was struggling to focus on the huge guy in front of him, whose grip had tightened.

'It's not a debate,' she said firmly. 'We're going home.' She wrestled Zac loose from the giant hand, mouthed an apology to the bar staff and hauled her husband out of the melee. As they reached the door, she glanced back to Rix and Ana, who were now arguing. Plunging into the cold night air, she put her arm around Zac to support him. 'Let's get you home, love. That nearly turned nasty.'

'I'm not scared of him. Or her,' he shouted, hawking up spit and projecting it into the road. 'She thinks she knows the truth.'

'What about?' said Etta, her concern rising.

Zac mumbled something incoherent, then stopped and bent double. She had just enough time to step away before he vomited all over the pavement.

·

It's time for the third one. Another who turned a blind eye, who kept a secret for years to protect themselves. I'm looking forward to confronting them, seeing the confusion as they realise what's happening. It's a terrible thing when someone you think you know turns out to be different – an enemy rather than a friend – and you discover your trust was misplaced. I should know, I've been there. Then again, they never really knew me. Not back then, and certainly not as I am now. Given how much they've had to drink tonight, I'd be surprised if they know what's going on at all. But even a booze-soaked brain has its survival instinct, the sense that danger is real. It's just a lot slower than normal. By the time they react, it'll be too late. I should get moving; I don't want them already passed out when I knock on their door, asking for help. On the other hand, I quite like the idea of waking them up for their own death. They've been sleeping too long.

CHAPTER FOURTEEN

Friday, 8 December 2017

Boateng turned down the blues on his car stereo, then popped a couple of ibuprofen into his mouth and washed them down with a swig of black coffee. His head was throbbing and he was confident that, if a colleague on traffic duty pulled him over for a breath test, he'd still be over the limit. The memory of how last night had ended was hazy. He recalled a lot of dark ale, a couple of arguments, Faye Rix and then, after that, nothing. He'd found his trousers in the laundry, his shoes outside the back door. Etta had filled in the blanks over a breakfast he couldn't touch for nausea. She'd suggested he call in sick, but he'd insisted on going to work. He couldn't wait around for the hangover to subside. He planned to check the address he'd found in Troy's diary last Sunday, and he still had to lead Hayworth's murder investigation as well as cover the existing Spearhead cases. The thought of it made the pain behind his eyes deepen. Of course, all that was on hold until after his current task: finding a way to get Troy's blood analysed. If he could confirm Troy had been administered the same injection as Hayworth, it would at least be proof they were dealing with two murders and one killer.

Boateng parked up behind the Waterloo campus of King's College London and pulled the evidence bag out of his glove compartment. Crossing to the entrance of the nondescript beige building, he clocked the London Eye peeking over the top of the vast IMAX cinema. Back in August, he, Etta and Kofi had been up inside the Eye, looking out. Today, he felt like it was observing him. He showed his warrant card at the desk, signed in and took the lift up. King's Forensics was the go-to toxicology lab for the Met, pioneering techniques that could've solved a thousand cases for generations of detectives in the capital, had the technology existed at the time. Now, he was hoping to commission a test he had no grounds for requesting. If he were caught, it could be the end of his career.

The young technician to whom he had been directed looked startled and stressed. Perhaps that was standard in an overworked lab. Boateng took in the white coat, plastic eye protectors, hairnet and security pass: Kamran Abas. His smooth skin and gelled hair made him look about fifteen, although the bags under his eyes suggested the weariness of someone much older.

'I'm DI Boateng. This is the sample I called you about,' he said, flashing his warrant card in one hand while thrusting the bag towards the technician with the other. No handshake.

Abas recoiled slightly, possibly at Boateng's breath. He hadn't taken the package yet. 'It wasn't sent with the original request from Dr Volz.'

'That's because this one is from us. Lewisham MIT. Dr Volz's sample was from her post-mortem in Greenwich.'

Abas cocked his head. 'Why do you need two samples analysed?'

Boateng feigned slight irritation, though he'd expected some resistance. He needed to convey urgency without pissing off the technician. 'Because one lot came from his body – that's Volz's sample – and the other came from the crime scene.'

'I didn't see anything about a crime scene blood sample. The guy was a burns victim, right?'

Boateng bit his lip; Abas was too sharp. 'The blood was found in a later examination of the victim's car. It wasn't at the main crime scene. But if the blood contains the same drug traces, it'll tell us more about when, where and how the substance was administered.' He knew his improvised explanations couldn't hold up to much more scrutiny.

'Should I check with Dr Volz?' asked Abas.

Damn. Boateng was still holding the evidence bag in front of him like a ticking bomb he wanted to hand over to a disposal expert. He fought down a wave of nausea. 'You could, if you've got time. But she only did the post-mortem; she doesn't know the investigative detail. And she doesn't work at the mortuary on Fridays.' He didn't know if the last part was true. 'It's just a case of running the same toxicology report on two samples rather than one. I'm not asking you to do any extra tests. Usual turnaround time.'

Abas looked at his watch. Did he have somewhere to be, or was he checking the date?

Boateng played his trump card. 'It's a live murder investigation.'

Abas hesitated a moment, then took the bag from his hand. 'Monday OK?'

'Any chance of squeezing it in over the weekend?'

'I'm working Sunday. No promises.'

'You're a legend, Kamran.'

'It's Kam, Detective.'

'Call me Zac.'

Boateng felt a swell of triumph as he returned to his car and set out for Lewisham. His headache had even faded enough for him to chuck an up-tempo jazz CD in the stereo. He was halfway down Old Kent Road when his mobile rang. It was Kat Jones. He turned down the music slightly and put her on speakerphone.

'Zac, can you talk?' No intros; that wasn't like her.

'Yeah, go on.'

'Another body's been found.'

His good cheer vanished like the light in a power cut. Even with a hangover, he was already processing her words. 'What do you mean, "another"?' Though he understood what she was getting at.

'I'm sorry, Zac.'

He waited for her to speak again; she was trying to break it to him gently.

'It's someone else you know.'

Boateng pulled up across the street from the quiet Victorian redbrick terrace in Streatham. Parked outside the house where Ana-Maria de Souza had lived were two police vehicles and the unmarked grey van coroners used to transport bodies to the mortuary. He stared at the van, briefly imagining himself lying in the back of it. Then he forced down the rest of his cold black coffee, grimaced and got out into the damp, heavy air.

He was met at the door by an officer he recognised, their paths having crossed on another murder case. The rugby player's frame of DCI Dave Maddox filled the front doorway. He had the same shaved head and few days' stubble as the last time Boateng had seen him, when Lambeth MIT had been first on the scene at a murder connected with Boateng's case. Here, Maddox was on home turf and was, Boateng guessed, senior officer attending. His tie was loose around his neck, the top button undone. It was a look that said he was obliged to dress formally.

'DI Boateng.' Maddox rasped a hand over his chin. 'They told me you'd be coming. You knew her?'

Boateng nodded. He could feel his fingers trembling, though whether from booze, caffeine or fear, he couldn't tell. 'Worked borough together in Kennington, sir,' he replied. 'Nearly twenty years ago.'

'Drop the sir.' Maddox reached into his pocket and brought out a packet of cigarettes. He offered one to Boateng, who declined.

The DCI clamped a fag between his lips and spoke from the corner of his mouth. 'You sure you want to see her?'

Boateng blinked and nodded.

'Personal or professional interest?' Maddox pulled out a lighter. 'Both.'

'Second Met suicide in as many weeks. You'd think it was contagious.' He emitted a small laugh as he raised the lighter, but it died on his lips as he saw Boateng wasn't joining in. 'Sorry,' he added. 'Were you close?'

'In a way. Do you mind if we get this over with?'

'OK.' Maddox put away the lighter and dropped the cigarette back in its box. 'Come in.'

Boateng followed him through into the hallway. 'Where's her partner?'

'Being interviewed at the station,' said Maddox over his shoulder. 'He's in pieces. Poor sod found her this morning when he came in off the night shift at Brixton prison.' They passed an open door; inside, two officers were checking shelves and paperwork.

'Hang on.' Boateng stopped. Glanced at his own shoes, then at Maddox's. 'You're not using overshoes and gloves?'

Maddox turned, looking down his crooked nose at Boateng as if he'd just been insulted. 'It's not a crime scene, is it?'

'You sure about that?'

'Eh?' Maddox narrowed his eyes. 'Listen, mate. I've been Job twenty years. Twelve officers I've known personally have topped themselves in that time. And another thirty that I didn't know. And that's just in the Met. Suicide is a police disease. It's what kills us – more often than the rest of the population. And I know a case when I see one.'

Boateng knew the stats on police suicide didn't tell the whole story. His psychology degree had taught him that people have all sorts of reasons for ending their own lives. For police officers, work could be the main reason for their suicide, totally unconnected, or anywhere in between. Often, those left behind simply didn't know. But right now, Boateng did know better than to tell a senior officer from another borough what his job was. Maddox's certainty did nothing to assuage the dread pooling in his stomach. He needed to see it for himself. 'OK.'

Maddox sighed. 'Look, I'm sorry that someone you knew did this to herself. Like I said, I've known others who've done the same. Call it an occupational hazard. It's the part of the work they don't put in the recruitment ads.' This time Maddox wasn't joking, and Boateng met his level gaze with a single nod.

They went through to the kitchen at the back and Boateng felt goosebumps rise on his arms and neck. Maddox stepped aside and he saw the corpse – his third in eight days. Ana-Maria de Souza was kneeling on the laminate floor, feet pressed against the back door. Her torso was bent forwards, arms hanging down, head bowed. Around her neck, a leather belt was pulled so tight it looked as if it had sliced through her skin. The belt buckle was at the side of her throat, the other end tied around the handle of the back door. Boateng moved closer and stooped to examine her face. One eye was closed, the other half open, blood pooling in the lower eyelid. Pinpricks of red were visible on her cheeks, evidence of veins bursting as she suffocated. Her lips were blue and swollen, a dark tongue protruding slightly between them. He could smell the alcohol coming off her. Boateng had seen two cases of hanging before, but never a partial hanging like this, the body in contact with the ground.

'She probably died of asphyxiation,' said Maddox, gesturing to the ligature formed by the belt. 'Not enough force to break her neck, but it doesn't take much weight to cut off the windpipe. See this sort of thing in prison,' he added.

'Any evidence of disturbance, struggle, intruders?' asked Boateng.

Maddox snorted. 'Do you think we'd be walking around here if there was?'

'Got to ask the question.'

'Your DS said you were out with her last night,' said Maddox, a hint of suspicion in his voice.

'We were at Troy McEwen's funeral.'

'You knew that guy too?' Maddox pursed his lips. 'Unlucky.'

'Yeah, well.'

'How did she seem?'

'Fine, you know, considering the occasion,' said Boateng. 'We had a few drinks.'

'A few?'

'Alright, a lot. I don't know how much she'd had. We were in the pub from three o'clock and I'm pretty sure she was still there when I left.'

'What time was that?'

'I don't remember,' replied Boateng sheepishly. 'I can ask my wife. Late.'

'So, she goes to the funeral of her old colleague, gets depressed, has a skinful, comes home, her bloke is out at work for the night, no one to console her, she drinks some more' – he gestured to a gin bottle on the side – 'and hangs herself with her own belt. Maybe she's been thinking about it for years, maybe the funeral triggered it, maybe it was impulsive after the booze.'

'She didn't seem depressed.'

'Some people hide it pretty well.'

'Yeah.' A hazy memory came to Boateng of de Souza and Rix shouting at one another. 'In the pub, before I left, she had an argument. With a journalist called Faye Rix.'

'OK.' Maddox looked unconvinced, but produced a notebook and scribbled a few words.

Boateng shifted slightly to study the exposed skin of the neck, searching for an injection mark that would support the hypothesis which had formed in his hungover brain before he'd even arrived: that de Souza was the third victim of the same killer. As he moved, something caught the light and he got closer to inspect it, his face just inches from the body. The object was so fine that he lost it and had to move back and forth so it caught the light again. It was trapped under the belt, one end curling up. In the same moment, he knew what it was and where it had come from.

A single long, red hair.

Boateng turned to Maddox. 'Hope you've got a spare evidence bag in your car. Sir.'

●

Sergeant Ana-Maria de Souza. Dead. Suicide? Kat Jones was beginning to doubt it, and wondered if Boateng was thinking the same. She was questioning their theory for Hayworth's murder, too. The team's investigation into the Spearhead hate crimes and National Right suggested a revenge motive for someone to murder Hayworth. Much as she hated to admit it, PC Evans may have been on the money with that theory. But with de Souza's death, things had changed.

Now, there were three bodies in the space of eight days, all of whom had a connection to this incident she'd found in the files from nineteen years ago. She'd done some more research and was developing a new theory of her own. Revenge, yes. But not for a hate crime committed today. For the deaths at Cleaver Square in May 1998. She'd begun with the people who survived the gun battle in the house. Of those, there were now three left: Boateng, convicted criminal Vic Walker and the child of the murdered couple, who had been twelve at the time.

Jones looked up Walker on the Crimint and PNC databases, finding that he'd received two further convictions for violent crime since serving his Cleaver Square sentence. He'd been released from prison for the third time earlier this year, though she could find no current address. She needed to speak to him. If he wasn't involved, then he was in danger. He deserved to know. The other possibility had dawned on her more slowly, like mist lifting as streets warmed under a winter sun. The kid.

His name was Joseph Young, born February 1986. He'd be thirty-one now. She found notes from an aborted interview with him at Kennington police station, which simply stated that he refused to say one word after the event. He was entirely mute throughout their attempts to get him to describe what had happened in the house. A child psychologist had interviewed him, with the same result: silence. Or 'selective mutism', as they called it. Another, later document by the investigating officer mentioned him being taken into care by social services after his parents died, there being no other living relatives who could be located to look after him.

Where was Joseph Young now?

She had to talk to Boateng. He could be in danger too.

●

Jim stood on the Millennium Bridge, dimly aware of the grey Thames water flowing underneath him. Normally, he liked watching the river: it was therapeutic; a break from watching people. But he couldn't afford such a break today. His eyes had been fixed in the direction of St Paul's Cathedral for the last twenty minutes. Eventually, he spotted the squat shape of his boss, wrapped in a thick Churchillian overcoat, marching towards him. The big man liked to 'walk the bridges', as he put it, during his lunch break; his only concession to the need for exercise. He didn't even slow down as he reached Jim, who fell into step with him.

'There's a third body,' said Jim immediately. His boss didn't want any small talk.

'Another one of the five?'

'Yes.' Jim glanced sideways. The big man didn't look shocked or concerned, just stoical, as if Jim had merely confirmed something he'd expected.

'Which one?'

'Ana-Maria de Souza. Police officer. Initial reports suggest it's a suicide.'

'Like McEwen, you mean?' By which his boss meant not a suicide.

'Probably.'

'Did Boateng do it?'

'I don't think so. He was blind drunk last night when it happened.'

'You sure? People can fake that. Bloody good alibi.'

'Unless he faked puking over his wife's shoes, it was real.'

'Hm.'

They continued walking in silence, reaching the end of the bridge, and descended the ramp to ground level, turning left towards the timber, wattle and daub of the Shakespeare's Globe theatre. Jim liked walking alongside the big man; it meant he couldn't stare at Jim's cleft lip.

'Have they determined time of death, yet?' asked the boss.

'Not that I know of.'

'So could it have been Boateng before he got pissed up?'

Jim considered this. 'Maybe.'

'Either it's him or there's a fifty-fifty chance he's next.'

'He went to the scene this morning. De Souza's house.'

'Is he investigating it?'

'No, it's in a different borough.'

'Why did he go?'

'I don't know, sir.' Jim felt like he was saying that a lot this week.

'Do you know where we are?'

Jim shrugged. 'South Bank.'

The boss stopped and indicated an alleyway. 'Bear Gardens. Hundreds of years ago, they used to bait bears here. People like me would join people like you to watch fighting dogs bite, claw and torment a bear. We'd all pay to see it, bet money on it. Those bears were more powerful than any dog or any man. They were usually chained up, unable to defend themselves properly. The bears would get angrier and angrier, and some were so strong they managed to break their chains. What do you think happened when they did that?'

Jim kept quiet; he guessed this was a rhetorical question.

'They killed people. In Tudor times, they thought it was God's judgement on the wicked if a bear broke loose.'

'Right.' Jim wasn't sure where the boss was going with this.

'We've poked and prodded a bear and now it's broken its chains. It's loose in the ring and goring people to death. It's my fault that it got out. And when the bear realises that we were among its tormentors, paying to watch, it'll come for us. For me.'

'Sir.' A neutral acknowledgement seemed the safest response.

'Be prepared.'

Jim instinctively brushed a hand over the 9 mm pistol in his shoulder holster. 'Always.'

CHAPTER FIFTEEN

'Thanks for squeezing me in.' Boateng sank back into the chair.

'No problem,' replied Summers. 'It's part of my brief to prioritise sessions with front-line staff, and' – he seemed unsure how best to express his idea – 'it doesn't get much more, um, front line than what you've been through in the last week. So, what would you like to bring to the session today, Zac?'

'Ana,' he stated. When he'd called Summers to arrange the session, he had told him about de Souza's apparent suicide. 'I can't believe she's gone, too.' He was silent a moment.

'Another suicide by someone you knew. It's a lot for anyone to cope with,' offered Summers. 'How are you dealing with it?'

'Not brilliantly.' Boateng rubbed his eyes. 'I'm stressed, on edge. Haven't been sleeping properly the past week. I feel as though I'm making mistakes. Sooner or later one of them is going to be serious.'

'What do you mean?'

Boateng ignored the question. 'I didn't know Ana that well, especially not in recent years. But finding her like that this morning affected me more than I expected.'

'Seeing someone familiar to you in that state would have a significant impact on anybody.'

'Maybe.'

'I'm interested that you said more than you expected?'

Boateng nodded and sat quietly a while. 'I can see myself in their place,' he said, at length. 'It started with Troy, and after Ana that sense is even stronger.'

Summers leaned in, waiting for him to explain.

'I've been around death a lot in this job. In some ways, you get used to it. Like, immune. But when Troy passed, it made me think about my own life. How he and I weren't that different. Things we'd been through, work we'd done. I had this weird feeling that I might die too.'

'Sounds like you identified with him. What did you make of that?'

'Well, I guess I was scared. More than I've ever been. And I realised that you can die in your forties. No one's immortal. Along with Amelia's murder, it made me ask a lot of questions. About what I'm doing, why I'm doing it, you know?'

'It sounds to me like you're in the process of working that out,' suggested Summers. 'Perhaps you already have the answers.'

Boateng closed his eyes. A sadness was rising, overwhelming him. His throat tightened. He was going to cry. He knew Summers wouldn't judge him, but still he resisted the tears.

'I'm just wondering, Zac, what else you meant by more than you expected? I don't want to pry, but it sounded like there was something more there. Behind that statement.'

Zac's eyes flickered open. Summers would be able to see they were moist – the eyes of a man losing his grip. Holding on wouldn't do him any good. 'I think, um, it made me realise that I could be a target too.' His right leg was jiggling.

Summers considered this. 'What makes you say that?'

'"Your sin will find you out."' He knew the Biblical quotation sounded random, but the words had been on his mind after Rix had uttered them in the pub.

'OK. Can you tell me more about that, please?'

'I don't think de Souza killed herself either.'

'Why not?'

Boateng realised the only solid proof of that theory was the red hair he'd found on her body. Lambeth MIT were meant to be questioning Rix, and he'd sent Jones along to join them, add a few questions about her indirect connection to Spearhead and Troy and see if any of it linked up. 'I told you last time we met that I thought someone else might be in danger. Well, I reckon they were, and I didn't do enough to protect them.'

Summers tilted his head. 'I must say, you're making me feel quite concerned, Zac. If someone's life is at risk, I may need to break our confidentiality.'

'It's about what happened years ago,' Boateng blurted. 'At Cleaver Square.' He hadn't meant to say it, but now it was out. OK.

'What happened there?'

'I don't know how to explain it,' replied Boateng. He'd said too much.

'It can be really difficult to express complex feelings, I know.' After a long silence, Summers rose, fetched a pad of paper and a pen and offered them up. 'Perhaps if you wrote it down, that might help?'

Boateng flicked his eyes from the paper to Summers, and took in the counsellor's earnest expression. 'OK,' he mumbled. He wiped his eyes on the back of his hand, took the pad and pen and began writing.

●

Jones was late. The traffic between Lewisham and Brixton had been terrible, roadworks everywhere. Solid single-lane traffic meant that even if she'd put on the blues and twos, it wouldn't have helped. And in any case, she disliked officers who did that when it wasn't a real emergency. Sirens wailing, everyone moving aside, just so they could pick up a takeaway before it got cold. By the time she had arrived, parked and jogged into Brixton police station, she'd begun to sweat. After what seemed like ages, DCI Dave Maddox came down to meet her. She remembered seeing him at the industrial estate murder scene last summer. He'd come off a night shift that time, but he didn't look much fresher today. Maddox was a massive bloke with thick forearms, a broken nose and a shaved head. He didn't have the bulk of Evans, but they both belonged to a definite Met type: hard man. He looked her up and down, tacitly assessing her body, then invited her through the staff door behind the reception desk. When he stopped and faced her in the corridor, Jones realised she wasn't going to be invited up into Lambeth MIT's office.

'Sorry I'm late, sir.' She got straight to the point. 'Where's Rix?'

'Gone.'

'What?'

'She left about fifteen minutes ago.'

'Er, why, sir?'

'Faye Rix cooperated fully with our inquiries. We were interviewing her as a witness, not as a suspect.'

Jones tried to master her frustration. 'What did she say?'

'She told us about the argument in the pub with de Souza. The altercation got a bit physical and her brother had to separate them. That explains why de Souza had a couple of Rix's hairs on her clothing. Nothing more than that to it, and certainly not enough to suspect her of murder. There was no other connection between them. Besides, her brother gave her an alibi for the time of death. Rix confirmed what your boss said about de Souza drinking hard until kicking-out time.'

'Right.' She knew Boateng would be pissed off about the dead end and her missing Rix at the station, but she could at least try to salvage something from the trip. 'And were you able to put our questions on Op Spearhead to her, sir?'

'Yeah.' Maddox flipped a pocket notebook open. 'She used to share a flat with this guy Leo Rogers.'

'Liam Rogers.'

'That's the one. Said she found it through an ad on SpareRoom. Never met him before that. Didn't much like the guy, thought he was a bit weird. Moved out of there and in with her brother six months later.'

Jones was trying to process this. 'That's it?'

Maddox snorted. 'What else d'you want? A polygraph?'

'Sorry, sir. Thanks for asking our questions.'

'See yourself out, love.' Maddox had already turned and begun walking up the stairs before she had a chance to respond.

'What a bellend!' exclaimed Malik, before taking a large swig of lager. Jones gave him a smile of acknowledgement across the high table. The pub they'd chosen in Blackheath was Friday-night busy, the overheated air filled with dozens of conversations against a backdrop of cheesy Christmas songs that were compulsory in December.

'Needed a more senior officer.' Connelly set his Guinness down and searched in vain for a stool. 'Krebs wouldn't have taken any shit from him.'

'It's nothing to do with seniority,' said Jones defensively.

'Kat's right.' Boateng sighed. He looked knackered. 'Maddox just didn't want us jumping in on his turf. Some people are like that, no "we" in team, or whatever that phrase is. You'd be surprised how rare it is to see boroughs cooperate on cases. And when I spoke to Maddox at de Souza's house, he'd already made up his mind it was suicide.'

'So Rix is in the clear for de Souza and Spearhead?' asked Malik.

'Looks that way,' replied Boateng. Jones couldn't resist making a noise somewhere between disappointment and disgust. 'My sentiments entirely,' he added. 'Don't worry though – she's still on our ops board. Maddox can't tell us what goes on that.'

'I'd pin her up there even if she wasn't connected to the case,' smirked Connelly.

'Perv,' said Jones.

Connelly held up his hands. 'I just appreciate a fine, flame-haired woman, that's all. The lass probably has Irish roots if you go back far enough.'

'Her hair's *dyed* red, Pat,' said Malik, shaking his head.

'Ahh.' He waved away the logic. 'Anyway, innocent until proven guilty.'

'If you're a good-looking woman?' she scoffed.

'I never said that.' Connelly gave a broad grin and sipped his Guinness.

Boateng drained his lime and soda, then pulled on his flat cap. 'Sorry, guys, I've got to head back. Need to read my lad a story before bed. Not really in a drinking mood either, after the past twenty-four hours.'

They said their goodbyes and Jones watched her boss walk out. He was slightly stooped, she thought. She hadn't had a chance to talk to him yet about Cleaver Square and share her theory about Joseph Young, the surviving child from the incident. Maybe she could call him…

'So, plans for the weekend?' Malik's attempt at casual was comically sweet. Jones knew he was hoping for some opportunity to hang out with her. She felt a bit sorry for him. Right now, the only man she could think about was Summers. Didn't have the heart to tell Malik she'd arranged a date with the police counsellor for tomorrow night. She was just deciding how to answer sensitively when a roar of laughter burst across the pub from a nearby table. They all turned to look; Jones recognised a group of constables from Lewisham. PC Evans was in the pack, twice the width of everyone else. They were gathered round something, pointing. As the group shifted and parted slightly, she caught a glimpse of Jason Leather on the other side of them, holding a beer bottle, at the edge of the group. He wasn't sharing the joke, whatever it was. His eyes locked on to hers and instinctively she looked away.

'What's so funny then, lads?' called Connelly as the laughs subsided.

'Check this out,' replied one, and the three of them took their drinks over, Jones somewhat more reluctantly than her teammates. The source of humour was a copy of Lewisham station's 'Badvent Calendar', a PR effort based on the twenty-four-day countdown to Christmas. Behind each door was the mugshot of a wanted criminal from the borough, listing their name, age and offences.

'Swear I saw that guy in the street today.' One officer tapped the face in door five. 'If I'd known, I would've arrested him.'

'He'd have you, no problems,' said Evans. 'Need to get down the gym.'

'I'd use a Taser.'

'Didn't you fail the assessment?'

'Probably electrocute himself!' retorted another, to more grunted laughs. Jones wasn't up for this. She wondered how fast she could finish her pint and leave. She was swallowing a mouthful of beer when she heard her name called. It was Evans. He moved towards her, beer in hand.

'Where's your boss?'

'Gone home.'

He cocked his head. 'So, what happened with the woman who did herself in last night?'

'If you're referring to Sergeant de Souza, there'll be a post-mortem, but the main concern is how her partner's doing.'

Evans sniffed. 'Hung herself, didn't she?'

Jones frowned. 'How do you know that?'

'People talk.'

'Which people?' Was it just morbid curiosity fuelling Evans's questions?

'Not just in the station. It's on Twitter. Look.' He reached for his phone, tapped and showed her the page. Faye Rix had posted about the suicide by hanging, calling de Souza's death the latest in a 'spate' of suicides.

'Spate?' Jones wasn't sure how two constituted a spate. Where was Rix getting her information?

Evans pocketed the phone, finished his pint and slapped the glass down. 'Coward's way out.' His breath was heavy with alcohol.

'Excuse me?'

'Spineless.'

'How can you say that?' She raised her voice.

'Come on,' said Evans, as if she was the one being unreasonable. 'I'm just voicing what we're all thinking. There are some that just aren't cut out for the Job. Can't hack it. Better for us if they're out of the game.'

'You insensitive prick,' she yelled at him. 'Those two had done twenty years' service each. They were suffering, they had problems and no one helped them.' Though she had a new, alternative theory about their deaths, Evans didn't know about any of that, and she couldn't believe his callousness.

Evans flashed her a fake smile. 'Survival of the fittest, isn't it?'

'No!'

'Face it, some people deserve to die. Was your old man up to the Job?'

Jones threw her pint into his face. Evans spat, shook off the beer, glared and wound up to hit her, but his hand stopped midway through the motion. Malik had blocked it with his own arm. Evans shoved him backwards and before Jones knew what had happened, bodies were surging in, Connelly was holding Evans back, officers were baying and shouting, the table tipped over and a couple of glasses were smashed. Retreating from the melee, Jones felt the panic growing in her chest as she watched the aggression unleashed. Still clutching her empty pint glass, she sprinted for the door and out into the freezing night.

*

Zac had a moment to himself. He'd put Kofi to bed and, with
Etta insisting on making him dinner, he'd shut the door on
his soundproofed music room and picked up his King Zephyr
saxophone. He wanted to take his mind off everything. But when
you'd seen the dead body of someone you knew just that morning,
it was easier said than done.

As he warmed up, the song 'Death Letter Blues' came into his
mind. He didn't know whether Eddie 'Son' House had actually
received the message he sung about, but it wasn't hard to see why
he'd thought of it. He set his fingering and began to recreate the
simple guitar riff on his sax, the tragic lyrics forming clearly in
his thoughts. House sang about letting people down, and not
realising how much they meant to you until they were gone. And
when their judgement day had come and the sun went down,
you were left alone. The song was about a lover, but Zac realised
it could apply equally to Etta, Troy or even Ana or his colleagues.
He hadn't been there for any of them, wasn't there for them now.
As he began to improvise around the tune, he wondered if he'd
end up alone or facing his own judgement day.

Zac had no clue who was behind the three deaths in the past
week. But he was certain that it wasn't over yet. No music could
keep that thought out of his mind.

CHAPTER SIXTEEN

Saturday, 9 December 2017

Etta was trying and failing to get herself in the Christmas mood. The run-up to it was always stressful with a child, but with just over two weeks to go, she wasn't feeling remotely festive. She'd even put some carols on while they had their traditional Saturday morning cooked breakfast. It hadn't helped. The only one who seemed excited about Christmas was Kofi, his boundless energy shifting here and there, but none of it rubbing off on her or Zac. Last night, she and her husband had spent the latter part of the evening together on the sofa, talking. He'd told her about his old colleague, Sergeant de Souza, found dead earlier that day. But he hadn't wanted to give details, nor had she probed for any. All he did was repeat his theory of Troy's death: murder, not suicide. She'd pushed him gently, but he didn't offer any proof. She'd asked about his counselling sessions; he'd clammed up. A fissure had opened between them, growing into a full-blown gap now, and she hated it.

'Can we get a tree today, Dad?'

'We're going to football, mate,' replied Zac.

'Can we go afterwards? Please. I want to choose it.'

'There might not be time, love,' she said gently. 'We're going for lunch with Grandma and Grandpa, remember?'

'About that…' began Zac.

She knew what was coming and couldn't stop herself from groaning. 'What about it?'

'I've got to go and meet someone. It's about what happened yesterday.' He glanced at Kofi; she knew he didn't want to say any more in front of their son.

'Ko,' she said. 'Go upstairs and clean your teeth.'

'But, Mum—'

'Now.'

As her baby scampered upstairs, she approached Zac. He was facing away, rinsing plates and stacking them in the dishwasher. Etta laid a hand on his shoulder. 'You've got to let me in, love.'

He didn't turn around. 'What d'you mean?'

'You've had some really traumatic experiences in the last ten days, Zac. I know you're getting the counselling, and that's great, but I'd love to know what's going on in here.' She stroked the back of his head and he stopped.

'I'm fine.'

'You're not,' she said firmly. 'I can see that. Anyone can.'

Zac didn't reply.

'This is exactly the time that you need us,' she continued. 'Me, Kofi, my parents. People around you who love you.'

He shrugged. 'You are around me.'

'It doesn't feel like we are.' She exhaled slowly. 'Why don't you come to lunch with us, eh? Give yourself a day off.'

Zac put down the plates, wiped wet hands on his jumper and put his arms around her. 'Sorry,' he said. No more explanation than that. She knew she hadn't just failed to change his mind about the family meal. She'd failed to penetrate the barriers he was building too.

⁕

Two weeks before Christmas and Brixton Market was heaving. Boateng had dropped Kofi back home with Etta after football.

Their exchange had been minimal, as transactional as handing over a package. He didn't want to enter into any more conversation about what he was going through. Not because he didn't trust Etta; not because he didn't love her. Because he didn't want to drag her into the mess he'd created nineteen years ago, just months before they'd met for the first time and started dating. He'd never told her, but it was getting together with her that had saved him from tumbling deeper into the abyss left by Cleaver Square. If there was any kind of threat to him now because of his actions back then, he had to keep his family as far away from it as possible. He was driven by the anguish of the day that their daughter died five years ago, the sense of having failed as a father, a protector. If anything happened to Etta or Kofi, he wouldn't be able to live with himself. That was, if he carried on living. Damn, he was turning into a gloomy bastard.

Boateng dodged the slop of soapy water sent across the pavement by the Albanian fishmongers and shouldered through the crowds into Market Row. At a wooden bench outside Chicken Liquor, he spotted DCI Maddox hunched over a basket of chicken wings. As Boateng slid in opposite him, Maddox pushed a second basket of Korean wings forwards. The DCI had called ahead to get his order, which meant he didn't have much time. DCIs never did.

'Thanks for meeting,' said Boateng, breath clouding in the air. He kept his flat cap and overcoat on.

'No worries. I needed a lunch break.' Maddox gave a small, lopsided grin. 'I gave your DS short shrift yesterday when she came to see Rix.'

'She'll live,' replied Boateng. 'You really don't think Rix is involved in any of it?'

'Nope.' Maddox bit into a wing and licked sauce off his thumb. 'Look, I'm not saying she's some paragon of journalistic integrity. But I don't think she's a murderess. And as for that connection to your other op, it was wafer thin.'

'Hm.'

'Well, interview her yourselves if you want.' He waved a hand, dropped a chicken bone onto the paper tablecloth.

'Appreciate it, sir.' Boateng tried not to sound sarcastic.

'Dave.'

'Right.'

'There is another reason I don't think she's involved, which is why I invited you here. Again, circumstantial, but I thought you'd want to hear it.'

'OK.'

'As you know, my lads checked some stuff around de Souza's house. Routine search, looking for evidence of debts, drugs, other problems that might contribute to suicide. Standard stuff a coroner would want to see at an inquest.'

'Sure.'

'We looked at her home phone. Sometimes there's a clue as to what happened, if the person called Samaritans or another helpline before, you know.'

'And?'

'She dialled a number just after midnight. We put it through a subscriber check, just in case.'

Boateng's heart was starting to beat faster.

Maddox picked up another wing and took a bite, spoke with his mouth full. 'That's where you come in. The mobile was registered to a guy whose last known address was in Lewisham. A wrong'un.'

'What was his name?' Boateng sensed he already knew the answer.

The DCI wiped his fingers and flipped the pages of a small notebook by his elbow.

'Vic Walker.'

As Boateng drove to Catford, he tried to pick apart the pattern. But it held fast, as strong and tight as Kevlar body armour. Any lingering doubt that they were dealing with a spree or serial killer was gone. He didn't know which term was more accurate – nobody seemed to agree on definitions anyway. Today, the FBI simply classified serial murder as two or more victims in separate incidents. What he was confident of now was the perpetrator's way of operating: their MO. They were picking off the people involved in the Cleaver Square incident of '98 one by one, and at each scene leaving a clue that led to the next victim. Rix had told him about a connection between Troy and Hayworth, and he'd received the email. At Hayworth's murder scene, his ledger pointed to de Souza. And her call record brought them to Walker. Was it all fake news designed for his benefit, including Troy's original text inviting him over? If so, did that mean that Rix's source was the murderer? He planned to ask her personally, and he wouldn't take no for an answer this time. They also needed to find Walker; according to the pattern, he was next on the list.

Boateng parked one street away from the main drag and checked the address he'd copied from Troy's diary. Unit 3. Some kind of warehouse? He walked up and down the road until he found the spot, marked only by a small plastic sign alongside the buzzer. The low brick building sat back on a pedestrianised pathway, flanked at the front by a halal butcher's and a slot machine arcade boasting £500 jackpots. Boateng tried the door of Unit 3: locked. He rang the buzzer: no reply. The lights were off inside the place and it appeared empty. But it didn't look like a warehouse. Peering through the windows, he saw that the interior resembled a meeting room: chairs stacked at the back, a flipchart at one end, folding tables at the other. What was Troy doing here? The address appeared in his diary just over three weeks before his death. Was there a connection to—

Movement in the reflection caught Boateng's eye. Something unnatural about it – the speed, the change of direction. He froze, watching as the dark shape shifted and disappeared from the window glass. He spun round and caught a figure passing into a walkway by the multistorey car park overlooking the street. Rix again? Or her brother? Boateng's gut told him he wasn't imagining it. He wasn't going to stand for this; it was the third time in a week someone had followed him. He broke into a run.

Reaching the car park walkway, he backed up and surveyed the three floors of the multistorey, but couldn't see the figure. He approached and scanned the ground floor. Nothing but silence, darkness and a few flickering strip lights over the scattered vehicles. Damn. Then a squeak of shoes from overhead. First floor. He dashed back, stepped up onto the railings and caught the walkway above. Pulled himself up on the metal barrier, jamming a foot on the base and leapt over, breaking into a run towards the sound. He rounded a corner and saw an exit door swinging shut. Boateng bolted at it, throwing the door open and plunging into the stairwell. Took the stairs two at a time going down. Burst through another door onto the ground floor and blinked in the blackness, searching for—

'Boateng. What are you doing here?'

He turned, eyes adjusting quickly. 'Evans?' He paused, caught his breath. 'Why did you run?'

'Eh?' The constable frowned.

'In here from the street. What's going on?'

'Don't know what you're talking about.' Evans raised the shopping bag at his side. 'I'm coming back to my car.'

'You were up on the first floor then you went back down.'

'No, mate.' Evans gave a brief chuckle. 'Why would I do that?'

'I swear…' Boateng was less sure of himself now.

Evans cocked his head. 'You following me?'

'No. Why would I do that?' Boateng smiled awkwardly.

'What brings you to Catford, then?'

'Christmas shopping.' Boateng spread his hands. 'Haven't found anything yet.'

Evans grunted. Could it be a coincidence that he was here? Boateng remembered Troy's altercation with him, shortly before his death. Then he turns up a hundred metres away from the address in Troy's diary.

'Actually, there was something I wanted to ask you,' said Boateng. 'Did you know Sergeant McEwen when you worked in Bromley?'

'The poof that blew his own head off?'

Boateng fought back his anger, tried to keep control. 'You knew him?'

'We worked in the same station. Why?'

'He was my friend,' said Boateng firmly. 'We went way back. Only, I hadn't seen him over the past year. How would you say he was, you know, in himself?'

'*In himself?*' Evans smirked. 'What d'you mean?'

'His mood, his behaviour. Did he have any arguments with anyone?'

Evans shrugged.

'Someone said you had a fight with him,' said Boateng.

'He tell you that?'

'Nope. Like I said, I hadn't seen him. What happened between you two?'

'Wouldn't call it a fight.'

Boateng pushed his head forward. 'What would you call it?'

'Why do you want to know?'

'He was my mate. I want to know if anything might've affected him.' Boateng wished he'd thought this through beforehand. He was freestyling, and it was too easy for Evans to avoid incriminating himself. Then again, it was entirely possible their altercation had no bearing on Troy's death. On his murder.

'Can't help you, sorry.' Evans coughed. 'Look, I know I've got a bit of a temper on me. Always have. I speak out of turn sometimes, and a lot of people don't like it. But at least everyone knows what I think. Not a lot of people are that honest.'

'Does that honesty extend to broadcasting your homophobia?'

'It was a figure of speech. If he was into that, good luck to him.'

Boateng took a step forward. 'Did you threaten him?'

Evans's chest seemed to inflate, his jaw clenched. 'If you're trying to pin the responsibility for his suicide on me, you can fuck right off.'

Boateng held his ground. This was the kind of courage that would make Troy proud.

The two men stood glaring at one another. Eventually, Evans cracked a smile. 'Hope you find what you came for,' he said. 'See you later.' He turned and walked away, leaving Boateng staring into the shadows.

◆

Amazing what exercise can do for you. After the frustrations of the Spearhead and Hayworth cases, plus the disaster of the pub last night, Jones needed a release. She had her date this evening with Summers to look forward to, of course, but before that, a serious gym session was in order. She'd caught the bus into Lewisham and was relived to find the work gym virtually empty. She put drum and bass on her headphones and nailed some cardio – a 5k run in twenty-one minutes – then bashed out a few weights. Finished with some pull-ups; her target was to do five in a row. She managed two and a half. Not bad. Now, grabbing an energy drink up in the office after a hot shower, her muscles tingling, she felt great.

She pulled open a desk drawer and extracted the documents she'd printed off about Joseph Young, the child who'd survived the Cleaver Square incident. Flicked through, reminded herself of the silent interviews, the social services referral. It was time to talk this over with Boateng. She called his mobile from the desk phone.

'Boateng.' He spoke over lilting jazz, the volume of which quickly dropped.

'Zac, it's me.'

'Kat. How's it going?' It sounded like he was driving.

'Yeah, good, I'm in the office.'

'Putting me to shame.'

'No, I've been in the gym.'

'Like I said.'

She laughed. 'Listen, Zac, I've been looking into our cases. Hayworth, de Souza – I know she's not a murder case or in our borough, but there's the link to Hayworth. Anyway, I had a dig on the system and found a report from '98 of a home invasion burglary in Kennington. Cleaver Square.'

'OK.' He sounded sceptical.

'Well, as I'm sure you remember, you and Troy McEwen were there too. Not all of the notes are available, but I just thought' – she didn't know how best to put the point to him – 'that it might all be connected. Three of the people from that event die in the space of nine days. It can't be coincidence. We were looking at criminal connections or maybe even revenge associated with Spearhead for Hayworth's murder, but maybe it's neither. What if all three deaths are about Cleaver Square?'

Boateng was silent for a while. Then he said, 'I think you're on to something.'

She exhaled, relieved. 'So, maybe Troy and de Souza didn't kill themselves.'

'Right now, you and I are the only people who are considering that.'

'So, I was thinking to myself, who might be behind it? Someone who knows about Cleaver Square, maybe even someone who was there. This Victor Walker guy?'

'We need to find him. Can you work tomorrow, Kat?'

'Sure.'

'Thanks. I'll see you in the office, then. Enjoy your—'

'Wait, Zac. One other thing. What about the boy who was there, Joseph Young? By my calculations, he'd be thirty-one now, and he might have a reason to, you know, given that both of his parents died...'

'Good idea, Kat. Logical motive.'

'Were you thinking the same thing?

'No.' His reply was swift, definite.

'Why not?'

'Because Joseph Young died in 2004.'

CHAPTER SEVENTEEN

As Boateng drove to New Cross, he reflected on how it had all started with a silent 999 call. Back in '98, when a Met operator had received a silent call originating in Cleaver Square, they'd judged it genuine – based on the caller's rapid breathing, they said afterwards – and passed it on to the local station at Kennington. It was a quiet Friday afternoon, so Boateng, Troy and Ana had set out to investigate. But they'd been completely unprepared for what was going on inside the house. Boateng knew he was lucky to have made it out alive; few did. He tried to focus on the present.

He'd already dropped by the address previously linked to Vic Walker – a flat off Lewisham High Street. But Walker was nowhere to be seen, and the current occupants – a young couple who told Boateng they were from China – had never heard of him. He took the landlord's details and followed up, but Walker hadn't given a forwarding address. That left his mobile phone, called from de Souza's house just before her death. Boateng had dialled it, blocking his own number, but got no reply. He decided to request tracking on it, tied to the Hayworth murder case, but didn't hold out much hope of it getting a serious look against terrorism targets or missing persons. The dead ends added to his sense of frustration. Boateng also knew that Etta's parents would probably be bad-mouthing him over the lunch he was missing, asking her where his priorities lay. And so long as he was keeping her in the dark, she couldn't really defend him. Damn. At least Jones seemed to be on his side. After the events of the summer, he knew he could trust her. But did he want to bring her into all this shit?

He left the car in a street paralleling the railway tracks behind New Cross station and headed into the Double Jab boxing gym. He followed the sound of distant music along corridors with photos of boxers young and old, posing proudly together. The beats grew louder until Boateng emerged into the bag room and hit a wall of dubstep. He imagined Etta training here, learning punching techniques, and smiled to himself. A handful of boxers were training on speedballs and heavy bags. A digital clock on the wall counted down, timing the sets. He spotted the red ponytail of Faye Rix in one corner. Her huge friend – the guy Jones said was Rix's brother – was holding the bag. She was blasting it with a flurry of blows, the speed and power of which surprised Boateng. At their first meeting outside Lewisham police station, Rix had told the big guy that she could look after herself. Now he knew what she meant. The clock hit zero, Rix stopped battering the bag and Boateng walked over and greeted her. He proffered a hand to the brother, but the guy just stared at him, letting it hang. Boateng cut his losses and dropped his arm.

'Is there somewhere we can talk?' he asked Rix.

'Right here's good,' she said. She was breathless, sweat droplets on her face and shoulders.

Boateng scanned the room. The music was probably too loud for anyone to overhear them. And he recognised that he had to do this on her terms. 'I need your help.'

She gave him a theatrical look of surprise. 'I thought you wanted me to "piss off", Detective. That's what you said last time we met.'

'I'd had a lot to drink.'

'You'd only arrived a few minutes before.'

Boateng coughed. 'OK, I spoke out of turn. I was upset. I'd just helped bury one of my best mates.' He leaned in slightly.

'Look, I know you're as interested in these recent deaths as I am. We're two of the few people who think they're connected. So, maybe we can help each other.'

'I'm listening.' Rix squirted a drink into her mouth.

'I want to know your source on the link between Troy and Hayworth.'

'I can't tell you that.'

'Just hear me out. It won't come back to you, I promise. Your source relationship will be protected.'

Rix smirked. 'You can guarantee that?'

Boateng nodded.

'How?'

'Because it won't be part of an evidence chain.' Boateng glanced from Rix to the brother; he was paying attention to the conversation but, as usual, wasn't saying a word.

'So, what – you're investigating this off the books?'

'Not exactly. Let's just call it personal interest.'

'In covering your own arse?'

'In finding out what happened to my friend.'

Rix stared at the ground, then at Boateng, before flicking her eyes to her brother. 'Alright,' she said. 'Suppose I agree. What will you give me in return?'

Boateng had anticipated this. 'I'll tell you my theory of what's going on here.'

'Go on then.'

He took a deep breath. 'I believe the same person murdered Troy McEwen, Dez Hayworth and Ana-Maria de Souza. I reckon they made Troy's and Ana's deaths look like suicide. And I don't think it's over yet. That's why I want to know the origin of that information about the contact between Troy and Hayworth.'

Rix nodded slowly. 'A serial killer.'

'If you want to use that term, yes.'

She glanced at her brother again. 'That's what I would call it. Better headlines. But why? I mean, why is he choosing those victims? Is it because of what happened in '98?'

'What happened in '98?' Boateng wanted to see what she knew.

'You tell me.'

He didn't reply.

Rix narrowed her eyes. 'What proof do you have that it's a serial killer?'

'None so far.' Boateng sniffed, held eye contact.

'So why should I believe you?'

'It's your choice whether you believe me or not. I'm telling you something off-record, about our investigation, which is not in the public domain.' He checked over his shoulder that no one else could eavesdrop. The music continued to boom out. 'I could face disciplinary charges if my boss found out I'd been speaking to you.'

'You said just now it was off the books.'

'Still unauthorised contact with the media about a live murder case.'

'What good is that to me without any proof? I can't write about it, can I?'

'Not yet.'

'Not yet? So it'll be my exclusive?' Rix studied him a moment before breaking into a wide, feline grin. 'OK. And if you get the urge to unburden yourself any more, there could be some reward in it for you.'

'Don't take the piss,' said Boateng. 'Come on then, what's your source?'

Rix bit the Velcro of her glove strap and tightened it with her teeth. 'Email.'

'Email?'

'Yeah. I got a forwarded message from Troy McEwen's address on the night he died. Then another message the following morning with a night shift report from Croydon police attached, describing how you found the body.'

'Who did you pay for that?'

'No one.'

'Bollocks.' He wasn't buying it.

'What can I say? Somebody wanted me to know.'

Boateng scratched his jaw. 'What address was the police report from?'

'Guerilla Mail, with a scrambled ID. Just letters and numbers.'

'I know the kind.' A temporary address; he tried to process this. 'So, someone who knows their way around a computer?'

'Seems so. I tried to reply but the address had already expired.'

He nodded. In talking to Rix, Boateng had hoped to gain some greater control. Instead, his powerlessness was growing. 'I have to get home,' he said distractedly.

'Alright. Safe trip back to Brockley. Tressillian Road, isn't it?'

'How did you know—'

'Your wife told me.' Rix smiled again. 'She's great. You want to look after her.' As Rix's brother took up position again behind the bag, she resumed her stance and began jabbing it, building up to some big hooks that connected with loud slaps against the vinyl.

Boateng looked up at the big digital clock on the wall. It had started counting down again.

⁂

Kat Jones had made the mistake of arriving early for her date with Tom. That wasn't cool – now she wouldn't be able to make an entrance. But the danger with being later than advertised was a lack of seats, awkwardly trying to find somewhere or picking another place if there were no tables to be had. That was even less cool. At least now they had a place to sit and some privacy when Tom arrived.

Kat also wondered if she'd judged her outfit correctly. She'd gone for leather leggings and an off-the-shoulder top, teamed with some slim-heeled black pumps. Hoped it wasn't too showy, too suggestive. Then again, she had a great figure and Tom wouldn't have seen it in her boring work clothes.

The LP Bar in New Cross was already quite busy, filled with local students and hipsters starting their Saturday night with a cocktail. Kat ordered a bottle of beer and was trying not to drink it too quickly, trying not to check her phone too often. Her watch read 7.05 p.m. Just as she was wondering whether to text Tom to say she'd got a table, he walked in. She stood and leaned towards him, planting a kiss on his cheek. He smelled nice. Not just his aftershave, but the pheromones or whatever it was that told you this was a compatible mate. She felt her face flush slightly and offered to get him a drink. 'My round,' she added, hoping the implication of a second one was clear.

Kat listened, rapt, as Tom described an upbringing on the south coast, a small and stuffy boarding school, some time out travelling in Latin America before realising that psychology was where his interests lay. He'd enrolled on some courses and had done his degree through the Open University while working, then moved into counselling training. He'd worked a lot in prisons, with offender rehabilitation, before volunteering for the Met. Tom's desire to help people was something she could relate to; it was part of her own professional motivation. When he asked, she wasn't sure whether to mention that her father had moved her to join the Met; she didn't want Tom thinking he was still in a counselling session. But, in the end, she had felt comfortable telling him. His attention was full, magnetic, and Kat wasn't aware of the bar, the music, the crowd or anything except those bright, green eyes. Before long, she was opening up to him about all sorts: the casual sexism of older colleagues, the tension between being an investigator and a politician as you got more senior, and her respect for her boss.

'He's a good guy,' Tom observed, taking a swig of beer.

'One of the best,' said Kat proudly. 'Hang on, do you know Zac?'

Tom didn't reply.

'Wait, is he having sessions with—' She stopped herself. 'Sorry, that's indiscreet. None of my business.' It made sense: with the trauma that Zac had been through, he'd have been referred to a counsellor as part of routine wellbeing policy.

'I shouldn't have said anything.'

'No, don't worry about it.' Jones sensed a shift of atmosphere; she was keen to get back to their earlier easy conversation. She finished her beer a bit too quickly and asked Tom if he wanted another.

'My turn,' he smiled, getting to his feet.

Kat watched him walk to the bar and immediately get the attention of the young woman serving. She looked down again, automatically reaching for her phone so that if he glanced over, she'd seem busy.

'You alright?'

The words were loud enough to leave no doubt they were directed at her. Kat glanced up to see Jason Leather standing next to her table. His long hair was down around his shoulders, but his uniform of heavy metal T-shirt was the same. She stared at the image briefly: a naked woman, cuffed and collared. Did he think that was a good look? Without asking, he pulled up a free bar stool and sat, awkwardly higher than her.

'Not the music I would've chosen,' he said in that flat, nasal voice.

'Er, I'm kind of having a—'

'Hello.' Tom paused at the table, a beer bottle in each hand. 'I think I've seen you at work. You're a colleague of Kat's, right?'

Great, now Tom would think she was responsible for inviting him to sit down. Jason's move was what her male mates would call a cock-block.

'If it was my bar,' Jason continued, oblivious, 'I'd play Mayhem. Norwegian black metal band. Even after the lead singer blew his own head off with a shotgun, they were still the best.'

Kat exchanged a glance with Tom, whose expression was a mixture of confusion and amusement. Tom handed her the beer, and under the wall light next to the table, she noticed some small white marks on his hand, like mini blotches or scars. She turned her attention back to their uninvited guest. 'What, er, it's Jason, right?' she said. 'Who are you out with?'

'No one,' he replied. 'This is my local. They know me here.'

I bet they do, she thought. *The weird guy with long, greasy hair who drinks alone.*

'I live in the flat above the convenience shop next door.'

'Right.' Kat swigged her beer; Tom did the same.

'You know they got a photo of it,' added Jason.

'What?' she asked. How could she get rid of him? They couldn't leave; Tom had only just got drinks.

'The shotgun suicide.' Jason's gaze lost focus. 'Incredible. I mean, like, unbelievable. Can you imagine seeing that happen for real? They even put a photo of it on a band T-shirt. I've got one – limited edition. Bought it online off a guy in Oslo. It's sick.'

'I'll take your word for it.'

'I mean, how often do we stop to think about death?' said Jason, finally looking at them in turn.

'Well, quite a lot actually,' she replied. 'I work in a Major Investigation Team.'

'No, he's right,' interjected Tom. 'We do tend to block out death, I think because most people are scared of it. There's even a psychology theory about it.' He was trying to be diplomatic, Kat could see. That was sweet, but she had no desire to prolong this interruption.

'Can you imagine what it must be like to know you're about to die?' asked Jason, without pausing for an answer. 'The singer of Mayhem called himself "Dead". Used to bury his clothes then dig them up and put them back on, so it looked like he'd just climbed out of a grave.'

'Probably smelled like it too,' suggested Kat. Tom smirked and raised one eyebrow.

'So, what about this woman who hanged herself then?' asked Jason. 'The copper. Did you see it, up close?'

'Ah, no, it's not our—'

'Used a belt, didn't she? Must've been a slow death.' He smiled, which seemed totally inappropriate. As Kat was wondering how to respond, Jason's phone rang and he stood, walking away to answer.

She leaned towards Tom. 'Christ, sorry about that. He just came over. I couldn't stop him.'

'Don't worry about it.'

'Shall we go somewhere else?' she asked.

Tom smiled, his cheeks dimpling, and nodded. Her heart beat a tiny bit harder.

·

Three out of five. Two left. Both must have worked out what connects the previous victims. Boateng is trying and failing to investigate it; the other one will have seen the news by now. I love the thought of them scared shitless because they think someone is coming for them. The experience is all too familiar: heart palpitations, adrenalin and cortisol on overdrive, insomnia. Things I dealt with for many years, wanted to get rid of but couldn't shift. Let someone else have all that; someone who deserves to feel that way.

The downside is that fear will make them more vigilant. An extra check before they cross the road, a double lock of the door at night, a second glance at anyone they pass who they don't know. But I know these people. I don't need to go looking for them. They'll come to me. In fact, the next one is probably already on his way. He just doesn't know it yet.

CHAPTER EIGHTEEN

Sunday, 10 December 2017

Zac stared out of the living room window at the snow that had fallen overnight. It always looked nice at first, blocking out the city's grime and decay. Everyone would take photos of their favourite things painted white and post them on social media. But within hours, the city would grind to a halt: trains stuck, roads closed, arrangements cancelled. That was one problem with living within walking distance of the office: no excuse to stay home. Not that Zac was intending to skive off; if anything, he needed to work harder. And given this killer's method, home was probably the most dangerous place for him.

'Can you help me, Dad?'

He turned to see Kofi holding a small cardboard angel; he recognised it as the one his daughter had made the Christmas before her death.

'That's Ammy's,' he observed.

'I want to put it up there,' said Kofi, pointing to the tip of their bare Christmas tree. Zac had promised his son they could decorate it together today, though he already knew he'd need to break that promise in order to find Vic Walker.

'Sure, come on.' Zac squatted down and Kofi climbed onto his shoulders, one hand cupping his dad's chin for stability. He was getting heavy now. His eleventh birthday wasn't far away;

soon he would be too big for this. At least then he could reach the top of a Christmas tree on his own.

With Zac holding his legs, Kofi set about tethering the angel to the tree with some pipe-cleaners. 'My sister's an angel now, isn't she?' said the boy out of nowhere.

'Ah, she's...' Zac paused, unsure how to reply. He didn't believe in a spirit world, but he could understand how the thought might be a comfort to his son. 'What do you mean by angel?' Zac recognised he was using one of Summers's 'tell me more' questions. The listening style was rubbing off on him.

'Well, she's in the sky and watches over our family. She protects us from bad things that could happen.'

'Who told you that?'

'Grandma and Grandpa.'

'Uh-huh.' Zac didn't want to contradict Etta's parents. He chose his words carefully. 'We still have to make our own choices about things, though. It's not like we can do whatever we like and not expect any consequences.'

'I know, Dad.'

'OK. Done?'

'Think so.'

Zac lowered Kofi to the ground and they stepped back to inspect the angel. 'Looks good. Now, let's get the rest of these decorations up. That'll be a nice surprise for your mum.'

As Kofi picked up a length of tinsel, Zac wondered how long he could put off going in to the office, and what time he could realistically expect Jones to arrive on a Sunday with no overtime pay. Then his phone rang. He didn't recognise the number.

'Zac Boateng.'

'Yeah, it's Kam Abas from King's Forensics.'

Zac hadn't expected a result so soon. He turned back to the window, his gaze sweeping over the snowfall. 'Appreciate the call.'

'About your samples,' began Abas. His tone suggested something was wrong. 'First off, they're different.'

'How?'

'Blood type. One is O positive, the other's A positive.'

'OK.'

'You know what that means?'

Zac tried to sound surprised. 'One's from Hayworth, the other isn't?'

'Correct. The one you supplied to me isn't his. You said it was from his car?'

'Er, yeah.'

'However, there was a match on that second sample, the A-positive. The DNA profile from it was identical to someone already on the system.'

Zac waited.

'An officer called Troy McEwen, recently deceased.'

'Jesus.' Boateng knew that some officers' DNA was stored on individual police force databases, to enable identification of investigators who may have contaminated crime scenes. 'Thanks, Kam. Should give us some angles to work. Anything else?' He hoped that the testing hadn't ended there; if the two samples were initially found to be from different people, it removed the stated rationale for detailed toxicology analysis of both.

'As it happens, yes. And that's where it gets interesting. Despite being from different people, both blood samples contained detectable quantities of a chemical called succinylmonocholine, or SMC. In Dr Volz's sample, it was low but present. In your sample, it barely registered, but there was no doubt that it was there. Another day or two and it would've vanished altogether.'

'OK, great.' Zac paused. 'What's SMC?'

'It's the metabolite of a muscle relaxant called succinylcholine, also called suxamethonium chloride. Abbreviated to sux.'

'Can we call it sux?'

'Sure. Now, sux is most commonly used in anaesthetic, so it's found—'

'It knocks you out, right?'

'Not exactly, I'm coming to that. It's one part of anaesthetic.'

'Which part?' A grim thought was already developing in Zac's mind.

'The part that paralyses you. Without the other components, a shot of sux renders you immobile, yet completely conscious.' Abas cleared his throat. 'And fully able to feel pain.'

'Christ.' Zac didn't know what else to say. His imagination was already firing on Troy's last moments. On Hayworth's. And, he'd bet, de Souza's.

'It's fast-acting,' continued Abas. 'You inject it, and within seconds the muscles lose tension. Less than a minute later, the person is totally paralysed. But you need to get the dose right, relative to someone's body weight. Too little and they can still move. Too much and their lungs stop working, they die from lack of oxygen to the brain. You'd need to keep the person alive with artificial respiration until the drug wears off. It only lasts for minutes before it needs to be topped up, or the person regains movement.'

Zac had grabbed his tablet and was already googling 'sux forensics'. The search hits made for interesting reading. 'Says here it's been used in a few murders before.'

'I believe so.'

'Where could someone get hold of it?'

'Through a vet, maybe a hospital. Probably easiest to buy it online, if you know where to look. Listen, I've got to get back, but I thought you'd appreciate the heads-up before I email the full report. Since it's a live murder case.'

'Thanks, Kam. I owe you.'

'I know better than to believe a detective when they say that. Good luck.'

Zac rang off and dialled Jones's number. The young technician had it right. It was very much a live murder case. And he was going to need a lot of luck.

·

Jones couldn't stop thinking about Tom Summers. The date last night had gone well, but at the end, she'd leaned in for a kiss and he hadn't reciprocated, just given her a peck on the cheek. Did that mean she'd done something wrong? It only made her want him more. She needed a distraction from him. Coming into the MIT office to hear Boateng's briefing on the toxicology breakthrough could work.

'Sux?' she repeated. 'That's the murder weapon?' She googled it and began browsing the search hits.

'Not directly, but effectively, yeah.' Boateng rotated his chair towards her. 'It's what allows the killer to incapacitate the victims, then murder them however he wants. Take his time, arrange the scene, make it look like suicide, make them suffer.' He thought of Hayworth being burned slowly, and took a breath. 'Whatever he needs to do.'

'But he still has to get the substance into their bodies. We think he's injecting them, right?'

'Yeah. Bruise on Hayworth's body suggests so, and I reckon we'd find a similar wound on de Souza.'

'How does he do that without them realising and struggling?'

'The victims must feel comfortable with the killer there. Either they're employing some kind of cover story, or—'

'It's someone they know.'

'Right. Killer gets up close and then bam! Before they realise, there's a needle in them.'

'And then it's too late.' Jones read off the screen. 'Carl Coppolino, a doctor in the US, murdered his wife with sux in 1967.' She clicked and scrolled. 'A Republican politician from Nevada, killed by her husband in 2006... There's a theme emerging here.'

'It's not all couples.' Boateng pointed to his own monitor. 'A serial murderer in Japan in the nineties. Practised his sux injections on dogs. And a guy from Hamas assassinated in Dubai in 2010.'

'How's our killer getting the sux, then?'

Boateng twirled a biro in his fingers and tapped it on the desk. 'Lab technician's view was that he's probably sourcing it online.'

'Multiple or bulk purchasing for the quantities needed. Should leave computer forensics evidence. We dealt with these kinds of leads when I was in Cyber Crime. There might be a payment record, delivery address. We could check with online suppliers. Start above ground then look at the dark web.'

'That's a lot of work. And they might not even be getting it online.'

'So we check with hospitals. Vets in the area, too.'

'Yup.' He leaned back, blew out his cheeks. 'Be a damn sight easier if we had a suspect, then we'd just focus on their online activity.'

'Vic Walker?' she suggested.

'Maybe. I've requested the trace on his mobile, and we've issued his picture to all boroughs as a person of interest.'

'You don't sound convinced it's him.'

'I think he's involved somehow, or about to be involved.'

'Who else could it be?' Jones held out her palms, inviting a name. Boateng was silent. 'I've read everything I could find about Cleaver Square in '98,' she continued. 'No next of kin could be located for the Young family after the incident. And like you said, the son, Joseph, died in '04.'

Boateng nodded. 'I agree; it looks like Walker. Unless there's a relative out there that no one knows about, he and I are the only living people connected to that crime. But I don't see him as being the mastermind. The brains of that home invasion was a guy called Arun Gray. He was shot dead at the scene. And if it's Walker, why now, nineteen years later?'

'Blackmail?' she suggested. 'He falls on hard times, decides to start demanding money from the others. They don't pay, he kills them. Or someone was threatening him, he concludes it relates to Cleaver Square, kills the others to protect himself.'

'That would include me.'

'Yeah.' Jones hesitated. But she had to ask. 'What happened that day, Zac?'

Boateng seemed to zone out, his eyes losing focus, jaw clenched.

'Zac?'

'Joseph Young died in Guatemala,' he said. 'I followed up on it myself, got a translation of the post-mortem. He fell off a cliff while he was travelling. No one knew if it was an accident – a cliff dive gone wrong – or suicide. I never met him at the time. He was found hiding in the house after we were taken away. Media kept his picture out of the papers because he was a minor. Apparently, the poor kid didn't say one word in interview, exhibited all the outward signs of trauma and depression. I read a report six months later from the child mental health service. Joseph's mutism continued, he had insomnia, bedwetting, even developed some kind of stress-related rash. I felt so guilty, I couldn't bring myself to go and see him in care.' Boateng shook his head. 'What could I have said to him?'

Jones dodged the invitation to sympathise; now wasn't the time. 'Is it possible,' she ventured, 'that he didn't die? That there was a mistake? Joseph Young would have one of the strongest motives imaginable for these murders, wouldn't he?'

Boateng bit his lip. 'I get what you're saying. But don't forget – Occam's razor.'

Jones smiled. Her boss had introduced her to the philosophical term earlier this year. The explanation with the fewest steps was most likely.

'Walker came out of prison earlier this year,' continued Boateng. 'Enough time for someone to blackmail him, or vice versa, and for him to plan this out before starting.'

'I didn't get the impression you thought it was him,' countered Jones. 'You said he was *involved*. Not responsible.'

'I don't know what I think any more.' Boateng shrugged and spun his pen again.

'What happened to Joseph Young's post-mortem report?' she asked.

'Probably tossed out or shredded years ago. I had no reason to keep it.'

'Shall I request another copy via the Guatemalan police?'

'Why?'

'In case there's something we missed.'

He snorted. 'You mean something *I* missed?'

'Come on, Zac. There's new cause to check it. Leave no stone unturned.'

'I do say that. OK, go for it.'

Jones began searching for the details to make a consular request via the Foreign Office pertaining to Joseph Young's death. She was already trying to work out how they could tackle the issue of sux suppliers, and wondering how Boateng was going to explain all this to Krebs, particularly his unauthorised toxicology request. They worked side by side in silence for a few minutes, until the question she was scared of asking returned.

'Zac?'

'Hm?'

'Do you think… Is it possible…'

'What?'

'Could you be a target, too?'

Boateng didn't say anything, but his face told Jones the answer. He took a deep breath and seemed about to speak, then his phone rang. He confirmed his name, made a few affirmative noises, then asked 'Whereabouts, exactly?' before thanking the caller and ringing off.

'Better get Connelly and Malik in,' he said. 'Duty team have reported a serious assault. Somali-run money transfer shop in Lewisham, last night. Victim's alive but hospitalised.'

'Oh my God.' Jones frowned. 'Is it a new Spearhead attack?'

'Maybe. And this time there's something we haven't had before.'

'What's that?'

'A witness.'

CHAPTER NINETEEN

Monday, 11 December 2017

Etta strode into the kitchen and found both her boys there. It was 8 a.m. and neither one looked ready for Monday morning in their respective institutions.

'Ko, you haven't got your uniform on yet.'

'I know, Mum, I'll do it.' He bit into his toast and immediately took a large gulp of orange juice.

'Wait till you've finished chewing before you take a sip of your drink.'

'OK, Mum.'

'You're still in your dressing gown, Zac.'

Her husband grinned. 'Thought I was the detective in this family.'

'Very funny. Starting late?'

'Let's just say I'm not in a rush to get in.' Zac swigged his coffee and poured some from the cafetière into a mug for her.

'Aren't you working a mur—' She caught herself, remembering their ten-year-old son was in the room. 'An important case?'

'Yup.' He began putting items into Kofi's lunchbox. 'But once I go in, I'll have to tell my boss something she's not going to like.'

'You've decided to resign from the Met and become a full-time chef?' Etta allowed herself a smirk, which her husband returned. He was clearly stressed, but his mood was a little lighter today. 'You're taking Ko in though, right?'

'Course.'

'Great.' She chose an apple from the fruit bowl, dropped it into her handbag. 'I'll pick him up from school, but I'm out tonight.'

'Oh?' Zac went over to the fridge and began pulling out an armful of sandwich ingredients.

Etta sighed briefly; he'd forgotten already. 'Boxing. Monday nights.'

'With the journalist?'

'Faye might be there, yes.' She tutted. 'I'll probably have to apologise again for your behaviour in the pub, of course...'

'What did he do?' Kofi sat up straight and stopped chewing, eyes wide at the prospect of Daddy behaving badly. 'What did you do, Dad?'

'Never mind.' Zac glared at her, shook his head.

'I hope she is there, in fact. I might learn some punching techniques off her.'

'Can you do punching, Mum?' Kofi mimicked a right hook. 'Pow!'

'Only at the boxing gym, Ko.' She finished her coffee and went over to kiss her son on the forehead, then her husband on the lips, drawing him in for a quick hug. He was extra cuddly with his thick dressing gown on. 'See you both later.'

Kofi waved his toast at her. 'Bye, Mum.'

'Go safe,' said Zac. He didn't normally say that.

Etta paused in the doorway and glanced back at him, wondering if that was code for something. She flashed a smile. 'You too.'

⁕

'You did *what?*' Krebs's voice was already at an eight. Wouldn't take much more for it to reach ten. Then everyone on the entire floor would know about his bollocking. He reckoned she had an eleven on the scale too, maybe reserved for occasions like this. 'Please tell me you're joking, Zac.'

'No, ma'am.' He held her gaze for a moment then looked at his shoes. Deference was probably his best chance to deal with the inevitable.

'You took a blood sample you personally collected from Troy McEwen's house to King's and talked to a lab technician – no, *lied* to a lab technician – about its provenance in order to get it tested. I can't believe it.'

'I'm sorry.' He coughed. 'But, it did reveal that—'

'Not now!' She'd reached ten. Krebs stood and chopped a hand in his direction. 'I don't want to hear that. You've broken the rules on gathering and processing evidence. You've done it outside of any recognised or authorised investigation. You've collected material from another borough of London without informing our colleagues there.' She was numbering the offences on her fingers. 'And you've done all of this after I expressly told you not to get involved.'

'With respect, ma'am, you only said that I should take some compassionate leave, and see the counsell—'

'Quiet!'

That was eleven. Krebs ran both hands over her face and through her hair. 'We've got to tell King's, obviously. They'll probably be required to run an audit on the supply of forensic samples to the lab. They'll have to review their policies, make sure the emergency systems aren't open to abuse. Think of the hours that's going to take, the cost. The loss of scientist trust in us. Because of you.'

Boateng said nothing. Krebs was getting hold of her breathing. She paced across to the framed photo of her and Met Commissioner Cressida Dick, then returned slowly to her desk and sat down. 'You can sit, too.'

'Thank you, ma'am.'

'I've covered for you a fair bit, Zac, because I believe your heart is in the right place, and you deliver excellent results. But this is too big for me to paper over. When this is all done, you might have to face disciplinary procedures over what you did, and it won't be up to me to decide on that.'

He frowned. 'When it's done, ma'am? Not now?' he added tentatively.

Krebs inhaled deeply and let her breath out slowly. 'Yes. You might have bent the regulations beyond even the most elastic of limits, and it's possible that your evidence is flawed, given the conditions under which it was obtained. But two bodies in a week, historically linked, both of whose blood contains traces of sux metabolite? Angry as I am, I won't overlook that.'

Boateng relaxed his posture slightly. 'And Sergeant de Souza, ma'am? Should we get Lambeth to ask for the same toxicology on a blood sample from her body?'

'Yes.' Krebs leaned back in her chair. 'But I need you to explain something before I can request that. The day after Sergeant McEwen's death, you stood here and told me he'd been murdered. You had no evidence. Now you've got hold of some that you couldn't possibly have known about at the time. Are you going to tell me what the hell this is about?'

Boateng hesitated. Now was the moment. He swallowed, composed himself.

'Back in '98,' he began, 'Sergeant McEwen, Sergeant de Souza and I were working borough together out of Kennington station. We were all PCs back then, pretty green, not long passed out of Hendon. We attended a silent 999 call at a big house on Cleaver Square. Home invasion burglary in process, four guys. They were armed. We weren't prepared at all.' He glanced up to check Krebs's reaction, but she was inscrutable, staring at him over steepled fingers. 'We made some mistakes, it was chaos. We were lucky to leave with our lives. It was thanks to Troy that Ana and I made it out. Unfortunately, the same wasn't true for Mr and Mrs Young, the hostages.'

'Two civilians died?'

'Yes. And two of the attackers.'

'Who was responsible for those deaths?'

'Troy shot one of the burglars after taking control of his weapon. Self-defence,' he added. 'The others were killed by the hostage takers.'

She frowned. 'The perpetrators shot one of their own, then?'

Boateng blinked, nodded.

'My God.'

'I believe that someone is taking revenge on us all for that day,' said Boateng. 'Hayworth was one of the group, and I think a guy called Vic Walker could be next.'

Krebs raised her eyebrows. 'Could Walker be the killer?'

'I don't know, ma'am. Whoever's doing this is quite sophisticated. Seems beyond Walker's skill set, but I could be wrong. Maybe I'm underestimating him. There was a son, but...' He shook his head. 'It's impossible.'

'What is?'

'The Young's son, Joseph, survived the attack by hiding. He was the one who dialled 999. But he died in '04, so it can't be him.'

'Hm. Maybe another relative, then?'

'Maybe.'

'And why the supposed suicides?'

'Could be trying to throw us off. No one treated Troy's death as murder.'

'Except you.'

He nodded. 'And Lambeth aren't doing anything about Ana's apparent suicide either. If there was a clear sequence to the three deaths, with identical MO – as most serial murderers employ – we'd have been all over it much quicker, allocated greater resources, joined up across boroughs. More chance we'd stop the killer before he completes his plan.'

'Which is what, exactly? To kill Walker and then' – she hesitated – 'you?'

'I believe so.'

'If you thought it was connected to Cleaver Square, why didn't you say so earlier?'

Boateng flushed with shame. She was right. 'I…' The truth was, he didn't want people asking questions about Cleaver Square. 'I was scared. To bring it all up again, to talk about the mistakes we made.'

Krebs leaned forward. 'That's not a good enough reason, Zac.'

'They were some pretty big mistakes.'

'Saving yourself?'

'I just…' He faltered. Right, again.

'Well, when we catch this person and they stand trial, I dare say it'll all come out in the wash. A defence barrister will get everything they can on it.'

Boateng closed his eyes at the prospect. He knew it could be the end of his career.

'Right now though, Zac, you've got a killer to catch. Better go and brief your team.'

•

Jones wrote the name 'Abdi Osman' on the Op Spearhead board, filling in the key details of the attack on him: date, time, place. She wrote 'Witness' alongside it and marked the word with an asterisk. Osman's wife had seen the attack on him from an upstairs window and had called the police. She was very frightened, and stressed with looking after four children on her own while her husband lay in hospital. But they needed to speak to her. Jones thought about other potential witnesses to the Spearhead attacks. Could be worth visiting Antony Webb in his psychiatric unit, too; perhaps he'd be more relaxed and forthcoming now.

After the attack on Osman and theft of cash from his money transfer business, community leaders were becoming much more vocal and the Lewisham MP had demanded to know what the

Met was doing about the attacks on migrant businesses. Desperate and under pressure from Krebs, they'd called on Dale Rogers this morning – following up the DNA lead – but he had solid alibis for the attacks. Staff confirmed he was in the cinema during Mehmet Bardak's murder, a landlord remembered him watching a football match in the pub when Vikram Kumar was attacked and his parents vouched for him being at their house last night. Their best Spearhead lead, down the drain.

'You're certain it's the same guy that targeted Bardak and Kumar, then?' Connelly had sidled up to the board, his tone sceptical.

'How can you doubt it, Pat?' she replied. 'Three attacks in three weeks on Lewisham residents of BAME background, at their own businesses. It's a message on behalf of racists. They think they can do what they like after the Brexit vote.'

'I'm just saying, the money was stolen too. In fact, there's probably a greater financial motive than any other for hitting a place like Osman's. He deals in cash.'

'True, but if all you want is cash, why not target a bank or a building society? Or a post office?'

'Too much security.'

Jones had to concede that Connelly was right about that. 'Look, if the MO's the same – night-time attacks, with something like a baseball bat, followed by theft of money – then it's clear the attacks are linked. Right?'

'As rain.'

'So, whether this person is doing it because they're a racist or because they want extra cash – or both – is actually less relevant than the fact it's a serial offender. The reason only becomes a way to help us find them.' Behind them, she heard a desk phone ring and Malik answered it.

'And how do we do that?' asked Connelly.

'We start by interviewing the witness, then we go and see Webb again, and match up what each of them has to say.'

'Webb? That's a waste of time, Kat, and you know it. The guy's not right in the head.'

'You sound like Evans.' She added a note to the board.

'Jeez, thanks for the insult. As I recall, I stopped him smashing your face in the other night.'

Jones remembered her escape in the pub. 'Yeah, thanks for that,' she said quietly, then turned to the Irishman. 'But why are you giving me a hard time about Spearhead?'

'I'm not!'

'Oi, you two.' Boateng was standing behind Malik's desk. 'Stop arguing and get your shit together. They've pinged Walker's phone. We need stab vests, Taser, squad cars, the works.' He clapped his hands. 'Let's go.'

They sat outside the tyre and exhaust workshop in Lee, just south-east of Lewisham centre, watching the forecourt from across the road. Jones was in the passenger seat of the unmarked vehicle, Boateng alongside her at the wheel. They'd cracked the window to stop the inside steaming up, and Jones was trying not to shiver as the icy air seeped inside. Malik and Connelly were split between two patrol cars parked north and south of the garage, each accompanied by a uniformed officer.

'Will you recognise him, do you think?' she asked. 'I mean, you haven't seen Walker in, like, nineteen years.'

'I saw the mugshot from his last arrest. Fella doesn't really look any different.'

'What did you tell the others?'

'Just that it relates to the Hayworth murder case. I'll fill them in on the rest later.'

'And do we have anything to suggest that Walker is a suspect?'

'Nope.' Boateng bit his lip. 'That's why we want to speak to him as a "person of interest". It's not an arrest, as such.'

'Got it.' She reached forward and fiddled with the radio, keeping the volume low. Tried and failed to find something she liked. Boateng hadn't brought any of his personal music collection, unfortunately. She was always happy to let him DJ their car journeys.

'Hey, here he comes.' Boateng shifted in his seat as a short, heavyset man in his forties with light, close-cropped hair and a leather jacket strolled out of the workshop's open front, glancing to left and right as he emerged. 'Showtime,' he said, opening the car door.

'Vic Walker.' Boateng held up his warrant card as they crossed the road. 'Remember me? Boateng.'

Walker froze, turned and ran back inside the workshop.

'Go round!' Boateng yelled as he raced after Walker.

Jones broke into a run, boots splashing in the grey mush that the snow had left behind. She radioed their pursuit through to Malik and Connelly, demanded backup. Reaching the side of the building, she saw an open space at the back. Climbing onto the wall, she jogged alongside the workshop, one hand on the side for balance. She slipped once and caught herself, carried on. At the rear, she saw Walker running through a garden and gave chase in parallel. Jones had to climb a fence to get out into the street, and it let Walker gain ground on her. She could hear Boateng shouting off to her right, and the sirens of patrol cars converging.

Picking up her pace on the wet surface, she entered a low-rise housing estate, following Walker between the brick buildings and out into a park. Jones slowed, now unable to see Walker among the trunks and foliage. She edged forward, peering into the spaces between trees.

'Hold it,' said a high-pitched voice behind her.

She spun round to see Walker standing in the shadow of a large evergreen. It took her a moment to register that he was holding a pistol, and that it was aimed at her. Adrenalin coursed through her abdomen and her heart hammered inside the stab vest. A thought flickered in her mind that it was exactly that: *stab* proof, not bulletproof. She raised two shaking hands.

'OK. It's alright, Mr Walker.'

'You won't take me, too.' The voice was almost a whine. Jones heard his desperation.

'No one wants to take you anywhere, sir. We'd just like to chat to you, that's all.'

'What, so you can kill me as well?' His breathing was audible.

Jones swallowed. The pistol barrel was aimed squarely at her chest. She shook her head. 'No, we want to protect you.'

Walker stared at her; was he searching for some reassurance? 'I don't believe you,' he barked. Then he clicked the hammer back on the pistol and closed one eye. 'Fuck this.'

'Please,' said Jones, but the word came out as a whisper. She shut her eyes, thought of her dad. How he'd died in the line of duty. How she'd wanted to follow in his footsteps. But not like this. She braced herself.

But the next thing she heard wasn't a gunshot. It was an electric crackle, immediately followed by a strangled moan. She opened her eyes to see Walker collapsed on the grass, a wire in his back. Standing a few metres behind him, Taser poised and ready to deliver more volts, was Malik.

'Drop the weapon!' he cried. Walker released his grip, and as Malik issued further instructions, Boateng and Connelly moved in, first kicking the gun away and then cuffing Walker.

Jones let out the breath she hadn't even realised she'd been holding. She was rooted to the spot, her legs refusing to move. Her whole body was trembling.

●

Jim checked his pistol and replaced it in the shoulder holster. Drew his jacket over the top, pulled the ear defenders on and flexed his hands. He was alone. The indoor firing range and its antechamber were entirely underground. That stopped any gunshot noises finding their way up to street level, but it did give the place a claustrophobic feel. Very few people knew about this facility and even fewer were allowed to train here. Hard to keep these skills sharp in the middle of a city; people tended to notice when a gun went off. You needed somewhere out of sight – and earshot.

The boss had entrusted Jim to protect a secret. He'd told him to use force if necessary. Hence his need to be here. It was time away from Boateng, but he couldn't stay on the guy 24/7. Even the boss, with his standards, would admit that was unrealistic. Jim wondered how much Boateng really knew. Were they both effectively just puppets of bigger players and influences? Boateng had been a busy bee over the weekend. Jim had followed him to the meeting room in Catford on Saturday afternoon. The detective had found the place, but did he know what went on there?

Chances were, Jim would have to act first and ask questions later. Not his normal approach, but this wasn't a normal job. That was why training was doubly important. Reinforcing muscle memory to make the process automatic. Paying attention to every detail of the movement. He stood still in the cold air, the extractor fans on full blast to suck out the fumes that accumulated with round after round in the closed space. He focused on the end of the range, fifteen metres away. With no warning, a board at the end swivelled towards him, revealing a human-shaped target of white paper. And with no thought, Jim pulled his jacket open, drew the 9 mm pistol in his right hand and smoothly brought the left up to meet it. He fired four rounds, in two bursts of two, before the target disappeared. He'd set the machine to make it visible for two seconds.

Jim holstered the pistol and walked up to the target, hit the button to reveal it again. Two holes punctured the centre of the chest. The other two were an inch apart, in the target's head. Not bad for a first go. Another twenty-four attempts left. Then he'd need to get back to watching Boateng. That was a song, wasn't it? 'Watching the Detectives'. Jim reset the target and walked back.

CHAPTER TWENTY

Tuesday, 12 December 2017

'What do you know about the death of Sergeant Ana-Maria de Souza?' Boateng didn't produce any photographs at this stage or give any more detail; he wanted to see what Vic Walker would say. The lawyer alongside him was silent.

'Nothing.' Walker shook his head, eyes wide. He glanced around the interview room, at the recording machine, then his gaze travelled to Jones and back to Boateng.

'Do you recognise this number?' Jones pushed a piece of paper towards him. On it were printed the distinctive eleven digits of a mobile.

Walker squinted at it. 'Er, yeah. That's my number.'

'A call was made from Ana-Maria de Souza's home phone to this number at the time of her death.'

'If you say so.' Walker sniffed, then tried to sit up in his chair to assert what little physical presence he had.

'We don't say so, Vic,' said Boateng. 'The telecoms record says so.'

'OK. What, you think I killed her?'

The lawyer leaned across and whispered something to Walker.

'No one said that.' Boateng inclined his head. 'But we'd like you to explain. You picked up and the call lasted twenty-three seconds. What did you talk about?'

'Nothing!' Walker leaned back, folded his arms. 'The line was silent, like there was no one there. Or a mistake, whatever. I asked who it was, said hello a few times, but all I could hear was some breathing. Then I hung up. End of.'

'Why would that call have been made to you?' asked Jones.

'No bloody idea.'

Boateng clasped his hands. 'Why were you carrying a weapon yesterday?'

'It was a replica.'

'Doesn't matter. We've examined the pistol and it'd been converted to fire live rounds. And you produced it in public to threaten a police officer. That makes what you did an offence under the Firearms Act 1968, Section 1. With your record, Vic, you could be looking at a custodial sentence. Do you want to go back inside?'

'At the minute, I wouldn't mind.'

'Sorry?'

'Might be safer.'

'What d'you mean?'

Walker leaned forward in his chair and placed both palms on the table. 'It's obvious, isn't it?' He jabbed a finger at Boateng. 'You of all people should know. Cleaver Square job, '98. I've suffered cos of what happened that day. Had therapy in prison and everything, got it off my chest. How's your conscience?'

Boateng didn't respond.

'Hayworth and the first copper, I read about them,' continued Walker. 'Now you tell me another copper's dead. Face facts: it's you and me next, mate.'

Boateng cracked his knuckles. 'You're going to need to account for your whereabouts on the nights that all three of them were murdered.'

Walker sat back. 'Happy to.'

'Let's start with the night of Thursday, November thirtieth.'

The lawyer whispered something else to Walker, who nodded. 'I was at me mum's house.'

'And can anyone confirm that, other than your mum?'

'Maybe, dunno.'

'What about Monday, December fourth and Thursday, December seventh?'

'Same, probably. Either there or the pub.'

Boateng arranged a couple of papers. 'We'll need to look into that in more detail, of course.' He knew there was nothing else connecting Walker to the crime scenes. Just that phone call, which anyone could have placed – anyone who'd been in de Souza's house the night she was murdered. Though toxicology had still to prove it was murder. 'Anything else to add before we close?' he asked.

Walker glanced from him to Jones and back. 'Have I been charged with anything?'

'Not yet. You'll be held for the time being.'

He cleared his throat. 'So, can I stay here? On remand or whatever.'

Boateng caught a flash of fear in Walker's expression. He nodded. 'I'll see if there's a spare custody cell.'

•

As Kat Jones accompanied Boateng down the corridors of Lewisham hospital, she felt the pieces start to fall into place. They'd just finished the interview with Halima Osman, Abdi's wife, who described what she'd seen from the flat above their shop. One man in a black balaclava, black gloves, green camouflage jacket and jeans, beating her husband with a baseball bat in the small car park behind the premises. The black items could be the same clothing from which fibres were found at the Bardak and Kumar attacks, and the bat was consistent with wounds on both previous victims. It was looking like a single suspect. Dale Rogers might have had good alibis, but his DNA was on the fiver at the Turkish restaurant, and he and his brother Liam were still of interest, given their connection to National Right. Now, they were hoping to use Halima Osman's description to narrow down the CCTV search, see if they could identify a candidate for the latest attack and trace his journey backwards from the crime scene. Given the coverage in London, it was possible. Jones had known that technique to work spectacularly well. It could even lead them right back to the perpetrator's front door. She wondered whether a Rogers brother or another member of National Right would lie at the end of that trail.

She and Boateng approached the locked metal door outside the secure mental health ward. Boateng buzzed to identify himself. The door was released for them. He showed his warrant card to a nurse who directed him to a psychiatrist behind a long desk. The young woman was early thirties, bespectacled. Jones read her name badge: Dr Keynejad, the psychiatrist she'd spoken to on the phone. They introduced themselves.

'Antony has been quite settled today.' Keynejad kept her voice low. 'He's agreed to see you, but given what happened when he was in custody, I think it'd be better if you spoke to him in the communal area. Try not to cause him any distress, please.'

'Of course. Thanks, Doctor.'

'Come with me.' She led them through into a lounge with a television playing on low volume. A few ward residents were sitting, each on their own. Some were reading the papers, others watching the TV. One was pacing around, checking the windows. Webb was alone at a small table, piecing together a jigsaw. As they approached, his head jerked up and alarm flashed across his face, before dissipating as the psychiatrist smiled at him.

'Antony, this is DI Boateng and DS Jones from the police. Do you remember DS Jones?'

He nodded. Webb looked a different man. He'd clearly showered, combed his hair, and trimmed his beard. He was in a fresh sweatshirt and jogging pants.

'I mentioned they'd be coming today. Is it OK if they speak to you for a few minutes?' asked Keynejad. Jones liked her style; she was relaxed and friendly, yet seemed in control. Police often moaned about how hard it was dealing with the public. Truth was, NHS staff probably encountered stress more frequently than those in the Job, and they weren't specially trained to deal with it.

Webb nodded again and the psychiatrist stepped back. 'I'll leave you to it, then. But I'm just over there if you need anything. Alright, Antony?'

'Yes.' Webb held a jigsaw piece in mid-air as they sat down. 'Doctor Keynejad says you're not going to arrest me.'

Jones nodded. 'That's right. We'd just like to have a chat.'

Webb fitted the piece into the puzzle. 'I'm sorry I ran out last time. Hadn't been taking my meds. I'm back on them now, though. Haven't missed one since I came here,' he said proudly. 'My head was all over the place that day in the station.'

'Don't worry about it,' she said, and noticed how he relaxed at her words. 'We wanted to ask what you know about Mehmet Bardak, the Turkish man who was murdered outside his restaurant. You told us you'd read about him in the paper, but then you said that the government had killed him. What did you mean by that?'

'Oh, I…' Webb faltered. His mouth opened but no sound emerged.

'Did you see anything, Antony?' Boateng spoke gently, leaning forward slightly.

Webb picked up another jigsaw piece. 'Can I trust you two?'

She and Boateng exchanged a glance and both said he could.

'The night he died, I was hungry. I wanted a kebab. So, I walked round to the restaurant, but it was shut. Guess it must've been late. It's not one of those all-night places.'

'How late?'

'Don't know.' He studied the board, fitted the piece. 'They close at 10.30 p.m., so after that. Maybe eleven.'

'Sorry, carry on.'

'Well, I went to the side to check if anyone was still there. Thought I'd maybe get the leftovers, you know. Sometimes they give stuff for free if they can't keep it. You save money that way. Anyway, I heard this shout, then a noise. Like a crack. So I go to look and there's this guy standing down the side of the restaurant by the bins. He had something long in his hand, like a stick. And there's a bloke on the floor, not moving.'

'What did you do?'

'I hid. I was scared, you know?'

Jones pictured Webb wrestling with Evans outside the custody cells – the drama, smashed camera and her intervention – and realised that the whole confrontation there had probably started because Webb was frightened.

'Did you call the police?' she asked.

'No.' Webb cast his eyes downwards. 'I didn't have my phone. I just hid. I called when I got home, but that was later on. Too late.'

'It's alright, Antony.'

'Do you…' Webb swallowed. 'Do you reckon if I'd called earlier he might still be alive?'

Jones couldn't help wondering the same, but knew it was unlikely. 'Mehmet Bardak was hit around the head with a heavy, blunt object. He fell and hit his head on the ground, and we think that's what killed him.' She reached out a hand, placed it just next to his alongside the jigsaw. 'There was nothing you could've done.'

'I'm sorry,' said Webb in a small voice. 'Is this the man who's attacked other foreign people as well?'

'We think so.'

He shook his head. 'I could've stopped it.' Webb's eyes were wet, his mouth making tiny twitching movements.

Jones glanced at Boateng, who nodded for her to continue. 'You can help us now,' she said. 'Can you tell us what this guy you saw looked like, please?'

'He had a black mask on and an army jacket. That's why I said government the other day, when I was a bit confused, cos I thought, you know, the army's the government, isn't it?'

'You never saw his face?'

'No.'

'You said he was holding a stick,' interjected Boateng. 'How was he holding it?'

'Like this.' Webb extended his left fist to the side of his body.

'In his left hand?'

'Yeah, definitely like this. Left.'

'We'd like to take an official statement from you about this please, Antony. And when we find this man, would you be willing to appear in court to say what you've told us?'

Webb didn't reply. He reached into the jigsaw box and took another piece, turned it and placed it into the puzzle. Now, Jones could see what it was: a map of Britain. Webb slowly fitted one more piece, scratched his chin, then sat up straight in his chair. 'Yes.' He took a deep breath and clenched his jaw a moment before nodding. 'Yes, I would.' He placed a finger on the jigsaw map. 'This is my country. And everyone's welcome.'

※

Boateng knew he'd have to work late. Bribed himself with a pint with the team at a pub in Blackheath, then it was back to the station to catch up on notes, statements, decision logs and all the other admin that underpinned an investigation. He'd called Etta earlier, and though he could tell she was disappointed, he knew she'd understand. Not the first time he'd needed to burn the midnight oil on a murder case. His team had been putting in the hours, and Boateng recognised that his private work on

Troy's and Ana's deaths had taken him away from giving them the support they needed. Now, the two apparent suicides were linked to Hayworth's death in a single investigation spanning three boroughs. His instincts had been proved right. Alongside Op Spearhead, though, that meant a lot of paperwork to be done. He'd already brought his team up to speed with the events at Cleaver Square – most of them, at least – and his theory on the deaths. Now they were all on the same page.

'So, what do you think, boss?' Connelly took a quick sip of Guinness. 'Is this fella Walker responsible for it all? Makes sense, doesn't it? It's only the two of yous left from that business in '98.'

Boateng grunted, both hands wrapped round his ale. 'I'm not sure. He seemed a bit scared when we interviewed him this morning. Said that he and I would be next.' He shook his head. 'What did you think, Kat?'

'Hm?' Jones turned back to them. Boateng realised she'd been gazing out of the window.

'She's dreaming about her new boyfriend.' Connelly's face lit up at his own joke, his thick eyebrows animated.

'Pat,' began Malik, his tone hard.

'It's OK, Nas,' said Jones. 'Actually, since you're interested, I have been dating someone.'

'Who?' blurted Malik. Boateng registered the mixture of anxiety and disappointment on his face. It was clear he was even more smitten than he had been six months ago when Jones first joined the team. Boateng felt for him.

'Is it someone at work?' asked Connelly. Jones hesitated and the Irishman wagged a finger. 'Knew it. I'm not a detective for nothing,' he grinned. 'Who's the lucky fella, then?'

'Piss off,' she replied, with the hint of a smile. She obviously did want to tell people about it. That suggested it was a guy she was proud to be with, not like some of the other dates she'd told him about. He was happy for her.

'Well,' said Connelly, 'if it's someone in the station, that's not going to stay secret for very long now, is it?' He winked. 'Wait a minute.' He held up a hand to get their attention. 'I've got it. It's Evans, isn't it?'

They laughed, although he noticed it faded more quickly for Malik.

Eventually, Boateng finished the pint and said his goodbyes, waving off both the inducement of another drink and the jeers about working too hard. He pulled on his overcoat and flat cap, touched fingertips to his forehead in a small salute, and left.

Walking back towards Lewisham centre, Boateng thrust his hands into his pockets to keep out the cold and picked up his pace. Winter was well and truly in control of London, and the shortest day of the year hadn't arrived yet. It would get darker before it got lighter. He thought he heard a shoe scuff the pavement behind him, and turned, but there was no one there. Still, he had the feeling that he was being watched, felt another set of eyes on him. Maybe the faintest perception that another body was nearby – moving, breathing. The sensation had become all too frequent in the past couple of weeks.

There it was again. A slight scuffing noise.

He was nearly at the junction with Lewisham High Street, where – whatever the hour – people would be walking, cars circulating. Boateng accelerated towards a bend in the quiet road, then ducked into the space between two shops. He waited, and fifteen seconds later, a smaller figure in a hooded sweatshirt under a thin black Puffa passed him. He'd had enough of this shit. Boateng stepped out behind the person.

'Hey!'

They continued walking, head bowed, and Boateng was forced to jog to catch up. He placed a hand on the shoulder and the figure whipped round. Boateng's heart thumped in his chest as he saw the black balaclava, and he took a step back. 'Who are you?' he growled.

A gloved hand reached up and lifted the balaclava over the chin, mouth and nose, and Boateng recognised the face.

Jason Leather.

'Why are you following me?' barked Boateng, squaring his shoulders.

'What?' Leather frowned. 'I'm on my way in to work.'

'At eight thirty at night?'

Leather shrugged. 'I've got some stuff to finish up. They want the installation finished by first thing tomorrow.' He snorted a small laugh. 'Software's not going to install itself.'

'Software?' Boateng didn't know what else to say.

'Sure it's not you that's following me?' Leather gave a lopsided grin.

'I'm going to work too,' said Boateng, defensively. He nodded in the direction of the station. 'Come on, then.'

They finished the journey in awkward silence, punctuated by Boateng's attempts to get Leather talking about his work, his background, anything. But the IT engineer only grunted, said the occasional yes or no. Nothing beyond one syllable, and in the end Boateng gave up. At the doors of the police station, they swiped in and went their separate ways. Boateng remembered Walker was in the cells. He strolled over to the reception desk.

'Alright? Who's on night shift at the custody suite?' he asked.

The uniform behind the desk clicked a mouse and checked his monitor. 'Evans, sir,' he replied.

'Cheers.' Boateng turned to leave.

'By the way,' said the uniform. 'There was a journalist here earlier. Red-headed woman. Said she was hoping to get an interview with a detainee called Vic Walker. I told her to come back another time. She was on about speaking to the press officer out of hours, getting it authorised now because of a deadline, something like that.'

'Do me a favour, will you? If she comes back, give me a call. And can you let Evans know I might be coming down to the cells later?'

'Sir.'

Boateng scribbled his extension and went over to the lift. Then changed his mind and took the stairs. He could use the exercise, particularly with the inevitable run of Christmas gluttony starting soon.

Settling at his desk, Boateng wondered when he should pay another visit to Walker. Maybe they could chat a bit more about 'back then'. An 'intelligence' conversation, off-record, no lawyer, no notes. See if there was anything else he'd be willing to say that might help find the person behind this. Assuming, of course, that it wasn't Walker. First, though, he had a shedload of paperwork to get through. To paraphrase Leather, it wasn't going to fill out itself.

＊

There are two more on my list. And I can't believe they're both here in this building, tonight. I didn't expect that; it's almost too good to be true. Each knows he's a target, but they probably think they're safe right now, inside a police station. Especially one as large and imposing as Lewisham. To some extent, they're right. The front desk is always staffed, and beyond that there are cameras, locked doors, swipe cards, panic buttons and the rest. A set of security measures designed to protect noble, honest police officers against outsiders who'd wish them harm. It's not exactly an easy place to walk in off the street and murder someone. But I'm not out there, trying to get in. I'm here. When they realise that, it'll be the most terrifying thing they've ever experienced: their refuge isn't safe at all. And by then, it'll be too late for them to do anything about it.

CHAPTER TWENTY-ONE

Wednesday, 13 December 2017

It was dark outside, still too early for the grey winter light to filter through. Boateng had come in as soon as he got the call. He jogged up the steps into the back entrance of Lewisham police station and made his way straight to the custody suite. He was met at the door by the tall figure of Krebs, who wore a pair of nitrile forensic gloves. She hadn't given any details over the phone when she summoned him, but he knew it was bad news. His pulse was already thumping in his ear.

'We're trying to determine how this happened,' she said quietly, handing him a pair of gloves. 'Follow me.'

They entered the suite and proceeded past the desk towards the cells. As they walked under the doorway, Krebs raised her finger and indicated above them. 'Bloody camera was broken. Smashed in a scuffle last week, apparently. Hadn't been fixed.' She shook her head, didn't need to say more. Boateng knew she'd be thinking about the fallout of whatever negligence, bureaucracy, maintenance cutbacks or other forces had conspired to keep the camera out of action. That part of it wasn't up to Krebs to explain. But the fact she was here meant there was something that fell within her responsibility as head of the MIT. Something that had occurred inside a cell. And he guessed they weren't wearing gloves because a detainee had a touch of food poisoning. She stopped just outside the one open door in the corridor and turned to him.

'What's happened?' he whispered urgently.

'See for yourself.'

He stepped into the doorway, his gaze immediately travelling between the two white-suited SOCOs to the body on the bed. The head wasn't visible, but Boateng recognised the diminutive shape of Vic Walker. He lay on his back, fully clothed, arms slightly raised at the elbows, the wrists cocked. Boateng knew the early signs of rigor mortis meant he'd been dead for a few hours at least. One of the SOCOs shifted position and Boateng caught sight of the clear plastic bag over Walker's head. He glanced back at Krebs, who stood at the threshold to the cell, impassive. Moving closer, he noticed that around Walker's neck, the open end of the bag was not secured. There were droplets of moisture inside it, over the face. He beckoned Krebs in.

'Suffocation,' Boateng stated. 'Oxygen supply cut off by the bag, so he's breathing more and more carbon dioxide until…' He trailed off, imagining the fear that he knew would have taken hold of Walker after less than a minute without oxygen. The panic as he desperately tried to get fresh air, somehow. The terror when he realised there wasn't any. Then the encroaching darkness as his consciousness faded, permanently.

'Suicide?' asked Krebs. Boateng couldn't swear to it, but he thought he detected a hint of hopefulness in her voice. The alternative was perhaps worse. Harder to explain.

'Murder.'

Krebs drew in a deep breath and muttered something to herself before fixing him with a stare. 'You're sure?'

'Ninety-nine per cent of plastic bag suffocations are self-administered,' he replied. 'Either suicide, as you suggested, or accidental – kids playing, teenage dares, asphyxiophilia.'

She narrowed her eyes.

'A sex thing, which has gone very wrong if we're the ones finding them.'

'Right.'

'One per cent of plastic bag deaths are homicide,' he continued. 'It's a problematic choice of method. See, when the CO_2 in your blood starts to rise, you devote every ounce of strength you've got to tearing the bag off your head, biting or clawing a hole in it, whatever you have to do to live. So, if it's a murder, the victim needs to be restrained and the bag probably has to be secured somehow over their head. Tape, string, a belt around the neck, something. But you can see there's nothing fixing the bag to Walker's head. If it was suicide, a survival reflex would've kicked in and he'd have torn it off, even if his intention was to kill himself. Which I don't believe it was,' he added.

'But he hasn't been restrained,' observed Krebs. 'So how did someone murder him with a plastic bag?'

'Probably the other way to stop someone moving. Drugs.'

Krebs stared at the body. Boateng wondered if they were thinking the same thing.

'My guess is that you'll find a needle mark somewhere on him in the post-mortem,' he said. 'And I bet those same sux metabolites will show up in toxicology.'

'Could he have administered the drugs to himself and held the bag over his own head?'

'Unlikely,' replied Boateng. She was still clinging to the suicide theory. 'When he lost muscle control, he wouldn't have been able to keep an unsecured bag tightly enough in place.'

Krebs folded her arms. 'Remind me why he was in our cells.'

'We located him as part of the investigation into Dennis Hayworth's death. When we approached him for a chat, he pulled a gun on DS Jones. A converted replica,' he added. 'He was Tasered and arrested. We interviewed him yesterday about the three deaths connected to Cleaver Square. He denied all knowledge of them, beyond what he'd read in the papers.'

'Alibis?'

'His mum, mainly. We hadn't checked it out yet.'

'How was his mental health?' asked Krebs.

'Fine. I mean, he was scared, if anything. Seemed quite content to spend the night here.'

'Ironic.'

'It would've been very difficult for him to get a plastic bag and sedative drugs into the cell. The searches are pretty thorough.' He looked back to the body, where the SOCOs had moved in for closer inspection. One was checking Walker's trouser pockets.

'We have to get hold of the custody officer.' Krebs spoke as much to herself as to him. 'Someone called PC Mike Evans. A new officer here. He had the last recorded contact with Walker at 8 p.m., collecting his dinner tray. Evans clocked off at 7 a.m. It was the morning shift who found him when they brought his breakfast at 8 a.m.' She looked sideways at him. 'You're confident it was murder then, Zac?'

Boateng nodded, his jaw set. So, a window from 8 p.m. last night to 8 a.m. this morning without documented contact with Walker. And no CCTV of the custody suite.

'Has anyone spoken to the other detainees?' he asked. 'The two on either side of Walker may have heard something.'

'Not yet.'

'And no other witnesses, I'm guessing?'

She shook her head.

Boateng quickly processed the facts. Someone inside the station had killed Walker. In other words, the murderer of Troy, Hayworth and Ana had been here last night. It also meant that there was only one person left from Cleaver Square now. Him.

'Ma'am.' One of the SOCOs was sealing a small, transparent evidence bag. She handed it to Krebs. 'This was in his coat pocket.'

Krebs took the bag and turned it over. The item inside looked like a piece of paper.

'What's this?' she asked. 'Suicide note?'

The SOCO shrugged.

Krebs studied the paper. She frowned, glanced at Boateng. Hesitated, then read aloud, 'Your sin will find you out.'

He swallowed. 'Not the first time I've heard that phrase recently.' He moved alongside her, read it too. Then read it again. His face grew hot, his hands clammy. 'It looks like…' He couldn't finish the sentence, because he couldn't believe what he was seeing.

'Indeed, Zac. That's what I thought too. I've seen enough of it in recent years to recognise. On your ops board, your notes. Is it…' Her voice rose, the question implicit.

'Yes,' he replied. 'That's my handwriting.'

'I'm sorry about this, Zac. I'm sure you understand why we have to do it this way. The procedure has to be followed in any situation like this.' Krebs shot him the briefest look of sympathy across the desk, then leaned over and started the digital recording machine. She announced the date, time and persons present.

'Could you please account for your whereabouts between the hours of 8 p.m. last night and 8 a.m. today?'

Boateng blinked.

'We're conducting the same interview with everyone else who was in the building during those hours,' said Krebs, perhaps by way of encouragement.

'Surely I'm not a suspect?'

Krebs just smiled. Clicked her pen.

He blew out his cheeks. 'OK. I was in the pub in Blackheath with my team until around eight twenty, then I walked back here to finish up some admin. I stopped working around ten forty-five and went home. I was there until I got your call this morning.'

'So, you got home at…?'

'Eleven or so.'

She inclined her head.

'My wife was at home,' he added in response to the unvoiced invitation to offer an alibi. This was unbelievable. He knew why it needed to be done – protocol had to be observed – but he should be out there working out who had done this, not sitting here, a mug on the wrong end of an interview.

'Can you describe your relationship with Victor Walker, please?'

'Relationship?' Boateng couldn't hide his frustration. He cleared his throat. 'I didn't have any relationship with Walker. Our paths crossed when I was part of a team that arrested him back in 1998, as you know, but we hadn't been in contact since.'

'How did you feel about him?' asked Krebs without looking up.

'I—' Boateng collected himself. 'What do you mean?' he asked calmly, though he knew very well what Krebs was getting at.

'Would you say there was any hostility between you? I mean, you interviewed him at length yesterday for a crime that would have put him back in jail, and he was a person of interest in your existing murder inquiry. Even before he pointed a gun at one of your closest colleagues and threatened her life.'

'If you're asking whether I liked the guy, then no, I didn't. Not especially. But let's get it on the record that I didn't kill him.' Boateng sat back, crossed him arms.

'OK, thanks. No one was suggesting that, of course. How do you account for what appears to be your handwriting on the paper in his pocket?'

'I can't. I didn't write it.'

'But it seems to be your handwriting, Zac.'

'Looks like it, yeah.'

'Mm.' Krebs asked a couple more questions before terminating the interview and stopping the recording. 'Sorry about that,' she said, though Boateng sensed she was treating him slightly differently since the discovery of the note.

'Listen, ma'am,' he began, his anger rising. 'I told you about the Cleaver Square incident. I think someone is trying to set me up here.'

'Nobody's accusing you of anything, Zac,' she said pleasantly. 'You know better than anyone in this station that these things need to be explained and accounted for. A man has died in our custody and no one seems to know how it happened. That's extremely serious.'

'Mm.' Boateng tried to keep his temper under control; she wasn't listening to him.

'And rest assured, we're checking the computer log to see who swiped in, cross-checking it with the camera in reception. Dr Volz is coming to make an assessment of the time of death, working off body temperature, which should help to narrow the window.'

'Will she be checking for an injection site on the body, too?' He spoke quickly. 'Requesting toxicology?'

'I'm sure.'

'Good.' He tried to relax. The phrase on the note came back to him, and he remembered who had said it to him in the pub after Troy's funeral. 'Did a journalist called Faye Rix come in last night?' The duty officer on reception hadn't notified him of Rix's arrival, but that didn't mean she hadn't visited.

Krebs pursed her lips. 'People are in and out of this building all the time. As I said, we'll be checking the visitor log as well as staff entry and exit around the time of death.'

That didn't give him much confidence. Whoever was orchestrating this was too clever to be caught out by something like that. He suddenly realised that the note was part of the pattern he'd spotted before: each body carries a clue that points to someone else. That person becomes a focus of investigation, a potential suspect. Until they're murdered too. Dread was creeping through his guts.

'I need to get back and follow up on this,' he told Krebs, scraping back his chair and standing.

'Ah, I wanted to talk to you about that.' She stood so that she was taller than him. *Classic power play*, he thought. 'Given your presence in the building last night, the fact we've had this interview, and further interviews are still to come, it'd be better if you weren't working on this case.'

'But it's linked to the others!' he protested. 'Anyone can see that.'

'Perhaps. Still, can you imagine the PR impact if it came out that an officer with possible evidential links to a murder—'

'I didn't write that note,' he interjected.

'Even so, if there was an inquiry, we can't be seen to—'

'I get it.' He snorted. 'Can I work the other cases?'

'Yes. Just don't…' Krebs pursed her lips, selected the diplomatic phrase: 'Go too far away.' She laughed awkwardly.

*

Kat Jones looked up as Boateng crossed the office and dropped heavily into his chair at the desk next to her. He looked seriously pissed off. 'How'd it go?' she asked.

Boateng shook his head. 'Jokes. I reckon there's maybe ten per cent of Krebs that believes I might actually have done it, despite the scene fitting the pattern of the other three murders.'

Jones spun her chair towards him. 'Come on, Zac. She can't genuinely think that? Surely it's just the routine she's got to go through.'

'Maybe. I remember how I grilled Hayworth about Troy, then I basically accused Ana of knowing something about Hayworth's death. We leaned on Walker about receiving a call from Ana before she died. Now it's me in the sequence. No one knows anything about the previous death that pointed to them. It's all bullshit, just a set-up.' He spoke through gritted teeth. 'I should've seen it coming. Damn!' He slapped the armrests of his chair and leaned back. 'Krebs has got a point, though. That note on the body is tough to explain.'

'Someone faked your handwriting.'

'Yeah, but who?' Before she had a chance to respond, he spoke again. 'Kat, can you get some background on Faye Rix, please?'

'Already have.' She flashed a smile and some of the tension dropped from his body.

'Christ, you're gonna tell me what I'm thinking next. Probably before I know.'

He slid his chair across to her desk as she clicked and dragged a couple of windows on her computer screen. 'Faye Rix has got a reasonable online profile, as you might expect from a freelance journalist,' she began. 'Website, blog, investigative pieces, quite a few published articles on alleged police corruption. She's had stuff in a couple of national papers. And she's a pretty good boxer, too.'

'So I gather.'

'Here's the thing. Rix is thirty-one.'

'OK.'

'But she's only existed since 2005.'

'Eh?'

'The first nineteen years of her life don't seem to have happened. So, I'm thinking maybe she changed her name? Left an old life behind. Could even have been a late adoption out of foster care.'

'You sure there's nothing? I mean, prior to '05, it was harder to put stuff online about yourself, there wasn't much social media, she wouldn't have been working…'

'There's nothing. She literally did not exist before then. Births, school enrolment, national insurance, none of it.'

'So, who was she befo—' Boateng froze. 'You said 2005?'

'That's the earliest reference to her I can find.' Jones raised her eyebrows slightly.

'Are you thinking that—'

She cut him off. 'Yeah, it's crazy, right?'

'Faye Rix is the reincarnation of Joseph Young.' Boateng voiced her thought, but the scepticism in his tone was clear.

Jones shrugged in a way that suggested anything was possible. 'She's linked to the victims, somehow or another. The email from Troy, same as the one you received. Indirect connection to Hayworth through Rogers and the flat. Hair on de Souza's body after their fight. She knew Walker was here – she wanted to come in to interview him, right? And check this out.' She clicked a link and a new window popped up. 'She wrote a piece in 2014 about how someone had died in police custody back in '99, practically accused the force of committing murder. Cites an unnamed source close to the Met. This stuff is like a vocation for her. Exactly the cause Joseph Young would've had.' She sat back and nodded, satisfied with the evidence.

Boateng skimmed the piece then turned to her. 'I don't know. That's one hell of a leap. Joseph Young fakes his own death at eighteen, has a sex change and reinvents himself as a red-headed female investigative journalist? Why the sex change?'

'We don't know anything about Joseph Young. Maybe he never felt comfortable male.'

'Occam's razor.' He tilted his head. 'Anyway, they found Joseph Young's body at the bottom of a cliff in Guatemala.'

'I admit, it's not the simplest explanation, but it fits. I think we should do a proper interview with Rix about these murders.'

Boateng inclined his head. 'Agreed, but on what grounds?'

Now she was less confident – carried away with the theory before thinking through the evidential components. 'Um…'

'Apart from the hair on de Souza – which probably came from the argument in the pub – the strongest thing against Rix is that she quoted the same phrase that appeared on the note found on Walker's body. But it's a pretty common phrase, and the note is in my writing. That's not enough. She says she knew about Hayworth's murder before anyone else because she got the same email as me. And we haven't even determined yet whether she was in the station last night. She might have a titanium alibi for Walker's death.'

'So you're saying we wait?'

'We find out if she was here when Walker died. In the meantime, let's build the intelligence case. Find out who her brother is – Adam, the big guy. What's his story? But don't lose sight of other options too. We want theories led by data, not data that we force into our theories, remember?'

She sighed, knew he was right. 'Yeah.'

'And let's get a move on,' he added. 'I may not have much time.'

CHAPTER TWENTY-TWO

'How do you want to use the time today, Zac?'

Boateng sunk into the soft chair, let himself relax in the low lighting and calmness of Summers's room. He'd taken a break from the investigations he could work on, following the principle Etta always championed: give yourself permission to switch off. Boateng had excused himself from the phone calls, emails, conversations, meetings, forms and briefings of an active multiple murder investigation. He'd worked through lunch anyway, and knew he'd probably be late home. They needed the list of people in the building last night, then they could cross-reference it with known purchases of the sux drug. That was their best chance on this. *His* best chance. In the meantime, he planned to follow any other leads as far as possible before heading home to Etta. Might miss Kofi's bedtime story, but if he didn't sort this mess out, there was a lot more he'd be missing. Boateng knew he had to take care now, watch over his shoulder. For the moment, though, he needed a friendly ear.

'Just, um, keep talking, really,' he replied.

'Sure. What about?'

Boateng cleared his throat. 'Expressing how I feel.' He knew it sounded naff. Connelly and the others would take the piss if they could hear him.

'And how do you feel?'

'All over the bloody place.' Boateng tutted at himself. 'Like a wreck. Or a shell.'

'Difficult emotions can leave people feeling a bit... hollowed out, you know.'

'That's it. Hollow.'

Summers clasped his hands. 'Tell me more about that.'

'I hoped it'd get better,' said Boateng. 'Thought I'd get a handle on it, that it was just losing Troy that knocked me so badly. That things would get easier. Now the opposite's happening.'

'It sounds very stressful.'

Boateng couldn't blame him for the platitude. Though he'd opened up to Summers more than most – even Etta, of late – the counsellor still didn't have a clue what was really going on. He just had to interpret Boateng's words in the sessions and do his best to explore them.

'I didn't imagine I could get worse than I had been over the last week or two. Then this morning, well...' He briefly assessed the confidentiality: Walker's death would become common knowledge soon, so it didn't matter too much. 'Someone I was very interested in died.'

'I'm sorry to hear that.' Summers dipped his head. 'You said "interested", Zac. What kind of interest?'

'Professional. Someone connected to my case. We made the arrest, brought him in here.' He noticed his voice was getting softer, less distinct. 'And he died.'

Summers paused. When he spoke again, he'd lowered his voice to match Boateng's. 'It sounds like you might feel some level of personal responsibility for what happened to him.'

'I do.' Boateng could sense his cheeks and throat getting tight; knew there was no point trying to play the hard man. He pressed his lips together, felt them twisting.

'And I can see that whatever it was, it's upset you.'

'It wasn't my fault,' he whispered, screwing his eyes shut. Hot tears were squeezed out and ran down his cheeks. He quickly wiped them with his shirtsleeve and let out an involuntary sob. 'Sorry. I just feel so... guilty.'

'That's OK, Zac,' said Summers gently. 'Let it come out. Then there's a chance to resolve the conflict you're experiencing.'

'They—' His voice caught, and he shuddered like the tears had taken control of his whole body. 'They think I did it.' He began to cry, and realised he was whimpering like a dog left alone. He sniffed deeply. 'But I didn't,' he gasped. 'I was only trying to help. That's all I ever wanted to do.'

'Of course.'

'Someone's trying to make it look like me. But it's not...' He faltered.

'Just take your time. You're doing really well to connect with the emotion here.'

Boateng covered his face with his hands and felt himself leaning forwards, drawing his knees in, curling up like he was defending himself. But it was more foetal position than pugilist stance.

◆

Jones cranked the treadmill up to fourteen kilometres per hour and extended her stride length as the belt whirred under her feet. She touched the phone inside her arm band, turned up her staple workout drum and bass. Let the uplifting chorus of 'Higher' by Sigma wash over her. Glanced at the mirror in front of her, vaguely considering that Tom might come in for a bit of training after work. How could he not love the two-tone Gymshark leggings and sports top she was rocking? Instead, she saw the hulking frame of Evans bowling into the weights area. He didn't appear to have noticed her. He wore a small vest top and tapered tracksuit bottoms, clearly keen to show off his upper body. The guy was big, no doubt, but the ripples and popping veins looked pretty disgusting. It wasn't a turn-on. And athletically there isn't much use for that kind of size. Some guys in the Met were just too obsessed with weights and protein supplements to bother with cardio training. All guns and guts, never mind learning how to actually chase, catch and control a suspect.

Still, she'd done that the other day, and where had it got her? A gun in the face. She felt a stab of panic. Then she recalled what Boateng had said about Evans being the last person to record any contact with Vic Walker. She slowed the running machine, stepped off and took out her headphones. Composed herself, then went over to Evans. He was sliding twenty-kilogram plates onto a bar on the floor. She noticed some white streaks on the back of his hand; maybe surgical scars, or wounds from his military service? Before she could consider this any further, he registered her presence and glanced up.

'Evans,' she said, trying to keep her voice neutral. The memory of their altercation in the pub was still fresh. Her throwing beer in his face, him raising his hand in response…

'What do you want?' He applied a collar to the end of bar and tightened it.

'You were the last person to see Vic Walker alive?'

Evans grunted. 'Another coward that did himself in.'

She wanted to challenge his choice of words, but this wasn't the time. 'Actually, his cause of death hasn't been determined yet.'

'Plastic bag over his head, wasn't it? Pretty fucking clear.' He chuckled.

'How did he seem to you, when you spoke to him?'

'I didn't speak to him. Just gave him his dinner, shut the door and left him alone to wank himself off or whatever he wanted to do in there. Anyway, I've been through all this with that lesbian boss of yours.'

'If you're referring to DCI Krebs, she's—'

'She is a lesbian, isn't she? There's nothing wrong with me saying that. It's a fact.' He planted his feet and squatted above the bar in position for a deadlift. 'By the sounds of it, this guy Walker had it coming to him.'

Jones shook her head. Even if Evans was right about Walker, it was pointless trying to talk to him. Turning to leave, something on Evans's arm caught her eye. A circular bruise on the bicep. She studied it for a moment. She'd seen a photograph recently with a very similar mark. It looked like the site of an injection.

Showered and dressed, Jones was walking up the back stairs to the MIT office. She planned to put another shift in before the end of the evening; Boateng would appreciate that. She thought about the bruise on Evans's bicep: an intramuscular injection. Had he had a vaccination or other routine medical jab, or was he taking something like testosterone? That might account for his temper, the outbursts, his unusual level of muscle. She'd read something about steroid abuse among amateur weightlifters, and the psychological issues associated. Perhaps Evans was injecting himself with it; the image made her wince. She pushed through the fire exit door and entered the office from the rear side. The mechanism closed smoothly and quietly behind her. Then she froze.

Jason Leather was sitting at her desk, using her computer. There was no one around him. She spotted the headphones trailing from his ears, and as she crept forward, she could hear the tinny rasp of his dark metal music or whatever he called it. Getting close enough to see the screen, she peered over his shoulder. He was reading what appeared to be a list of file names, several of which she recognised from current investigations.

'What the fuck are you doing?' she said, loud enough to be heard over the music.

Leather started and whipped round, pulled the earphones out. He blinked, took off his little round glasses, swallowed. 'Essential maintenance on the shared drive.'

'From *my* computer?'

The initial shock was gone from his face now. He pressed some keys to return to the desktop sign-in screen, rolled the chair back and stood. 'I have to do it on everyone's machine. You weren't here, so I—'

'Thought you'd help yourself? Why were you reading my files?'

'I wasn't.'

'Bullshit. I just saw you.'

'I can assure you, I have full authorisation to be carrying out this work.'

She stepped around him, pulled the chair towards her and sat down. 'Yeah, well ask next time. OK?'

Leather replaced his glasses and scuttled away, out of the MIT office. Jones noticed he'd left his spring-loaded hand-grip thing on her desk. She pushed it to one side and studied her screen. Perhaps he was telling the truth. He had been on every MIT computer at some point over the past couple of weeks. Maybe it was just a bit of Boateng's paranoia rubbing off on her. Jones made a mental note to tell her boss anyway.

○

'I'm in here, love,' called Etta from the living room when she heard the front door open. She tried to keep her voice down; Kofi was asleep upstairs. Zac didn't come in immediately. She took a sip of wine and said his name as loud as she dared. There was some movement in the hallway and then the sound of two bolts being drawn across – top and bottom – a latch going up and a chain slinking into its dock.

Zac poked his head through the doorway. 'I'll just do the back door too.' Before she could respond, he was marching through to the kitchen.

Moments later, he returned, flung himself down on the sofa next to her and leaned in for a kiss. She noticed that he held on to her a bit tighter than usual, and for a little longer. When he released her, she handed him a glass of wine and chinked hers against his.

'Everything OK?' she asked.

'Yeah, fine,' he replied breezily. 'Just another long day.'

'Me too.' She took a drink and studied him for a few seconds. 'Only, you seem a bit more, um, security conscious than usual.'

'I'm only making sure the doors are locked properly for the night.'

'You don't normally put all the bolts and the chain on.'

'I do.'

'Zac.'

'What?'

'And you told me to "be safe" or whatever the other day. What's going on?'

'Nothing.' He raised the glass to his lips, holding her gaze slightly too long; he always did that when he was hiding something. Overcompensating.

'Come on.' She was losing patience. 'Don't treat me like an idiot. If there's some kind of threat to you, me, Ko or all of us, I have a right to know about it.'

'It's fine.'

'What do you mean, "it's fine"? There *is* a threat to us?' She could hear the volume and pitch of her voice rising.

'No,' he said hastily. 'Just precautions. Look, if I thought there was—'

'Don't lie to me, Zac.' The skin of her face felt hot.

'I'm not lying, just trust me when I say that—'

'We are not losing another member of this family.' She raised a finger and noticed her hand was trembling. The strength of her own words had surprised her. 'If we're in danger, you need to—'

'I'm sorry,' he growled. 'OK? I'm sorry I lost our daughter, sorry I let her run ahead, sorry I couldn't revive her. Sorry for everything.'

'That's not what I meant.' Etta put down her wine glass and reached out to him. 'Come here.'

'It's all my fault.' He tipped his head back on the sofa, briefly closed his eyes.

'Amelia's death was not your fault.'

'I…' he began, then cut himself off. 'This is something else.'

'What?' she said gently.

He took a gulp of wine and his head lolled towards her. She noticed how dark-rimmed his eyes were, the filigree of blood on their whites. 'Someone died last night. At the station.' Zac drank some more.

'Who? An officer?'

'A suspect.'

'My God. How?'

'Murdered.'

'And you're investigating?'

'No, that's the point. I'm not allowed to. He was my suspect. They think I was involved.'

She scoffed, frowning. 'Well, that's ridiculous. Surely they don't believe you had anything to do with it?'

'They're interviewing everyone who was in the station around the time of death.'

'OK. And you were there. But there can't be any evidence linking you to it, so you're in the clear.'

'That's the problem.'

She frowned. 'There's evidence?' Her voice went up another notch. 'What the hell, Zac?'

He laid a hand on hers, squeezed it. 'I've been set up. I'm sure it'll be dismissed once there's a proper analysis, but for the time being, I have to be careful.'

'Including bolting all our doors?'

He sighed. 'Someone murdered this guy and tried to make it look as if I was part of it. I think the same person might try to…'

'Come here?' She caught the shout, checked herself. Remembered her mindfulness. 'Shouldn't we have some official protection?'

'A patrol car has added us to their route.'

'Were you planning on telling me this?'

'I didn't want to worry you.'

'Zac! For God's sake.'

'Sorry. It's a standard measure. There's no specific intelligence on a threat against us. Look, we don't need to change our routine or anything. Just, you know, be careful. And don't open the door to strangers.' He tried to smile. 'Or anyone, for that matter.'

She shook her head at the absurdity of it. 'Thanks for the security tip, Detective.' Etta raised her glass and drank slowly. 'I'm not in the habit of doing that, anyway.' She put the wine down and leaned into him, felt his warmth. This wasn't the first time in his twenty-one years in the Met that something he'd been working on had placed his family in danger. She accepted that; at times her legal work raised similar issues – personal threats that had to be managed. And she trusted Zac to protect her and Kofi.

But there was still something he wasn't telling her.

CHAPTER TWENTY-THREE

'OK, so who's on the list?' said Boateng.

He rubbed his eyes and poured himself more coffee. Another sleepless night. He'd been up three times, or was it four? Watched over Etta, looked in on Kofi, double-checked the doors were locked and bolted. Lay awake, staring at the ceiling. Wondering how tiny choices can lead to such dramatic, life-changing outcomes. Thinking about when – not if – this killer would come for him. Knowing that his best chance of survival was to catch them first. The next step was working out who was in the building when Walker died, two nights ago. Krebs was personally managing that investigation, and had told Boateng to keep a distance, but he knew it was their best lead on the other three murders, so he'd asked Krebs for a copy of the list. Boateng sensed that she harboured a few lingering doubts over his possible involvement in Walker's death. But it was impossible to overlook the connections with the other murders and so, eventually, the DCI had obliged.

Malik scanned the printout. 'Well, you, boss. For starters.'

'Thanks, Nas.' It wasn't public knowledge that a note with Boateng's handwriting had been found in Walker's pocket, and he wanted to keep it that way. 'Next?'

'PC Mike Evans. Was on night duty in the custody suite. Says he followed protocol on things like breaks, but admitted that the suite may have been unattended for periods of time. Claimed he was having digestive issues.' Malik made quotation marks with his fingers for the last two words.

Connelly sniggered. 'The thought of that big fella shittin' himself is pretty funny, you have to admit.'

'Not if it gave someone the chance to kill Walker,' said Jones.

'I thought you'd have been glad about that.' The Irishman grinned. 'After all, he nearly shot you.'

'Well, thanks to Nas, he didn't,' she said.

Malik beamed at the recognition, before his expression changed quickly as something occurred to him. 'This sounds mad, but any chance it could've been Evans?'

'You've changed your tune,' said Connelly. 'Last week you thought he was the best thing in law enforcement since RoboCop.'

'Yeah, well,' muttered Malik, glancing at Jones. Boateng had heard what happened in the pub on Friday night after he left. He knew none of them particularly liked Evans, but could he be their murderer?

'It's possible, Nas,' said Boateng. 'He ticks a few boxes. You said that according to the stories, Evans had killed before, when he was a soldier. I found him reading a book about snipers and military intelligence operations, capture-or-kill stuff. He's physically capable, no doubt. And he's about the right age for...' He struggled to voice the theory.

'The reincarnation of Joseph Young,' said Jones.

'What're you two on about?' scoffed Connelly.

'We need someone with a motive for murdering these people connected with Cleaver Square, and Kat came up with the idea that the kid who was there that day isn't dead. But we need to keep all the options open. And we can't let our... how can I put it? Strong personal views of Evans bias our judgement. Who else?'

Malik consulted the document. He read a couple of names that Boateng didn't know, young beat coppers who were on night shift. Four Trident detectives who were running an arrest operation in the early hours. There was nothing immediate that suggested their involvement or connection to Walker, though he asked his team to speak to them anyway. But the mention of Trident – the Met's gang crime specialists – reminded Boateng of his unfinished business from the summer, relating to Amelia's murder and a man known only as Kaiser. He tried to push this thought to the back of his mind and concentrate on this situation. The time would come for that, he knew it. Then Malik reached a name that they all recognised: Jason Leather.

'He was walking in at the same time as me,' offered Boateng. 'Said he had some kind of software installation to finish before the morning.'

Connelly glanced around the office to make sure they couldn't be overheard. 'Well, he's a weird one alright. I think that's the technical term. Candidate?'

'Don't know,' replied Boateng. 'Plenty of people are weird. Far, far fewer are killers.'

'He's had access to basically our entire investigation on Hayworth.' Jones gestured to the ops board. 'Not to mention the IT systems, including our databases. There's a kind of, um, rage about him, too.'

'He does some obscure martial arts, apparently,' said Boateng, thinking how Leather's exterior belied his physicality. 'Got the computer skills to find a lot of things out and keep them hidden.' He paused a moment, considering the wisdom of his decision to ask Leather to identify the VPN router in Troy's house. Was the awkward IT engineer capable of four murders? Boateng's experience on homicide had taught him that it was a mistake to make assumptions about who was or wasn't 'a killer'.

'And he's obsessed with death,' added Jones.

'You seem to know a lot about the fella,' said Connelly. 'Been chatting him up?'

'He – let's just say he decided to tell me. I definitely didn't ask.'

'Who else is on there, Nas?' said Boateng.

'Duty officer on reception, couple of cleaners in the building, a counsellor called Summers, a maintenance guy who—'

'Tom?' exclaimed Jones and Boateng at the same time, then looked at one another.

'What's going on here?' Connelly seemed to scent a story – maybe two.

'Nothing,' replied Jones quickly, and Boateng noticed Malik frowning. Was Jones having treatment with Summers too? Then the more obvious explanation of why an attractive young woman would know the guy registered.

'Actually,' said Boateng, as much to protect Jones's privacy as to explain his own response, 'I've had a couple of sessions with him.' He cleared his throat. Hadn't intended to tell his team this, but he felt OK making the disclosure. 'After Troy died, you know, Krebs suggested talking to him and, well, it was pretty useful. I'd recommend it.'

'Good for you, boss,' said Connelly. He sounded sincere.

'Just a few more names on the list,' said Malik. 'The press officer was here, briefing that journalist, Faye Rix. She signed in with someone called Adam Rix. Husband?'

'Brother,' stated Boateng. He already knew they'd been in the building. Though the officer on the front desk hadn't passed anything on to him last night, he'd checked this morning. The press officer had admitted the Rixes through the back entrance. Boateng still didn't quite get the relationship between them. He glanced at Jones, remembering her off-the-wall theory about Rix being Joseph Young. He thought about the brother, his muteness, the documents describing how Joseph Young had refused to say a word to police after the bloodbath at Cleaver Square. Could it be him? He didn't want to throw too many ideas at his team, so settled for a general statement. 'Everyone who was in the building has to be treated as a suspect.'

'Including you, boss?' Connelly's bushy eyebrows rose. 'Aye, I'm only kidding.'

'Technically, you're right, Pat,' said Boateng.

'Rix is a possibility,' offered Jones. 'She's got connections to the previous murders, mostly indirect, but she's in amongst it.'

'Could be that she was just following the story of the connected deaths,' suggested Malik.

'She's pretty well informed on them, that's for sure,' acknowledged Jones.

'Well, it's not me tipping her off, in case you're wondering,' said Connelly. 'I've been hoping she'll pump me for information about it, but no luck so far.'

'Kat, did you find anything on Rix's brother?' asked Boateng, keeping the conversation moving.

'Yeah, a bit.' Jones took up her notepad. 'He's thirty-one, same as her. Twins?'

'Possibly, though if you've seen them together it's hard to believe. Go on.'

'Adam spent quite a few years in prison in his twenties for assaults of one kind or another. There are a couple of records showing that in interviews he was totally silent. Seems like the guy never says a word.'

'Lets his fists do the talking,' said Connelly, miming a punch.

'Very little history prior to '06 – his teenage years.' Jones flipped a page. 'None, in fact. And I couldn't find a record of his birth.' She paused. 'So, maybe he and Faye are adoptive siblings who changed their names.'

'Could be. We need to keep an eye on him. Nice work, Kat. Nas, is that all the names?'

Malik checked his list, nodded.

'So, the second part of our investigation is access to the sux drug. Pat, anything?'

'Nope. No vets or hospitals in the area have reported any missing, including private clinics. There are no commercial suppliers to the public inside the UK – you have to go overseas. I found a place in Germany that stocks it and will ship here. A few in the States as well. That's assuming it's being bought via the regular web and not the dark web, obviously.'

Boateng's head dropped in disappointment. He believed the sux was key to this investigation. Test results had already confirmed that Walker had been administered sux, and with Krebs's intervention, Lambeth MIT had requested the same toxicology for de Souza's blood sample; Boateng was confident that it would test positive for sux too. If they could find the point where a person of interest – namely someone who was in the building last night – intersected with the purchase of sux, they'd have their man. Or woman. He had to rally his team.

'Good work, guys. Let's widen the net here. Pat, I want you to track down the main suppliers of sux internationally and contact them. Do it through the embassy or the local police, whatever's quickest. Nas, can you help him?'

'Sure.'

'Find out who they've shipped to in the UK, particularly London, in the last six months. Kat and I will continue to run down the leads from the other murders. Alright, let's go.' He clapped his hands, but the words felt empty. This killer was too organised, too meticulous to be caught out through simple mistakes. They had a strict plan. And it was nearly complete.

* * *

Etta tried to concentrate on her punching. She had learned a combination: two jabs with her left hand, then a hook with her right. The bigger swing from her right glove felt satisfying as it connected with the bag. But it was hard work staying on her toes, keeping her guard up. The coach had said that in boxing, if you don't keep your guard up, you're exposed. You might catch a knockout blow to the head. Then it was game over.

During the past week or more, it seemed like Zac had his guard up. Literally, in the case of the doors and locks. And emotionally, too, when they spoke. It felt like there was a lot he wasn't sharing. Etta's suspicions had deepened when a uniformed officer had turned up at their house earlier, before Zac arrived home. The guy looked like he'd spent most of his life lifting weights. He'd politely shown a badge, introduced himself as PC Evans, and explained that their house was now on a patrol route for added safety. But there was something in the way he'd been looking past her, into the hallway, scanning the rooms. Asking about Zac. And he was alone. She hadn't told this guy anything much, and she hadn't invited him inside. But his manner had been odd. She'd mention the visit to Zac later. Was it connected to whatever he was hiding from her? Somehow Etta didn't think she'd get a straight answer.

She felt anger rise slowly inside her. Nearly twenty years they'd been together, but sometimes the shutters just came down around Zac and she didn't know him any more. That frustration was one reason why she'd made her excuses this evening and come out to boxing. Right now, it was the best therapy. Who did Zac think he was, keeping her in the dark like this? She deserved better. Her punches became harder, the rate quicker, her breathing heavier.

'Great technique,' said a deep female voice behind her.

Etta landed one last combination and turned to see Faye Rix standing there, muscular shoulders bared, the sleeve tattoo on full show, her hair pulled back in a high ponytail. Her hands were wrapped and gloves dangled around her neck.

'D'you want to spar a bit?' asked Rix. She jerked her head towards the door, in the direction of the ring.

Etta felt a little pang of adrenalin. She hadn't boxed against a *person* yet; it was still early days in her training. But what the hell. 'Sure,' she replied.

Rix led the way towards the ring.

Afterwards, with Etta drenched in sweat and glowing from the exertion, she and Rix took a seat and towelled down.

'Nice work.' Rix took a hefty swig from a sports drink and offered some to Etta.

She took the bottle and laughed. 'I don't know what I'm doing. I'm just trying to learn.'

'Looked pretty good to me.'

'Thanks.' Etta beamed, flushed with the praise. 'How long have you been boxing?'

'About twelve years. I started after… well, it was a new me. The old me wasn't a fighter, and I thought it was about time that changed.'

'I know what you mean.'

'You do?' Rix looked surprised.

'Yeah.' Etta paused, then decided to take the step. 'We lost our daughter five and a half years ago. Zac and I.'

'I'm so sorry.' Rix spoke more softly. 'What happened, if you don't mind me asking?'

'She was killed by a gang member who opened fire on someone in a shop, round the corner from our old house.' Etta thought back to the summer, to Zac's reckless solo mission to try to find the person who had done it. How that stubborn pursuit had nearly cost him his life. 'She only went there to get some sweets.'

'Oh my God.' Rix shook her head. 'So, you do know what I mean. Sometimes it feels like I'm the only one who's been through it.'

Etta felt a rush of sympathy for this tough young woman, and wondered if that was where her pain lay. There had to be a source of the fury in her boxing. 'You've lost someone too?'

'You could say that.' Rix broke eye contact, her gaze drifting back over the ring. 'So, what's your husband doing tonight?' Her tone was lighter now.

'Looking after our son. And probably doing some work. Or thinking about himself,' she added, knowing it was indiscreet, but not caring all the same.

'Work stressing him out?'

'Yeah, worse than usual.'

'How so?' enquired Rix.

'Well…' Etta lowered her voice. 'A suspect they were holding in Lewisham station died last night. And for some crazy reason they think Zac was involved.'

'No way. A murder?' Rix's eyes widened. 'So they don't know who did it? I mean, how the guy died?'

'Not yet.'

'Has your husband been interviewed yet as a suspect?' The journalist seemed visibly excited.

Etta hesitated, knew she'd said too much already. She shouldn't have told Rix anything, but she figured it would be news soon enough. Anyway, if someone had been murdered in the station, it was in the public interest for this stuff to be aired. Still, she felt a pang of guilt about betraying Zac – as pissed off as she was with him – and was trying to work out how to respond when a shadow fell over them. She looked up to see the huge, bald man who'd been in the pub after Troy's funeral and who held the punchbag for Rix.

Rix nodded up at him. 'I'm done. Give me two minutes to get changed.' She turned to Etta. 'This is my brother, Adam.'

'Nice to meet you,' said Etta.

The guy didn't reply.

'You know, I was planning a night off,' said Rix. 'But I think I might have a new story now.'

'Wait!' blurted Etta. 'You can't print anything I said there, I didn't mean for it to be—'

'It's OK.' Rix grinned. 'Don't worry. I won't mention you or anything like that. I'll just do a little bit of digging around the edges. Your secret's safe with me. Keep training.' She stood, began unwrapping her hands and walked towards the door. Her brother's gaze lingered on Etta for a few moments, his eyes slightly narrowed. Before she could work out whether the expression was one of curiosity or hostility, he turned and followed his sister out.

Four dead. If Vic Walker hadn't deserved to die, I'd almost feel bad about deceiving him. But I didn't feel anything much. Not when I entered his cell, knowing what was about to happen. Not when I watched his expression change from surprise to pleasure and then to fear. Not when I placed the clear plastic bag over his head and watched it cling to the contours of his face, distorting his features and fogging as the wet air left his lungs. I'm even grateful to him; it was the secret he shared with me that led to all of this.

Boateng is the only one of the five that's left, and now it's his turn. I'm glad I didn't kill him earlier. If I had, his team might not have found Walker for me. And in some ways, because of what he did back then, it feels as though I've saved the most deserved death for last. Boateng knows the punishment is coming to him. He just has no idea who's delivering it.

CHAPTER TWENTY-FOUR

Boateng had shifted the sofa so that he could keep watch over the front of their house from the living room window. When she got back from boxing, Etta would want to know why he'd done that, and would ask more questions about security, no doubt. Boateng felt terrible. He'd considered asking her to take Kofi to her parents' house, but ultimately decided against it. If his family was here, in the home, he could protect them personally. And he'd do it with his life, if necessary. He thought of Amelia and how he would've done the same for her – if he'd had the chance. Kofi was asleep upstairs. Anyone who wanted to get to him would have to pass through Boateng. The doors were bolted, the windows locked. He was scared, but ready.

And yet, it didn't seem like the killer was an all-out attacker, a shock-and-awe tactician. Instead, this person got close enough to their victims to inject them before they realised what was happening. This would be someone with a familiar face. That was worse – being deceived, having let your guard down. So, his best defence was to keep his wits about him, suspicion high and trust low. He'd told his team earlier that everyone was a suspect. And he needed to remember that principle at every waking moment, which felt like ninety per cent of the day right now. The nervous energy was taking its toll on him, the constant alertness draining. Fear was part of the Job, but he'd never faced a threat so personal: this killer was coming for *him*.

Boateng heard the bleep of a car remote and doors locking, and spotted Etta's familiar beige winter coat appear from behind the hedge. As she walked up the path, he sprung into the hallway, slid the bolts back and opened the door. Looked over her shoulder before focusing on his wife and giving her a kiss. One final glance into the road as she stepped past him and the bolts were thrown back across. Etta registered this and gave a small sigh, but didn't say anything.

'How was boxing?' he asked.

'Great,' she said. 'Did my first ever sparring.'

'Serious?'

'Yeah. Oh my God, Zac, it was amazing.'

'So, how many fingers am I holding up?'

She smiled and flicked his hand away. 'Faye Rix was showing me how to do it properly. No head strikes. Not in the first go at sparring, anyway.'

'Rix? Was her brother there?'

'Yeah, he was. Why?'

'Never mind.'

'Zac, what are you not telling me?'

'Nothing, love.'

Etta stared at him, clearly unconvinced, before walking through into the kitchen. Boateng heard her running water into the kettle, switching it on. 'One of your colleagues came by earlier,' she called. 'Evans, I think his name was.'

He followed her through, trying not to make his interest too obvious. 'Really?'

'Yeah, said it was part of the extra security they'd put in place.'

'Mm.' Now wasn't the time to spook her any further, but he'd check it out at work. Particularly after confirming Evans was on their suspect list. 'That's good.'

She looked at him again as if expecting more, but he kept quiet. 'So, what've you been up to?' she asked eventually.

'Not a lot. I put Ko to bed, read him a story or two. Then just… chilling, you know.' He was anxious to change the subject from what he'd been doing, because it consisted entirely of keeping watch over the street from their house, like some paranoid recluse. 'I thought boxing was Mondays.'

'It is, normally. But they have an open session on Thursdays, so I thought I'd check it out on a different day.'

He froze. Stood still while he calculated.

'Zac?'

'That's it,' he said.

'What're you talking about?'

'A different day.' He marched across the flagstones, gripped her shoulders and kissed her firmly on the mouth. 'Thank you.'

'OK.' She smiled, bemused. 'What for?'

'I have to go out.'

'What? Zac, it's nine thirty.'

Boateng was already back in the hallway, grabbing his flat cap, scarf and overcoat. He took his car keys from the dish. 'I'll be back in a bit. Bolt the doors behind me, OK?'

'Zac, where are you—'

The rest of her question was lost as the front door closed behind him. The street was empty as he popped the car door, fired up the engine and pulled away.

Boateng arrived in Catford ten minutes later. He parked down the road from the address which had been listed in Troy's diary under Thursday, 9 November. He'd visited the place on a Saturday, but it hadn't previously occurred to him that the event listed by Troy might be weekly. A meeting of some sort, perhaps? It was worth another shot, and he felt good to be out of the house and chasing a lead, rather than sitting and waiting. That wasn't his style.

He approached the building slowly on foot, keeping close in to the wall and scanning the road around him. Couldn't see or hear anything unusual. The only noise came from the main street, half a block away. He could see lights on. The blinds were partially shut, but as he edged nearer he made out the shapes of people inside and heard the murmur of voices. Had Troy attended this same gathering five weeks earlier, only three weeks before his death? Boateng needed to find out what was going on inside. He crossed to the opposite pavement to see if there was a better angle through the back windows. Though the street was quiet, he instinctively glanced right as he stepped into the road. It was only a split second, but he registered the human form in the periphery of his vision. He whipped round as the adrenalin hit, but there was no one there. Just a line of parked cars.

He swore under his breath. This was happening far too often. Boateng had to find out if he was being followed. Doubling back, he walked quickly to where he'd seen the figure, at a row of gates bordering the back of some shop units. But there was nobody around. He paused against a wall, holding his breath to eliminate any sound or movement. Blood was thumping at his temples as he strained to listen. Moments later a sound rose alongside him. Footsteps, followed by a low grunt of effort. Boateng steeled himself as the person approached from the other side of a wooden gate. Arms taut, fists balled, he watched the gate ease open and a heavyset, middle-aged man emerge from behind it, carrying a box.

'Police,' hissed Boateng, stepping towards him. 'Stop right there.'

The guy jerked backwards and the container slipped from his hands. It crashed to the concrete with the shatter and tinkle of broken glass. 'Fuck's sake,' he spat. 'That's a delivery you've made me drop.'

Boateng stared. He'd let his paranoia get the better of him. 'Sorry,' he mumbled. 'You insured for stuff like that?'

'Thankfully. Who are you, anyway? What you doing at the back of my shop?'

'Detective Inspector Zac Boateng, Lewisham police.' He flashed the warrant card. 'Do you know what's going on in Unit 3 over there?'

'Them lot? Nope. See the same ones coming and going every Thursday night, though. Rest of the week it's different people. Wednesdays is always music, singing and whatnot. Tuesdays is a Boy Scout group, Monday—'

'Thanks. Do you know what the Thursday group is?'

'No idea, mate.' The guy squatted to examine the box.

'OK. Look, I'm sorry about your delivery.' He took out a card and handed it over. 'If there are any problems with the insurance, call me, OK?'

The man took it and nodded, surprised, before lifting the box and returning inside the back of the shop.

Boateng crept over to the back of the main building and took out his phone. He manoeuvred quietly to a spot behind Unit 3, where a gap in the blinds afforded a better view. There were around thirty people in the room, he estimated, almost all male. No kids. Boateng tried to work out who they were. A few middle-aged people, but the group was made up predominantly of younger guys in casual clothing. It looked as if most of them were white. Could this be Troy's extreme right-wing group? It was a crazy idea. Was he outside a meeting of National Right? Did he need to be careful? He selected the camera app on his phone and captured the group as those inside milled around chatting and clutching polystyrene cups, oblivious to his attention.

•

Jim stood inside the multistorey car park and peered through his mini binoculars at Unit 3. So, Boateng had found the meeting place. He didn't know how the detective had known to come here, or why he'd bolted out of the house just minutes after his wife had returned home. Maybe he'd received some new intelligence about the gathering. Jim tried to piece it together. How much did Boateng know about the group? Was he targeting someone inside it, someone else connected with Cleaver Square? Surely not. There was no one else left except Boateng. And the killer, of course. So what the hell was he doing here?

The uncertainty made Jim apprehensive. The boss would want to know what he'd been up to. If Jim couldn't offer an explanation, he'd look bad. Watching was one thing – and Jim did that as well as anyone – but the boss always wanted interpretation too. Turning the details into information. Not just what the target was doing, but why they were doing it too. And Jim didn't have a clue. He could picture the big man's face as he briefed him tomorrow. As Jim admitted ignorance and incapability. The boss's jowls wobbling like a bloodhound as he shook his head in disbelief. Jim's mouth felt a bit dry and he ran his tongue around the inside, over the scar that bisected his top lip. He adjusted the focus slightly on his binoculars and saw that Boateng was papping away on a camera phone. The detective wanted evidence, but to what end?

It was only yesterday morning that the body of long-time criminal Victor Walker had been found at Lewisham police station. The Met had done a good job keeping it out of the press, but it hadn't taken long for Jim to find out. When he'd briefed the boss, the big man had just sat there in silence, processing it somewhere inside that large domed head which caught the light beneath a thin comb-over. He'd asked Jim if he thought it was someone in the police who was behind these killings. And if not Boateng, then who? Jim hadn't known what to say. He didn't think Boateng was responsible. Watching him around his family, his colleagues, he seemed like a good bloke. Not a murderer. Having said that, Boateng was in the station when Walker died. Jim was aware that the boss knew all that, and a whole lot more besides. So in the end he'd just said, 'I don't know', and felt like a twat.

The big man had told him to keep watching, have his weapon ready, and await further instruc—

A sound caught Jim's attention and he swung the binoculars to the other side of the building. Two younger men had exited Unit 3 and were whispering to each other, walking around to the back where Boateng was crouching with his phone. Jim took in the details of their appearance and swiftly concluded who they were. He held his breath and began a quick cost-benefit calculation of whether he should intervene. The young guys looked like hard bastards. One of them was carrying a baseball bat.

This wasn't going to end well.

·

Boateng heard the low voices and scuff of shoes before he saw the men. It gave him just enough time to pocket his phone and get to his feet before two guys appeared around the side of the building. One was a shade taller than him, broad and beefy. The other was shorter but carried a baseball bat. Both men had close-cropped hair and wore dark jackets, jeans and work boots.

'What the fuck are you doing, boy?' demanded the shorter one in a slightly hoarse London accent. The sort of voice that always sounded aggressive.

Boateng instinctively backed off, his hands raised in the non-threatening pose that police self-defence instructors taught; appearing compliant but ready to strike or block, to protect his head. 'Sorry, lads, I was looking for the singing practice. Must have the wrong—'

'Bollocks. Someone inside said you were filming. Who are ya?'

Before he could respond, the larger one held out his hand. 'Give us your phone.'

Boateng had always told Etta, his friends and anyone else who would listen that if someone with a weapon asks you for something, you give it to them. Swallow your pride and just hand it over. Nothing you own is worth an injury. But Boateng also knew he had a problem with taking his own advice.

'No,' he said, simply.

'Give it here,' said the big guy, as the smaller one stepped to the side of him. 'Let's see what you've been doing.' They were blocking him against the wall and cutting off the route to his car. He had to think, buy some time.

'It's password protected.' He took another step away, created more space.

'So unlock it. Then give it to me.'

The hoarse voice came from his left. 'There are no cameras here, son. No witnesses neither.' He brought the bat up to his side, in position to swing. It was close enough for Boateng to see the wood grain and read the words 'Louisville Slugger' on the side. He knew that brand. Solid American hardwood. A bone-breaker. He tried to stay calm.

'Phone,' ordered the big guy.

Boateng had already realised he wasn't getting out of this without a fight. He could feel the tingle in his hands and feet, the pre-emptive tremble of his leg muscles. His gaze flicked between the two guys. He was waiting for the smallest signal, then he'd react and hope for the best. 'Come on, guys,' he said. 'I've just got the wrong place. I'll be on my way.'

Then it happened.

The smaller guy drew the bat back and Boateng rushed at him, closing the distance. The only chance with a blunt object was taking away the power in the swing at its source. He grabbed the base of the bat in both hands and spun the guy round, bending his wrist the wrong way against the bat. It came loose, but now the big guy was in the mix, grabbing Boateng from behind in a bear hug. Thick arms locked around Boateng's ribs and squeezed. He kicked out into the smaller man's chest then pulled the bat backwards as hard as he could, its base connecting with the big guy's ribs. He barked at the contact and Boateng slipped the bat inside his arm, ripping it upwards to break the grip of his hands. Now he had the bat in his control, but the two men quickly recovered and began to circle him. Boateng swung at the air a few times to keep them away. 'Stay there,' he yelled, trying to manoeuvre himself towards his car. But the men fanned out and Boateng realised he was pinned against the wall, his striking range reduced. Knew he couldn't take out both men if they came at him together. His heart was pounding, jaw set, top lip shaking, eyes wild. He heard more feet alongside the building, then raised voices, and guessed it was reinforcements. 'Get back!' he bellowed, but it was an empty threat. He'd lost the advantage. Now he was on the defensive again. He exhaled hard, steadied himself, and prepared for the attack.

The siren rose sharply, half a block away on the main street. The two men didn't even exchange a look; they just ran. Footsteps retreated into the building. Boateng heard doors open and close rapidly, the commotion receding as a squad car pulled up hard from the side road. Two PCs climbed out. Boateng pictured the scene from their point of view. A man standing alone in a dark street behind an industrial unit, soaked in sweat, heavy breaths clouding the air, baseball bat in hand. The PCs clearly reached the same conclusion he might have made: hostile.

One officer drew a Taser from his holster and began shouting instructions. Boateng threw the bat to the pavement as he registered the red laser dot over his chest. Held up his hands. Between jagged breaths, he managed to speak.

'I'm DI Boateng, Lewisham MIT.'

CHAPTER TWENTY-FIVE

Friday, 15 December 2017

After greeting his team, Boateng dropped into the office chair and groaned as his back and legs hit the seat. He hadn't realised that he'd picked up bruises in the fight until the adrenalin seeped away sometime in the small hours. Walking to work hadn't helped, either. It had just made his muscles and joints ache even more.

'Rough night, Zac?' Jones glanced sideways at him, her mouth twitching into a smile.

'Not like that,' he replied. 'I was working.'

'Alone?'

'Yup.'

'On what?'

Etta had asked him the same question when he'd finally returned home. After the squad car arrived outside Unit 3 last night, Boateng spent several minutes trying to convince the night shift constables that something was going on inside. By the time they'd agreed to knock on the door, everyone had dispersed from the front. The two guys who attacked him were nowhere to be found and there were no cameras out back. The officers said they were responding to a 999 call, but the caller had given no personal details. 'Adult male, slight speech impediment', was all that had been reported, based on the recording. It meant nothing to Boateng. He'd told everyone – Etta included – that he was there developing intelligence on a lead for the murder inquiry. When asked which one, he'd said Troy's.

'I'm not sure,' he replied at length. He took out his mobile, held it up. 'But I'm hoping some photos on here might tell us.' He fished out a USB connector from the drawers under his desk and plugged the phone into his computer. 'What've you guys got?'

Connelly shook his head. 'Nothing so far on the sux suppliers in America, boss. Couple of them have shipped to private healthcare clinics in the UK, but none of those clinics has reported anything missing from their stocks. We're waiting on a couple more replies, via the FBI.'

'Alright. Good work, Pat. The more we can eliminate, the better. How about you, Nas?'

'German police came back to us this morning. Their companies have done a lot more business with the UK – as you'd guess, given the distance and free trade – so we're going through the recipients now. There's a ton of them.'

'Nice one, Nas. First task is to check purchasers' names against anyone who was in the building when Walker was murdered.'

'OK.' Malik nodded and returned to his screen.

'I've been comparing the statements for Spearhead,' said Jones. 'With Antony Webb and Halima Osman, we've got two witnesses. They both describe a man with a wooden bat in an army or camouflage jacket, black mask and gloves. So far, so good. Then the accounts diverge. Bardak's assailant was taller than average, while Halima said the man she saw was medium height and heavyset.'

Boateng considered this. 'She watched it from an upstairs window. Could be the result of different perspective.'

'Maybe. But that's not the only discrepancy. Osman thinks the attacker was right-handed, and Webb swears he was left-handed.' She gave a sigh, frustration visible as her mouth tightened. 'Without matching DNA from the scenes, they're going to look unreliable. Defence barrister's going to have a field day – if the case even gets past the Crown Prosecution Service.'

'Hang on a minute, Kat.' Boateng held up a hand. 'It's great that you're thinking about presenting evidence to the CPS and taking it to trial, but we need more work on our suspects first. I suggest we go and speak to some of these other National Right lads, find out where they were on the nights in question. Maybe ask them about their political beliefs while we're at it. Shake things up a bit. Before that, though, I want us to go through the photos I took last night and compare them to our board here.' He jerked a thumb towards the Spearhead mugshots. 'Might take a while.'

Jones leaned back in her chair, tapped her pen on the desk. 'Fine by me. Can't do much else on the Cleaver Square murders until we know where to look on the sux.'

Connelly raised his head. 'Alright, we're going as fast as we can. You're welcome to get involved if you like.'

Boateng watched Jones check her reaction to the Irishman's sarcasm.

'Pat, I wasn't suggesting…' she trailed off. 'No rush.'

Boateng didn't agree. But before he could start ruminating on that again, his attention was caught by DCI Krebs marching across the MIT office towards his desk, waving a copy of the morning *Metro*.

'What is this, DI Boateng?' she cried before reaching him.

He glanced at his team but they only returned shrugs or tiny shakes of the head to show they were as ignorant as he was. Malik and Connelly wisely kept their heads down.

'Ma'am?'

She dropped the paper on his desk. 'Open it. Page nine.'

Boateng studied Krebs for a second, then followed her instruction and read the headline: EX-CON MURDERED IN MET POLICE CELL. He swallowed and cursed silently as he clocked the byline: Faye Rix.

'Would you care to explain to me, DI Boateng, why you appear in the article?'

'What?' He frowned at her, before scanning the piece and seeing his name: *Sources indicated that Detective Inspector Zachariah Boateng, who works in Lewisham borough's Major Investigation Team, may be connected to the death.* Was it a reference to his handwritten note on the body? How many people had access to that information? 'I don't know, ma'am. I…' He tried to think of an explanation. 'Rix was in the building when Walker was murdered. Perhaps we could ask the press officer? Maybe she over-briefed—'

'Walker's body wasn't discovered until the morning,' interjected Krebs, pinning the paper to his desk with a finger. 'And we've been to all sorts of lengths to keep it out of the media until we know more. Deaths in custody are extremely serious matters. Now the lid's blown right off. Have you been speaking to Faye Rix off-record?'

Boateng hesitated; he had spoken to her, just not about Walker. He recalled their argument at Troy's wake, then the conversation in the boxing gym. 'Well, we've had a couple of chats in the last few weeks, but I didn't—'

'Unauthorised contact with a journalist?' Krebs was visibly enraged. 'My office, now.'

Boateng felt his temper flare, tried to relax and rolled back his seat. Krebs turned on her heel and began striding out. 'Back soon,' he told his team. 'I hope.' He was halfway to the door when Malik's voice rang out across the open-plan room.

'Boss!'

He turned, saw the urgency in Malik's expression. Boateng called to Krebs, raised his hands in apology. 'Ma'am, just a moment, if I may. Operational matter.' He jogged back to their desks.

'I checked all the most recent arrivals from Germany,' said Malik. 'No hits for anyone of interest to us in the past month.

Then I sorted the older shipments, first by those who've had regular deliveries.'

'Good thinking.'

'This address came up. Fifteen separate orders of sux over the past two years, sent to this flat in Charlton. And the customer?' Malik rotated the monitor towards him, tapped the glass.

'Adam Rix.'

Twenty minutes later, Boateng and Jones were sitting in an unmarked car behind Charlton Athletic football stadium with eyes on the flat shared by Adam and Faye Rix. It was a sixth-floor apartment in a monolithic block called Valiant House. Maybe it was the name that had attracted them; they wouldn't think it was ironic. Malik and Connelly were in a second vehicle on the other side of the building. They were all waiting for the arrival of the TSG – Territorial Support Group – before proceeding with the arrest. Adam Rix was now the prime suspect for the murders of Troy, Ana, Hayworth and Walker. Krebs had paused her bollocking and channelled her energy into getting an emergency arrest warrant for Rix signed off by a duty magistrate. Of course, they didn't know for sure that he was in the flat. At 6 p.m. on a Friday, Rix could be anywhere. But the warrant enabled them to break in and search the place if necessary.

Once Rix had shown up on the purchasers' list for sux imports, coupled with his presence in the building on the night of Walker's death, there was little doubt over his involvement. After that, Boateng saw the rest fall into place: Adam Rix was Joseph Young, taking his revenge on those he held responsible for his parents' deaths. The mutism was a legacy of his childhood trauma. The refusal to shake Boateng's hand, the latent anger every time they'd met – it all fit. It also explained his – probably adoptive – sister Faye's interest in the case, and her source on the murders. Did she know her brother's true identity? He wondered at the MO: did Faye engage the victim in conversation while her brother ambushed them with an injection? Or did he restrain them while Rix administered the sux? Boateng found it hard to imagine Adam acting without his sister's knowledge. Either way, it was now just a question of finding the pair.

For the first time in more than two weeks, Boateng felt a sense of relief – even safety. He'd found the answer just in time. Rix wouldn't be able to get to him past colleagues and backup, not to mention the stab vest he now wore. Nevertheless, his analytical mind wondered why Adam Rix hadn't tried to kill him earlier. Perhaps he'd been waiting to catch Boateng alone, toying with him, or just enjoying watching him stumble around in the darkness. Well, now Boateng and his MIT had the upper hand.

Sitting in the car, he'd made two phone calls. One to Summers to cancel the session they'd planned for last thing that evening; the second to Etta to check she was OK. She'd tutted, laughed, said that obviously she *was* fine, since they were having a nice chat on the phone. His wife had been more interested in when he was finishing up and coming home for dinner and a drink. When he'd mentioned the discovery that meant Adam Rix was now their main suspect, she'd been shocked, but congratulated him. He could sense the relief in her voice too. She asked if they'd be arresting Faye as well. Boateng told her that was likely, and there may even be charges of conspiracy to murder depending on how the evidence fell. He'd be back for dinner as soon as they'd gone into Rix's flat. Even if Rix wasn't inside, units would keep watch on the place and check other locations, including the boxing gym, while comms experts searched for his mobile phone. That meant Boateng could take a break and go home, then head back in to question Rix when they lifted him. Etta had offered to cook oto, one of his favourite Ghanaian dishes. Boateng smiled to himself, imagining unwinding with her on the sofa after Kofi had gone to bed. A bottle of wine, some low music…

The radio bleeped and Jones gave their call sign. A matter-of-fact voice stated that the TSG was on its way to their location. Jones asked for their ETA. The reply crackled back across the Airwave unit.

Ten minutes.

Etta checked the clock. She hoped Zac would be home soon. He'd guessed around seven or eight, so she'd begged a favour off her parents and asked them to look after Kofi for the night. Promised her son a treat of Christmas shopping tomorrow in return, after his football. The privacy would give her and Zac a chance to relax and enjoy each other's company. They'd struggled, understandably, since the night of Troy's death. There was no point trying to apportion blame. What they both needed now was to spend time together with no distractions, no work or childcare between them. Important as those things were, their relationship deserved more attention.

Oto was a relatively simple Ghanaian dish that was one of Zac's favourites, and Etta wanted it to be part of a night that brought them back together. Her preparations were going well. She'd put the late, great funk-soul diva Sharon Jones on the sound system and was singing along to 'Stranger to My Happiness'. The sad lyrics about lovers being dishonest captured something of what she'd felt recently, while the cheery music showed that there was a way out. She'd selected the best plantains she could find in the shop, and was peeling, cutting and plopping them in a pot of water, ready to boil. Then she could get started on the chicken to go with it. Her work was in rhythm with the music, and she had a glass of wine on the go already. Perfect.

The doorbell rang.

Had Zac returned already? But why ring? He couldn't be locked out – his house keys were on the same bunch as those for his car. She looked through the peephole, recognised the face. Not Zac, but his colleague. She opened the door, hungry for news, thoughts racing as she tried to work out why someone else would come round. Had something happened to Zac?

'Everything's alright,' said the visitor, perhaps in response to her concerned expression. 'Zac's still at work.'

Etta breathed a sigh of relief. 'Thank God. It's nice to see you again. Come in,' she said. 'Cup of tea?'

'Sure, thanks.'

She walked down the hallway and the visitor followed. In the kitchen, Etta filled the kettle and switched it on, becoming suddenly aware of the physical presence behind her, too close. She turned, saw the needle. Felt the sharp stab in her arm. Tried to scream, but the music swallowed up her noise. In seconds her limbs were slackening, losing control. Then she was being guided to a chair, unable to resist. Her breathing slowed as the mask of a respirator was placed over her mouth and nose, the machine forcing air into her lungs. Zac's advice from the other night flashed into her fully conscious mind: *Don't open the door to strangers… or anyone, for that matter.*

Too late.

CHAPTER TWENTY-SIX

Kat Jones studied the cover sheet on the fax. She couldn't remember the last time she'd received one. There was a kind of old-school charm about it in a world full of emails, like receiving a letter through the post. Her Spanish wasn't up to much, but the origin of the missive was clear because it was written in English too: Guatemalan National Civil Police. The two other pieces of information that jumped out at her were the name of the subject, Joseph Young, and the year of the report, 2004.

The obvious next step – particularly at 8.30 p.m. on a Friday – would be to send it off for translation and get the full text back early next week. Chances were the post-mortem wouldn't offer much help on the Cleaver Square murders anyway. The sux deliveries to Adam Rix were basically a slam dunk, particularly when combined with all the other circumstantial evidence they had on him. Any medical detail in the report to indicate that the body found in Guatemala was not really Joseph Young would be icing on the cake. And that evidence might not even be clear until they had Adam Rix in custody and a doctor could examine him. Surely his arrest was just a matter of time: the warrant was out, local units had been briefed, they'd even passed his name and photograph to the border authorities.

Boateng had headed off a few minutes ago, announcing that he had a dinner date at home with his wife. Jones envied their relationship, particularly after her second date with Tom had failed to materialise and she found herself alone, again, working into

Friday night. But she was happy for her boss, getting a chance to chill after the past couple of weeks. He deserved it. Malik and Connelly had already packed up for the night and gone for a pint in Blackheath with others from the station. They'd invited her, but she'd politely refused, blaming paperwork. After the standard mockery, they'd left. That gave her the chance to look at the post-mortem in peace. She still harboured some hope of making a breakthrough by putting in the hours – particularly on how their current cases were connected – and winning the others' praise and respect. *Did you hear about Jones's work on those murders? She played a blinder,* they'd say.

She began flicking through the report, tapping a couple of key terms into Google Translate, deciphering others with common sense. Jones wasn't sure what she was looking for, but she had the feeling she'd know when she saw it. Photographs were interposed between paragraphs of text in the report, and she paused, studying each in turn. One made her stomach lurch: a close-up of Joseph Young's face after his fall off the cliff. He appeared to have hit his head against some rocks on the way down, or perhaps landed face first. One cheek was completely caved in, the skin livid under dried blood. Most of his teeth seemed to have been knocked out by the impact, a few stragglers protruding from the gaping hole above his shattered jaw. Jones typed and translated some more lines. Those teeth, along with the passport found in the shorts pocket, had confirmed the ID of the dead man as Joseph Young.

Jones picked up another wad of documents she'd printed earlier: Joseph Young's medical records from the English National Health Service. The privacy of medical information was sacrosanct, but the police and other agencies had a back door into the gigantic NHS Spine database, designed to assist them in the most urgent cases, where risk to life took priority over data protection. With no next of kin, and evidence connecting Joseph Young to a current murder inquiry, Jones had easily secured access to the records.

She'd scanned through them and was now checking photographs from the Guatemalan report against physical features noted in the NHS records.

Young's medical history was unremarkable until age twelve, when his family had been decimated. A raft of diagnoses appeared in subsequent months: post-traumatic stress disorder, mutism and depression, all signed off by a child psychiatrist. A GP had added secondary enuresis in there, which Jones had looked up. Another term she'd needed to check was 'focal vitiligo': loss of skin pigmentation, specifically on one hand and wrist in Young's case, leaving small white marks. She went back to the Guatemalan police report and checked a dozen photographs before she found a picture showing Young's hands. She examined the image, turned it under her desk light. No discolouration was visible, despite what was written in his record. She leaned back in her chair and considered this for a moment. Maybe the photos weren't high enough quality to show the scars. Maybe Young had recovered from the vitiligo in his late teens, or had cosmetic surgery to alter the white marks.

Maybe.

More likely, this was evidence that the body found in Guatemala was not Joseph Young. That meant that he probably wasn't dead. Which in turn meant he'd taken a new identity. Probably that of Adam Rix, since it was Young who had the strongest motive to avenge the death of his parents in Cleaver Square. This neat, satisfying chain of logic was immediately followed by a second realisation that hadn't occurred to her earlier, as if her brain had been processing it outside her awareness.

Jones had seen that scarring before. Recently.

She knew who the killer was.

And it wasn't Adam Rix.

Jim walked up the hill that led out of Lewisham centre and towards
Brockley. He was about a hundred metres behind Boateng, on the
opposite side of the road and masked by enough traffic, commuters
and darkness to ensure he couldn't be seen by his quarry. At first,
Jim had considered getting his car. But once Boateng started out
on foot in the direction of his house, it'd been pretty obvious where
he was headed. That enabled Jim to keep back and minimise any
chance of counter-surveillance. Although a lot of detectives didn't
even get basic training in that, he had to assume Boateng would
have, given the narcotics work on his file.

The detective looked exhausted when he'd finally emerged
from the police station. Unshaven, with heavy bags under slow-
blinking eyes. Not surprising, considering what happened last
night in Catford. Boateng was lucky to still be breathing. Jim had
elected to intervene with a 999 call in the end; the boss would
want whatever Boateng was doing to play out, to let them see
the bigger picture.

And yet, there was a lightness in Boateng's gait this evening that
Jim hadn't observed before. A new detail, which suggested some
development in his favour. Jim would simply continue watching
and find out what it was. But he didn't expect much more to
happen tonight; it seemed like Boateng was just heading home
now, probably for a quiet one with the missus. He'd follow him
back, check he was in for the evening, then call it a night. Start
again tomorrow morning, and keep going. However long it took.

Until the boss told him it was time for action.

*

Boateng was strolling home. Yup, strolling. That was the word
he'd use. He hadn't strolled in a while, but now his mood was
lifting and he was happy. He was safe, he was going to see Etta,
and he knew what they were having for dinner: oto, one of
his all-time favourites. Things were good. OK, so they hadn't

found the Rixes at their flat in Charlton, even after the TSG had arrived and smashed in the door. But four vials of sux were discovered in a cabinet below the bathroom sink, corroborating the purchase data Malik received from Germany. They'd driven back to Lewisham police station via the boxing gym in New Cross, but neither Adam nor Faye was there, either. Units were briefed and in position watching the flat, the gym and a couple of local railway stations, while a technical team was trying to geolocate either Adam's or Faye's mobile phone. When they were found, it was a case of sending in the arrest team and lifting them. Then the questioning could take place and the most challenging task would begin: making the evidential case for a murder charge. Rix had clearly been careful at the scenes, but the methods of dispatching his victims were certainly premeditated. Boateng and his team just needed to prove that materially. He'd run the ideas past Etta; her legal knowledge had often helped him when building a case for trial. But that could wait for another time. Tonight was about celebrating.

CHAPTER TWENTY-SEVEN

Kat Jones knew that what she was doing was neither official investigative protocol nor strictly advisable from a safety perspective, but at 9 p.m. on a Friday there wasn't really another option. Not if she wanted an answer to the question triggered by her comparison of Young's post-mortem report and medical records: *was it him?* She remembered Jason Leather's words when he'd turned up unannounced at the LP bar: *I live in the flat above the convenience shop next door.* Jones now stood outside, looking up at the first and second floor windows. Likely a split-level flat, since there was only one buzzer on the door. The lights were on. Jason was probably at home.

She knew that the sensible course of action would be to report her discovery to Boateng, plan the arrest, sit tight and then go in with backup – probably tomorrow. But something was driving her on. She couldn't resist the idea that this would cement her name in the MIT as a solid investigator, someone to be taken seriously. That pay-off was worth the risk.

Nevertheless, a heads-up to Boateng before she acted would provide the cover she needed. She took out her phone and dialled, but he didn't answer. The call went to voicemail and she left a message, telling him that she was following up on something that could be critical in their case, if her guess was right. Jones took the pepper spray out of her pocket, then concealed it in her jacket sleeve. She didn't know how Leather would react. Steeling herself, she took a deep breath and pressed the buzzer. Her pulse quickened as she heard someone coming down stairs. There was a pause, then the door flew open.

Jason Leather stood there, topless and out of breath, a sheen of sweat on an athletic torso that Jones would not have guessed lay under those gross black T-shirts. She registered screams, drums and thrashing guitars from the top of the staircase behind him. Leather's eyes were dead behind those little circular glasses, the loose shoulder-length hair lank and greasy. Jones felt a stab of adrenalin when she noticed what was in his hand. It looked like a samurai or ninja sword. She composed herself, studied the hand holding the sword, noted the small white scars. Another deep breath, pepper spray ready.

'Can I come in?' she asked.

Leather looked at her, his chest rising and falling. Glanced at his sword, and back to her. 'What for?'

She swallowed. 'There's something I have to ask you.'

●

Boateng slid his key into the front door and entered. There was no music, no movement, none of the pre-dinner energy he'd expected. Strange. He looked down the hallway into the kitchen: it appeared empty, although he could smell the cooking. He began to salivate.

'Etta?' he called. But the only reply was a faint, regular rhythm, like a machine moving back and forth. The sound came from the living room, to his left. Its door was shut. He turned the handle and cautiously pushed. As it swung open, he remembered that Adam Rix knew where he lived; Faye had even quoted the name of their street to him in the boxing gym. Had she and Adam—

The thought was interrupted when Boateng clocked the revolver lying on the coffee table. He froze, hands tingling. Heard the machine noise again, like a breath, before it stopped.

'Come in,' said a familiar voice. 'Slowly.'

As he took one step across the threshold, Boateng saw Etta slumped back in an armchair. She wasn't moving. A 9 mm pistol pointed directly at her head, the person holding it still out of his view in the L-shaped room.

Boateng's guts felt like they were moving inside him. 'What the fuck?' he cried.

'Don't do anything stupid,' said the voice. 'You're going to die. But if you listen to me, you have the chance to save her.'

It took Boateng a split second to place that voice, out of context. He did so just as its owner moved into his vision beside the armchair, keeping the pistol trained on his wife's head.

'Tom Summers.'

The counsellor flashed a smile. 'Hello, Zac.'

'You were Joseph Young,' stated Boateng.

'I left that name at the bottom of a cliff in Guatemala. Normally I like to plan things, but when that guy slipped and fell, I saw the chance for a new start.'

'You pushed him?'

'No,' chuckled Summers. 'I only murder people who deserve to die.'

Boateng glanced at his wife. 'Let her go, Tom,' he pleaded. 'She's nothing to do with it, with Cleaver Square, with my mistakes. Nothing. She's innocent.'

'Guilt by association, I say.'

'It's OK, baby,' Boateng said to her, before turning to Summers. 'Let her go or I swear I will kill you.'

'You're not really in a position to make that kind of threat, Zac. I have a fully loaded gun. The revolver there' – he nodded at the table – 'is for you. It's a six-shooter, as you can see. Five blanks, one real bullet. You're going to play a game of Russian roulette. But if you try to be a hero, I will execute your wife, then you, before you've had a chance to find that real bullet. I'll make it look like you shot her, then yourself. You've seen my work with the others. Imagine what your son would make of that.'

Boateng felt a rage swelling inside him, the frustration of impotence. The desire to rip Summers's head off for doing this to Etta, to avenge Troy in the process. But he caught himself, tried to think. There had to be a way out. For now, he recognised that Summers was holding all the cards. 'Alright. You're in charge.'

'Thank you,' replied Summers. 'Pick up the gun.'

Boateng did so and stood facing his wife, the revolver hanging in a loose grip at his side.

'You've probably worked out my method. Your wife has a dose of suxamethonium chloride in her body. She can't move, but she can hear, understand, and feel everything. Can't you, Etta?' Summers reached around her with his left hand and pressed a thumb into the side of her neck, where Boateng knew there was a pressure point. Her head rolled to one side, and Boateng saw her eyes water. 'She can just about breathe. So listen to me, Zac. Understand?'

'Yes.'

'You know why you're about to die?'

Boateng blinked. 'Cleaver Square.'

'Correct. Why don't you explain, for the benefit of your wife, what you did that day? May fifteenth, 1998.'

Boateng flicked his gaze from Summers to Etta and back. 'OK,' he said slowly. If this was a chance to buy time, he had to take it. 'It was late afternoon,' he began. 'A silent 999 call was passed from the operator to Kennington station. Troy, Ana and I responded. We turned up at 17 Cleaver Square in a patrol car. Ana went to the front, Troy and I to the rear. We climbed the garden wall and saw the back door was open. So, we went inside. Ana rang the bell, and a guy came downstairs, masked, with a pistol. He reached the bottom of the stairs, turned, and saw me in the kitchen. He raised the pistol at my chest and...' Boateng felt the emotion growing, a mixture of sadness and fear, his throat tightening. 'I thought I was done. I swear he was about to pull the trigger, and then Troy lunged at him from the side, grabbed the gun. I just stood still, frozen.' He looked to Etta for a reaction. Her face was impassive, but he caught a twitch in her fingers. Summers was staring at him and hadn't seen the movement.

'That's right,' commented Summers. 'You just stood there. Like a coward.'

Boateng's head dropped, his face hot with shame. Sweat was prickling his hands and armpits. 'Yeah,' he said quietly.

'Go on,' said Summers. 'Remember, I saw it. I'll stop you if your version is off the mark.'

'Troy grappled with the gunman, and I just watched them. Then Troy twisted the gun around, got his finger over the trigger. Next thing I knew it'd fired, and Troy stepped away, holding it, staring like he didn't know what he'd done. He was gasping. The guy staggered back, blood on his sweatshirt. The bloodstain grew and grew, and Troy shouted at me to give the guy some first aid. There was a noise from upstairs, and Troy just charged up there with the pistol. I opened the front door and let Ana inside. Then I heard shouting from above, followed by gunshots. I ran up, followed the noise into the bedroom.' He paused, shook his head. 'It was a damned bloodbath. Three people shot, and Troy standing there holding the gun. Mr and Mrs Young—'

'My parents,' interjected Summers.

Boateng nodded. 'Shot.'

'By your friend.'

'No.'

'Liar!' bellowed Summers.

'It was the burglar, Arun Gray,' said Boateng, holding his free hand up. 'He was the guy in charge. He shot your father, Joseph.'

Summers's eyes burned. 'You lied then and you're lying now. Troy McEwen killed my parents.'

'Arun Gray killed your father. Troy said he shot Gray after that to protect your mother, but Gray was standing in front of her and the bullet passed through him and hit her too. It was an accident.'

'Bullshit.'

Boateng didn't reply. He knew sooner or later the real discrepancy in the accounts was coming.

'So,' continued Summers, 'Troy McEwen shoots my parents and Arun Gray dead. Actually, my mother wasn't dead. She died later. You didn't save her, either.'

'I tried, believe me.'

Summers snorted. 'I don't believe a damn word that comes out of your mouth.'

'I swear.'

'Like you tried to save the guy downstairs? I watched him bleed to death.'

Boateng was silent. He felt like judgement was being passed on him. It was the truth. He and Ana had both panicked, made an attempt at stemming the blood flow, but the guy had already lost too much from his exit wound. They didn't call for a paramedic soon enough. Summers was right.

'And the worst was yet to come, wasn't it?' The counsellor raised his eyebrows.

Boateng tried to think of some way out, but nothing came to him.

'Wasn't it?' repeated Summers.

'What do you mean?' *Buy some time*, he thought.

'Don't treat me like a fool!' Summers pressed his thumb into Etta's neck again, and this time her body bucked slightly at the pain. 'Do you want her to suffer more?'

'OK, OK.' Boateng knew Etta was able to hear everything, that he was confessing something he'd kept secret, even from her, for nearly twenty years. 'Troy came back downstairs. He told us not to call for backup yet. We were all shitting ourselves, we had no idea what to do. It seemed like we'd only arrived thirty seconds earlier and four people had already died.'

'That's right,' added Summers. 'You didn't call for backup. Meanwhile, upstairs, my mother was bleeding to death.'

'We didn't know that.'

'You didn't check.'

'We did,' protested Boateng. 'Just—'

'Not fast enough, right?'

Boateng took a big jagged breath. He could feel tears in his eyes. 'I'm sorry.'

'It's too late for that.' Summers's jaw set hard. He had the pistol pressed to the top of Etta's head. 'And the story doesn't end there, does it? Tell your lovely wife what happened next.'

'We…' Boateng hesitated, saw Etta's feet shift. He remembered what the King's lab technician had said about sux wearing off in minutes, how it had to be topped up for the person to remain immobilised. If he continued to keep Summers's attention, maybe there was a chance. 'We didn't know what to do. None of it was meant to happen.' He felt a tear roll down his cheek and hit the corner of his mouth.

'Tell the truth,' said Summers. 'For once.'

'OK. But just take the gun away from her. Please.'

Summers considered this, then raised the barrel so it was aimed directly at Boateng. 'The truth,' he commanded.

'I'm sorry, baby,' he told Etta. 'We didn't know what else to do.' He shut his eyes. 'I took the pistol from Troy. By this point he was shaking. We couldn't think straight. I wiped the gun down and put it in the dead burglar's hand. Then we checked the scene. The ballistics fitted. We got our stories straight: there must've been an argument between the burglars, perhaps over the execution of Mr Young. Then they turned on each other, and Mrs Young was caught in the crossfire. That was our story. The part about Troy ambushing the burglar downstairs and the gun going off remained. It was self-defence. We just said it happened after the other shots upstairs. Then we called for backup and when reinforcements arrived, they found Dez Hayworth and Vic Walker on the top floor, unarmed, hiding. They'd been trying to open a safe. And they found you, Joseph.'

'Hiding in the pantry, looking through the little wooden slats in the door. You never knew I was there, but I saw what you did.'

'You didn't see what happened upstairs.'

'No, but I found out. Quite recently, in fact.'

'How?'

'I spent seven years working as a prison counsellor. Thought it might help me deal with what happened.' He shrugged without relaxing his grip on the pistol. 'For a few years, it did. Until a man called Vic came in for a session one day, a couple of years ago.'

'Walker?'

Summers nodded. 'He decided to unburden himself of something he'd seen once. Of course, he had no idea who I was. He told me how he watched a police officer burst in on a home burglary he'd done and start shooting. How he kept quiet about it at the time in exchange for a shorter sentence. I knew exactly what he was describing. Memories came back, rage I'd buried. I didn't sleep for days, thought I was going mad. Then everything became clear. The simplicity of it was beautiful. The man who shot my parents was still alive, and there was only one course of action I could live with. Serve justice to those who'd obstructed it. Took a while to get myself in position, but fortunately the Met is always happy to save money through volunteers. Once I had access to the systems, I could locate you all, plan it out. After I shot Troy, I texted from his phone to invite you over. I knew that if you found his body, policy meant your boss would be obliged to refer you to me. I enjoyed hearing about your pain, Zac. Your self-doubt, your inadequacies. It's a shame we won't have any more sessions.'

Boateng swallowed. He was sure Troy hadn't meant to kill anyone, least of all a civilian. But there was nothing accidental about their cover-up.

'So, you faked the evidence at Cleaver Square,' stated Summers.

'Yes.'

'And you lied in your testimony.'

'Yes.'

'All three of you.'

Boateng nodded. He felt so ashamed of it all. He owed Troy, that was for sure. The man had saved his life. But what was the price of that? Somehow, even now, the worst part for him was holding it all back from Etta.

'Now it's time for justice,' said Summers. 'Isn't that what you believe in?' He nodded to the revolver in Boateng's right hand. 'Put the gun to your temple.'

Boateng's pulse leapt and he felt his limbs start to tremble. He fought back tears, his mouth twisting, eyes screwing shut. Still trying to think of a way out.

'Do it,' whispered Summers.

Boateng placed the barrel to his head. It felt cold and smooth against his skin.

'Pull the trigger.'

He couldn't.

'You have to understand, this is the only way your wife has a chance to live.'

Boateng opened his eyes, blinked through the tears, looked at Etta. One of the two people who meant more to him than anyone else in the world. Her legs shifted, forearms flexed. 'What guarantee can you give me of that?' he said, his voice strangled.

'This is about you, not her,' said Summers, still aiming the pistol straight at Boateng's chest. 'Once you've shot yourself, I walk out of here. No one will ever see me again.'

Boateng dropped the pistol from his head so it hung in front of him, pointing at the floor. He scrutinised the back of the revolver's chamber, in case there was any clue which bullet was real. But there were no obvious differences. Summers would've thought of that.

'Put the gun back to your temple,' said Summers, calmly. 'And pull the trigger.'

Boateng realised in that moment that he had no choice. There was no backup coming, no alternative. He pressed the cold steel to his skin again. It was heavy, resting next to his right eye. He brought it away slightly, angled it up a bit.

Then he pulled the trigger.

It seemed like his ear had exploded, the bang deafening, leaving a high-pitched shrill tone that filled the room. He felt a raw pain at the side of his head, the flesh burning. He was disorientated, but alive. The round had been a blank.

'Lucky for you.' Summers tilted his head. 'Perhaps you'd guessed – I didn't want it to be over on the first shot.'

Boateng's legs felt weak. He had to save Etta, no matter if he died in the process. Every second that passed was a step closer to her regaining her movement. But he was running out of time.

'Now,' said Summers. 'Round two.'

CHAPTER TWENTY-EIGHT

Jim had been about to leave. He'd kept an eye on Boateng's front door for ten minutes after the detective had gone inside. Imagined him kicking off his shoes, pouring a drink with his wife, getting the dinner ready. Jim had let his own mind wander to food, prompted by the hollow feeling in his stomach. Things had been moving so fast, he'd barely eaten all day. Maybe he'd pick something up on the way home. A nice curry would do the trick. He'd begun to picture the rogan josh with slow-cooked lamb… then he heard the single shot.

It was so out of place that Jim thought his ears had deceived him. A car backfiring on a parallel road, perhaps? But there was no accompanying engine strain, no grind of gears. It had to be a handgun. And it sounded like it had come from inside Boateng's house. He got up from the park bench and moved closer to the terrace, keeping in the cover of trees. Peering through thick foliage, he scanned the windows at the front of the building: no movement, curtains drawn. Was it Boateng who'd fired? Who else was in the house? He had to react.

Jim reached inside his jacket.

Nothing Etta had experienced came close to this terror. There was something about being paralysed, about losing control of your muscles, which heightened the awareness of other sensations. She'd heard the bang and the high tone now rang in her ears.

She could smell burnt gunpowder, like a firework had gone off. But most acutely, she could see her husband holding a revolver to his head, tears filling his eyes. The skin and hair at the side of his head was broken and bloodied, but he was alive. He was looking at her. And she'd just heard Summers order him to fire again. Etta knew she couldn't take any more, she couldn't let this happen. Not to Zac, not to her. No one else was going to threaten her family.

The loss of muscle control had been one of the strangest things she's ever felt. Like someone had switched off her body, shutting down the automatic movements she took for granted. But now, steadily, sensation was returning. She knew that to shift too much or too quickly would alert her captor. Resisting the urge to stand, she gradually tested her body: fingers, toes, hands and feet. Slowly flexed the muscles in her legs and arms. Rolled her shoulders almost imperceptibly. Zac had raised the revolver to his own head again. Her eyes darted left. Summers had his pistol raised in both hands, his attention focused on her husband. Etta knew she had one shot at this. The longer she waited, the better her movement. But with Summers repeating his instruction to shoot, there was no time. She had to act. For her husband, for herself, for her family.

Gathering her strength, she glanced left at Summers again, checked his distance and posture. Balled her right fist. Then in one movement she stood and lunged with everything she could muster, throwing the punch hard into Summers's solar plexus. The hook connected with his body and sent him crumpling over. Her momentum carried her into him and sent him crashing to the floor, the pistol still in his grip but flailing to the side, pointing at the wall. She tried to move towards the gun, but the effort had drained her and her body wouldn't obey her brain. She half collapsed and watched as Summers began to recover, weapon twitching in his hand.

Then Zac was on top of him, gripping his wrist, wrestling with the pistol. Etta hauled herself to her feet, steadying herself on the armchair as Zac aimed a left-handed punch into Summers's ribs. Zac was above Summers and pressing his weight down on him. Summers writhed and the gun was suspended in the air, each man pulling it towards him. Zac landed another punch and Summers flinched, the gun slipping in his hand. Zac batted it away towards the far wall, out of reach for both men. Etta tried to think what she could do. She scanned the room. Something to help Zac. Then it came to her.

The revolver. Zac had dropped it on the other side of the room. She ran to it, picked it up. The handle was sweaty. It felt heavy and awkward in her hands.

She turned back to the fight in time to see Summers produce something from his pocket that he jabbed into Zac's thigh. Zac bellowed in pain and swung his fist again, but missed. His next punch seemed to have no power, and then his spine bent, the tension dropping from his neck and shoulders. Summers rolled over on top of him and clamped both hands around Zac's neck. Etta watched him squeezing hard, Zac's limp body unresponsive.

Her legs felt weak beneath her, but she stepped closer, aimed the gun at Summers's back as he sat astride her husband, growling as he strangled Zac. She heard a choke and gasp from Zac, and she steadied herself and tried to breathe. Her hands were shaking. Then she fired. The bang threw her backwards and off balance, but when she looked back, nothing had changed. Zac's body was immobile, Summers applying his full force around Zac's throat. She quickly fired again, trying to hold her arms steady. Nothing.

At the sound of the shots, Summers glanced back at her. He released his grip on Zac's neck and scrambled towards his gun at the far wall. Etta fired once more in his direction. Same result: another blank. That was four of the six bullets, wasn't it? She couldn't be sure. Gun smoke was clouding her vision, choking her. Summers stooped, picked up the pistol and turned towards her. She stepped forward and squeezed the trigger again.

The force of the blast flung her arms upwards and she stumbled, falling sideways into the sofa. When she clawed herself back up, Summers was lying on his back with a small hole in his abdomen. The younger man was still breathing, making a high-pitched moan like an injured dog. He held the gun in one hand and she watched his fingers tighten around its grip once more.

Etta dropped the revolver and raced over to Summers, stamping on his wrist before kicking the pistol aside. She moved across to her husband. Zac was immobile, staring straight up at the ceiling. At first, she thought he was dead. Then she put her cheek to his mouth and felt the slightest movement of air escaping from his lungs. But he wasn't breathing in. Frantic, she glanced around her. How could she help him? She stood, searching for something. Then she remembered: the respirator.

Etta snatched up the device from behind the armchair where it had fallen after she lunged at Summers. She held the mask over Zac's mouth and nose and began to operate the machine, the bag filling and compressing as it drove oxygen into his depleted lungs. Summers writhed next to her, gripping his wound, red liquid oozing over his hands. But she could only help one man, and there was no doubt who that would be. Summers could wait.

'It's OK, baby,' she said, continuing to pump oxygen into her husband's mouth. 'We're going to be alright.'

The faint sound of a siren rose in the distance. Could it be…?

Zac still wasn't breathing. She pressed the oxygen mask firmly over his face as the sound grew.

Then she screamed for help as loud as she could.

CHAPTER TWENTY-NINE

Saturday, 16 December 2017

Zac slowly opened his eyes and looked sideways towards the light. His wife's familiar form came into focus, picked out in the low winter sunshine that shone through the hospital window. He could see the trees and grass of Ladywell Fields below, could hear dogs barking and children shrieking in the playground. The whump of a football being kicked was followed by players' urgent cries. A normal day.

'How are you feeling, love?' asked Etta. He reached out instinctively and she grasped his palm with a warm hand.

Zac's smile became a grimace as he turned his head towards her. After the paramedics arrived at their house last night, he'd been taken to A & E at Lewisham hospital, examined and kept in overnight for observation. Fortunately, his larynx and trachea were intact. But doctors found second-degree burns over a patch of skin and hair at the right side of his head, a perforated right eardrum and severe bruising around his throat. This morning, it all hurt like hell.

'Been better,' he replied, letting his neck relax and his head drop back to the pillow as his eyes closed. 'You?' He knew his wife had been given the all-clear – physically, at least. His question was more about her emotional state.

Etta stroked his hand. 'I'm OK.'

'You saved my life.' He'd already told her that last night, as soon as the sux had worn off and he'd regained the ability to speak. 'Twice,' he added. First with Summers, then with his breathing.

'I was on autopilot. What is it they say, fight or flight?' He heard her give a small snort. 'Guess I chose fight. I still can't believe it all happened. In our home, too.'

'You never know how you're gonna react until you're in a situation like that. And I for one am glad it turns out you're a bloody hero.'

'I shot someone.' She paused a beat, as if letting the words sink in. 'God knows how that's going to affect me down the line. The image of it keeps coming back, totally clear. But right now, it just seems like something I imagined or dreamed.'

'You had no choice. Same as me when he told me to pull the trigger. I was scared shitless. But I saw you there and I… I just prayed it was a blank.'

Etta squeezed his hand. 'Thank you. Sounds weird saying that, but I understand why you did it. I could hear everything.'

Zac opened his eyes again, swallowed and let the pain subside marginally. 'I love you,' he said.

'Love you too, baby.' She leaned in and touched her forehead gently to his. The contact was sweet against the skin that wasn't covered in gauze and bandages.

'Listen,' he began. 'I'm sorry I didn't tell you what was going on. I thought I was protecting you, but I wasn't. I was just pushing you away, being selfish and—'

'Shh.' She kissed him once on the lips. 'It's alright.' Her eyes were moistening and she wiped them with the back of her hand. 'Just, whatever you're going through, Zachariah, don't forget about your family, OK? About me and Ko. We've lost Amelia, but we're not going to lose each other.'

'Never.' Zac knew there was no chance of forgetting his family. Especially his daughter. Or the fact that there was someone involved in her death still out there. He didn't voice this last thought to his wife. Her predictable reply would almost certainly be the right one: let it go, move on with life, remember all the fantastic moments they had together while Amelia was alive. Still, a little bit of him raged against that, equating letting go with giving up. The feeling burned, nagging, like the pain under his bandage. Covered over, but raw.

He snapped out of it when she kissed him again.

'I'm going to pick Kofi up,' she said. 'I know he wants to see you.'

'Can't I see him at home? Surely I'm going to be out of here soon.'

'They won't let you come home until the swelling in your neck reduces a bit, in case of what they call "complications". It's no bad thing – means they can change your burns dressings and sort your ear out, too.'

Zac glanced around the room. 'At least let me get up and put my own clothes on. Don't want him seeing me like this, some kind of invalid.'

She grinned, shaking her head. 'He'll think you're a hero, whatever happens.'

He didn't return the expression. 'What about you? After what I confessed to, last night.'

Etta sat back in the chair, weighing her words. 'I guess it's like you said, Zac. You never know how you'll react until the situation demands it.'

He frowned, sending pain shooting through his face. 'You mean, when the shit hit the fan, I panicked, tampered with evidence, lied and misled an investigation?'

'No.' She fixed him with a level gaze. 'I mean that when you had to, you protected your friend. You repaid him for sticking up for you and saving your life.'

'But was that the right thing?'

'Well, I think you did what came naturally. You protected what's most important to you. And for you, Zac, it's others. The people you love. I'm not talking as a lawyer, here. I'm talking as a human being.'

There was a knock on the open door and they looked up to see Kat Jones standing there. She wore a leather jacket with jeans, her head and neck swathed in a woolly hat and scarf.

Etta smiled and kissed him again before standing. 'See you in an hour or two.'

●

Kat fished in her purse, pulled out a bank card. 'Buy you a coffee, Zac? Since I didn't bring any flowers.'

'If you insist.' The nurses had let her accompany Zac to the café across the park from the hospital, with friendly but firm instructions to bring him back within an hour.

She placed the order and looked up at the sign hanging behind the counter. 'Ten Thousand Hands? So, what's the story of this place?'

Boateng nodded to the photograph of a young man on the wall. 'Jimmy Mizen. Sixteen years old. Murdered in Lewisham borough ten years ago.'

'They catch the person who did it?'

'Didn't have to. He turned himself in.'

'Your case?' she asked.

'No. I was still working drugs back then. Jimmy's family set up a charity named after him. The message is compassion, not revenge.'

'Great. Easier said than done, though.' She thought of the robbers who her father had been chasing sixteen years ago when he was hit by a car. She hadn't forgiven them. Jones took the coffees and they headed over to a corner table. 'That's what was motivating Tom Summers. Revenge. He led a double life for years.'

'We could never have seen it coming.'

'Couldn't we?' She was so happy that Boateng and his wife were safe – lucky to be alive after last night – but she felt bitterness and regret at the way she'd fallen for Summers. He'd probably only gone on a date with her to add to his cover of a 'normal' existence. *Once bitten*, she thought. 'That'll teach me to judge a book by its cover.'

'What's the latest on him anyway?' Boateng sipped his coffee.

'He's in intensive care after surgery. The ambulance got him to the trauma centre at King's.' She saw the anger flare in Boateng's eyes. 'Come on, Zac. When he's out of there, he'll be held on remand until he can stand trial. There's no way he's getting off a murder charge for those four deaths.' She jabbed a finger on the table.

'You sure?'

'Oh yeah, I didn't tell you. Jason Leather traced a bulk suxamethonium chloride purchase to Summers. I asked him for his help last night. Summers had gone to some lengths to hide it. He bought the stuff with cryptocurrency on the dark web, had it delivered to a PO Box he rents. Don't ask me how Leather found it, but he did.'

'What were you saying about books and covers?'

'Shut up.'

Boateng grinned. 'What made you think of Summers?'

'Medical records. Joseph Young's NHS history didn't match the post-mortem from Guatemala. The body they found had no vitiligo on the hands, where Young did have it. Then I remembered where I'd seen that recently and it fell into place. Hand scars are pretty common. Leather and Evans both had marks on their hands, but they were cut-type scars, not from depigmentation. Only one person we know had marks like that. Once I realised that Joseph Young might be Summers, I had to find some other evidence. I was thinking with my old Cyber Crime hat on, I guess.

Look at the electronic links. It was Friday night and everyone had gone home. Leather was the only person I could think of. I tried to call to let you know, but you didn't pick up.'

Boateng grunted a laugh. 'I was too busy finding out Summers's true identity for myself.'

'So, it's not a slam dunk yet. We need to tie him evidentially to the scenes, but that should be easier now we know what we're looking for. We can go back to his computer in the office, check what he accessed on the systems. And forensics recovered what they think is Troy McEwen's laptop from Summers's flat this morning.'

Boateng gave a slow and painful nod. 'He had Troy's phone and laptop. He sent the text that brought me to Troy's house the night he killed him. That'd also explain how he sent those emails to me and Faye Rix from Troy's account.'

Jones frowned. 'Rix didn't know any more about it than us, then?'

'Nope. She was just following the leads Summers was feeding her on the case. She wasn't bribing anyone, and she didn't commit a crime, as far as I can tell. Her link to Hayworth was circum-stantial. Like you said, she just had a passion for stories of police corruption. Summers knew she'd go for it, get it in the papers. Maybe he thought that would scare us, or muddy the waters, make us look at her and her brother as suspects.'

'What about the sux we found in the Rixes' flat?'

'I should've realised, it was a way of controlling their dog.' He shook his head. 'Rix told me it had behavioural problems. Vets use sux when they need to operate on animals. When we found it at their place, I think I just wanted Adam Rix to be the killer. But his aggression was only about protecting his sister. Truth is, the poor guy is probably dealing with his own issues, whatever they are.'

'Maybe the stuff that led to him being adopted late? If that's what happened.' They still hadn't confirmed if the Rixes were adopted; after Summers's identification as the killer, there was no longer a case for accessing their records through social services.

'That's a good bet,' replied Boateng.

Jones cradled the coffee cup in both hands. 'There's still one thing I haven't worked out. How did Summers forge your handwriting?'

'I used to write in our sessions. He had all the samples he could want. Probably practised at home. Just part of his plan.'

She stared into the cup. 'Psychopath.'

'No way you could've known, Kat.'

She glanced up to see Boateng studying her. He looked daft with those bandages round his head, but there was compassion in his eyes. The silence hung a moment.

'What a total bastard,' she said, eventually. 'It's scary how you can be so wrong about someone. Makes me want to never date anyone again.'

'Ah, I wouldn't give up just yet,' he said. Then raised his cup to her. 'You're a catch. Just, you know, pick a more normal bloke next time.' He winked.

Jones felt the smile twitch at her mouth. 'Maybe I should stick to internet dating.'

CHAPTER THIRTY

Wednesday, 20 December 2017

Boateng shouldered his way down Regent Street, the pavement thick with bodies despite it being the middle of a working day. He gripped Kofi's hand, the lad alternating between running and standing, staring open-mouthed at the elaborate Christmas windows. Etta was in the office today, so he'd brought Kofi out for a little shopping trip to London's best-known toy store. Knew he had to face it sometime. Compared to the past three weeks though, it seemed a pretty minor trial.

After Lewisham hospital discharged him on Sunday morning, Boateng had been determined to get straight back onto the investigation. There was a case against Summers to be built and presented to the Crown Prosecution Service, and they were still working on the Spearhead attacks. But Krebs – along with Jones, Connelly and Malik – had emphatically told him to butt out. Eventually he'd accepted their assurances that they had it covered, and let himself switch off for a bit. He'd tried to rest up, spend time with his wife and son, watch a few films. Call a friend or two he hadn't spoken to in a while. It had helped a lot. Still, he wondered how much longer he'd be getting flashbacks in his own living room. It was important, psychologically speaking, to 'reclaim' the place where a trauma had occurred. That was why he was determined for Christmas at home to be as normal as possible.

'Here we are, Dad!' yelped Kofi with a little jump of excitement as they reached the first huge window of Hamleys. 'What can we buy?'

Boateng stopped and followed his son's gaze. He had to admit the arrangement of dancing animals in a snowy forest was impressive, if you liked that sort of thing. He bent his head down, squatting slightly to get closer to Kofi's face. 'Remember, son, Christmas is about family, OK?'

The boy grinned. 'You say that every year.'

'That's cos it's true.'

'But it's about presents as well, isn't it?'

Before Boateng could reply, his attention was diverted. It had only been a second, perhaps not even that long. But there was something in the reflection of the window: stillness followed by a movement. The sense that the man was too far away to be interested in the shop. That he'd not been looking at the toy display, but at Boateng. That was the conclusion he reached in a moment before the blank, white face had been subsumed into the shoppers hustling past. When Boateng glanced over his shoulder, the man was gone. He stood up straight, clamping one hand on Kofi's arm and scanning the street. But it was a mass of people, and he couldn't pick out the man. He pulled Kofi nearer, shielding him from the crowd.

'What is it, Dad?'

Boateng told himself it was just the result of last Friday night. That if Rix or Summers had been following him at times over the past few weeks, it was over now. After a trauma, the brain was more likely to interpret ambiguous shapes and signals as threatening. It was called 'hypervigilance' – simply the body's attempt to keep itself safe – and it would probably go away in a week or two.

'Nothing, Ko. Come on.'

Boateng took one last look up and down the street before guiding his son through the shop door.

It'd been close. Jim thought he'd been rumbled by Boateng outside the toy shop. He couldn't get complacent. Even though the guy seemed more relaxed than he had been recently, that didn't mean Jim could switch off. He had to bring his A game every time he followed Boateng. After all, the boss would expect nothing less. And he wouldn't tolerate a cock-up.

Watching outside Boateng's house on Friday night, Jim had called 999 as soon as he'd heard gunshots. He'd seen Boateng and his wife emerge – him looking much worse for wear than her – and be guided into a paramedic rapid response car. Thirty seconds later, another body had been stretchered out and stuck in the back of an ambulance. Jim had no idea who it was. The two vehicles had departed in different directions and Jim didn't have the transport to follow either one in real time. He guessed that Boateng was heading to Lewisham A & E, and fifteen minutes later had spotted him and his wife there in the waiting room. Plenty of details, but not enough information. The other body had been filed under 'don't know' for when the boss inevitably asked.

Nevertheless, one thing Jim did know was that Boateng was the only survivor from the events that had taken place at 17 Cleaver Square on 15 May 1998. The boss was pretty exercised about that. He didn't like loose ends. When the Met police had announced yesterday that they'd charged a suspect with two recent south London murders, and were investigating this individual's role in two other suspicious deaths, it had put Boateng in the clear for those crimes, at least. Jim and his boss guessed that the killer was someone with a connection to the Young family, perhaps a distant relative. Maybe this was the person stretchered out of Boateng's house. Of course, they couldn't rule out an organised 'hit'. Whoever had done those murders, Boateng was still alive. It remained unclear what he knew about Cleaver Square, and therefore he still posed a risk for the boss. A risk that had to be removed.

It was strange to think that after so long spent watching someone, knowing their idiosyncrasies and habits, surmising what they'd eaten for breakfast from a stain on their shirt, estimating how long they'd slept the previous night from the bags under their eyes, knowing on any given day whether they'd shaved, had an argument with their partner or were pissed off with their kid, it would all come to an end. Well, that was the nature of the job. The boss had given the order, and now it was just a question of when and where Jim delivered it. It was a shame. In some ways, he'd got quite attached to Boateng.

CHAPTER THIRTY-ONE

Thursday, 21 December 2017

Boateng left his car round the back of Lewisham police station and, hurrying against the rain, made his way to the back entrance, past the caged-in, almost-bare Christmas tree, which had been voted the most depressing in the UK. At least they had the 'Badvent Calendar'. The thought gave him a moment's relief; he'd been on edge ever since Krebs had called half an hour earlier, asking him to come in. She wouldn't say what it was about over the phone. In the lift and corridors that led to her office, colleagues who'd heard about last Friday night stopped to ask if he was OK, clap him on the shoulder, or just nod silent respect as he passed. Boateng acknowledged them all, but his mind was occupied with trying to guess what Krebs wanted. He knocked on the open door and entered.

'Zac.' She stood, striding around the desk to greet him. 'How are you bearing up?'

'Fine, thanks.' He glanced past her to the desk, trying to spot any clue as to his summons.

'I heard you've got the medical sign-off,' she said, making eye contact before he could read anything.

'Yup.' Boateng touched his fingertips to the healing burn at his temple. 'And the specialist says that the tear in my ear drum is small enough to heal up fully. I'm ready to get back to work.'

'Mm, that's great.' She did the lip-pursing thing again, though Boateng already knew that his health wasn't her main agenda point. 'But I'm afraid I have some bad news for you. Sit down, please.' She motioned him to a chair and returned to her own behind the desk.

'Is this about the unofficial toxicology request I made to King's? Because if so, I know that was against regulations, but I'm sure that once the murder case is—'

'It's not about that,' said Krebs, cutting him off. 'That'll be dealt with internally by the Directorate of Professional Standards. In slower time.'

'OK,' he said cautiously. 'So, what's the bad news?'

'A DNA test has shown that Tom Summers was a first degree relative of the Young couple, who were murdered in '98.'

'That's good, isn't it? It strengthens the case for his motive.'

'I agree. But in response to that, Summers has told his lawyer that he witnessed at least one death in his home that day at the hands of police. He's alleging serious malpractice by the officers involved, including you, Zac.'

Boateng's jaw tightened.

'Tom Summers has already said he'll testify in an inquiry. The IPCC has accepted the case, and it'll be one of the first for it under its new structure as the IOPC in January.'

Krebs was right, this was bad news. The Independent Police Complaints Commission – or the Independent Office for Police Conduct, as it would soon be renamed – only became involved in the most serious cases of alleged misconduct. Career-ending stuff, if the complaint was upheld. And scrutiny would be twice as tough in January, with everyone keen to show that their new and improved model worked.

'You'll be required to give evidence,' she continued, tilting her head down slightly to underline the seriousness of his position. 'You know, I hate to see colleagues put through that mill, but I'm sure you'll agree that we need it. Too many officers in the Met got away with too much for too long before the IPCC started getting things under control in '04. We have to rebuild public trust in the force, we need to restore the faith of the community...'

Boateng zoned out for a moment while she was in politician mode. He was already thinking about what to say, what arguments to make, what lines to deploy.

'Of course, I'm sure you have nothing to worry about, Zac. You said that you made some mistakes in the emergency response at Cleaver Square, but who hasn't made an error in their job? We're only human. I'm sure the presiding commissioner will see that.'

He agreed with her in theory, but she was missing one crucial piece of information: what he would decide to tell the inquiry about that day.

∗

Kat Jones had to admit she'd started feeling Christmassy. She clinked her glass against those of Connelly, Malik and Boateng and took a sip. Felt the cool, refreshing beer glide down, savoured the delight of that first taste. It was well earned. Time to celebrate a big win, for once. She had barely been able to contain herself from spilling the whole story the second Boateng sat down in the pub with them. They'd chosen a quieter drinking spot in Brockley, near Boateng's house, to make it easy for him to get there, and away from the mob of drunken officers up the road in Lewisham or Blackheath, who by now would be losing track of the number of pints they'd had and singing along to the cheesy Christmas playlist. She didn't mind a bit of random karaoke, but when there was some proper news to share, it was best done in a place like this.

'Are you going to tell him then, Kat, or what?' Connelly's thick eyebrows performed a little jig as he raised the Guinness to his lips.

She held on a bit longer, then let go and allowed the smile to spread as she looked at her boss. 'We've nailed Spearhead,' she said proudly.

'No way!' exclaimed Boateng. 'Come on then, let's have it.'

She swigged the beer, taking her time. 'Well, quite a bit happened this week while you've been chilling at home.'

'Recovering,' countered Boateng.

'Skiving?' offered Connelly.

'Oi!' Boateng grinned. 'Go on, Kat.'

'Forensics established that the laptop found in Summers's flat belonged to Troy McEwen. On its hard drive they discovered an encrypted folder of documents. Took a day to open it, but they got in. It was a goldmine. Notes, profiles, recordings of conversations and meetings, photographs, you name it. McEwen had been working up a dossier on National Right. On his own, off the books.'

Boateng's gaze flitted around the table. 'He wasn't joining them. He was working against them.'

'Eh?'

'I knew Troy was having sessions with Summers – counselling. Summers told me that Troy had become interested in a far-right group, that he was having to protect the country by doing what the government wouldn't do, or whatever. Summers was trying to mislead me about himself by giving me something truthful about Troy. I didn't know what he was on about. I thought maybe Troy was signing up for National Right, that for whatever reason he'd radically changed his political views. Maybe Hayworth knew about him trying to gather evidence on the group, and that's why he sent the email threat to Troy.'

'It also explains the mysterious informant report about Liam Rogers being a part of National Right,' suggested Malik. 'If it was McEwen who'd put it on the system.'

'And the fact he was using some special internet router, a VPN, to disguise his online presence,' added Boateng.

'We ran Krebs through it all this afternoon,' continued Jones. 'She thought there was probably enough evidence there to get National Right proscribed by the Home Office.'

'Sweet.' Boateng sipped his drink before his brow creased, and he winced slightly. 'You said that'd solved Spearhead. How?'

'Well, among the profiles McEwen had compiled was one guy we know pretty well. He appeared in the photographs you took at the meeting room in Catford too. In the background, he's not immediately obvious, but zoom in and there's no question about it. Right in the mix, thick as thieves with all the others in McEwen's dossier.'

Boateng didn't speak; he just stared, wide-eyed, waiting for the name.

'PC Mike Evans,' she said with a nod.

'Damn,' he responded. 'No wonder he didn't want to have a cup of tea with me.'

It was her turn to look confused, but then she just laughed. 'We brought Evans in for an interview this afternoon. Hinted at the evidence we've got, suggested that it'd be the end of his career, his pension. We hadn't even started talking about Spearhead before he offered to name names. So much for his loyalty.'

'Serious?'

She nodded. 'Evans gave us the MO. He wasn't one of the attackers, but he knew them all, heard them talking about it at one of their little gatherings. They had one set of clothes between them, one bat, but a different guy for each attack. The three perpetrators all had cast-iron alibis for the two attacks they didn't commit – somewhere public with independent witnesses, like a bar – so we're left thinking it's not them, because everything else about the incidents is serial. They get a partner or family member to supply the alibi for the attack they did, and we can't get much further. Rogers was in the cinema with a dozen people vouching for him while another guy from National Right murdered Mehmet Bardak at the Turkish restaurant. So, even when Rogers's DNA turned up on a fiver at the scene, he was in the clear. He must've given the fiver to the guy that did it or left it in a pocket if he acquired the clothing. Evans said that Rogers did the third attack on Abdi Osman.'

'Bastards,' said Boateng, shaking his head. 'That's why they had different eyewitness descriptions.' He swilled his beer, processing it. 'So, Evans walks away from a joint enterprise prosecution?'

'Unfortunately, yes. He's off the hook. That was the deal we offered him. But he's agreed to give evidence in court. And you'll be pleased to know he's leaving Lewisham.'

Boateng snorted. 'Someone else's problem, then. Well done, guys. It's a massive result.'

She paused, glanced at the others, then ducked her head to read his expression more clearly. 'You don't seem that pleased, Zac.'

'No, no, I am. Believe me. I've just got some other shit going on at the moment.'

'Still, boss?' enquired Connelly. Jones couldn't tell if he was joking.

'Yeah.' Boateng lowered his voice. 'It's Summers. He's complained to the IPCC about what happened in '98, including my role, and they're set to start investigating in January. It's serious. Krebs has recommended I stay off until it's done in case a verdict biases any judgements on stuff I've been working. You'll have to keep putting those cases together without me for a bit.' He took a gulp of beer. 'Sorry.'

Malik shook his head. 'It's not right.'

'We'll see, Nas,' replied Boateng quietly. 'It might be.'

The conversation moved on and they chatted some more before Boateng gave his apologies and stood to leave, saying that he needed to get back for dinner with his wife. Jones knew that wasn't an excuse, but still, she could tell he was on edge. It was understandable. She hadn't ever been the subject of an inquiry. But much like dead colleagues, it was probably just a matter of time. Boateng had been through it all, and he was still standing. She waved him farewell and watched him walk out of the pub, shoulders hunched against more than just the freezing December night.

'Next round's on me.' Connelly pushed back his chair and stood, pointed at her glass. 'Same again, Kat?'

'Yeah, cheers.'

Gone was the Irishman's undermining tone. He'd been proved wrong about Spearhead, with her theory of racially motivated attacks vindicated. But rather than resenting her, he'd graciously accepted her win and was treating her more like an equal now. Maybe the old guard weren't so bad.

As Connelly walked over to the bar, Jones wondered if she should start a conversation about something specific, to deflect any kind of probe from Malik about Summers. But before she could think of a gambit, he spoke.

'You alright then?'

The question could be interpreted in several ways. But they both knew what he was talking about. She blinked slowly. Nodded.

'Cool,' he said. 'So, what are your Christmas plans?'

'Family,' she replied. 'My mum.'

'Yeah, me too.'

There was something so caring, so earnest in his face at that moment, she could have kissed him. Instead, she simply grinned and drained the last of her beer.

'Last working day tomorrow,' she stated. 'Christmas jumpers? I will if you will.'

'You're on,' said Malik.

∗

Etta opened the oven door and peered inside. The roast chicken pieces and sweet potatoes looked great, smelled even better. Chilled soul music was drifting out of the speakers, and Kofi was tucked into bed upstairs. All good. She shut the oven and glanced at her husband, who was slicing okra on the worktop across from her. His lips were moving almost imperceptibly, accompanied by tiny facial movements in response to whatever thoughts he was half voicing.

'You OK, baby?' she asked, walking over and stroking his shoulder. He stopped cutting the okra. 'Tonight's about us; we can just relax, do whatever you want.' She met his eyes and smiled, making the implication clear even to her distracted husband.

He returned his focus to the chopping board. 'There's going to be an inquiry,' he stated matter-of-factly. 'Into what happened at Cleaver Square back in '98. Summers took it to the IPCC. Krebs briefed me on it today, said I'll need to give evidence.'

She rubbed his back as he resumed slicing. 'OK. Wasn't there an investigation into it before, though?'

'Yeah, but when Troy, Ana and I all gave the same story and there was no one to counter it, we were off the hook pretty fast. But things have changed. The Met doesn't protect its own any more. I don't know, maybe that's right. The IPCC didn't even exist back in '98.'

'So what's different this time round?'

'An eyewitness, remember? Summers saw me move the gun into the criminal's hand. He watched me tamper with evidence, alter a crime scene, delay giving first aid to the guy after Troy shot him. Heard us discussing what to do.'

She wasn't sure how to respond. A brief silence lay between them.

'I'm screwed,' he said, putting the knife down and spreading his palms in defeat. 'I'll be hung out to dry.'

Etta put an arm around his waist, pulled him into a hug. Her gaze darted around his face, from the tension in his mouth and jaw, to the filigrees of blood in the whites of his eyes, to the healing burns at his right temple.

'What are you going to do?' she asked.

He exhaled slowly. 'Well, after everything that's happened with Summers, I feel as though I should just tell the truth. Get it off my chest. We were dishonest. I buried that for nineteen years. Don't know if I could live with it if I lied again just to protect myself.'

'What's the alternative to lying?'

'Tell the truth and risk losing my job. Oh, and my pension and my reputation.'

'Is it perverting the course of justice?' she asked.

'I know what you're saying, but—'

'That could be prison time, Zac.' A tremor of fear rippled through her and she held tight to him. 'Will all that stuff definitely happen if you admit what you did?'

'Depends on the commissioner.'

'Could you plead heat-of-the-moment rash decisions? The fact you'd thought you were going to die just a few minutes earlier?'

'Maybe.'

'Like I said before, I understand why you did that. You were protecting yourself, but mostly protecting your friend. I'm not saying I agree with what happened, but I wasn't there, so I can't second-guess it. And sometimes people do the wrong things for the right reasons.'

He nodded, stared at the kitchen flagstones beneath them. Held her, stroked her hair. Then, after a while, he lifted his gaze and met hers.

'I'm going to tell the truth,' he said. 'And face the consequences. I have a second chance to do the right thing, and I'm not going to let it go. I'll let the commissioner decide.'

Etta studied his expression, the determination in his features. She let herself briefly imagine the worst-case scenario. Then she took a deep breath, squeezed his hips, then reached up and kissed him.

CHAPTER THIRTY-TWO

Friday, 22 December 2017

Jim glanced in the rear-view mirror. Boateng had squeezed his car into a spot about thirty metres down the street on Tressillian Road; near his house, but Jim was confident he could close the distance before Boateng got through the front door. He'd observed the wife go out to work just before 8 a.m. and had followed the detective when he exited the house an hour later with his kid. Boateng had driven ten minutes south to Honor Oak, dropped the boy off at someone's flat on an estate, chatted to a woman on the doorstep for a bit, then returned here. Now it was time to act.

Jim had done one final briefing with the boss last night. The big man had told him that there could be no part of the Cleaver Square business left 'unfinished', as he put it. Sweat glistened on his scalp under the comb-over as he gave the go-ahead, a tremor in his fingers as he raised a glass of water to dry lips. He'd reminded Jim to be careful, but he needn't have. Jim had seen the body stretchered out of this very house just a week ago. Boateng was not someone to underestimate. Jim slid the pistol out of his shoulder holster, made a last check: loaded, ready. Those details always counted, particularly when you didn't know how someone would react to your arrival. He replaced the pistol in its covert holster. Patted his inside jacket pocket; he had what he needed in there, too.

Next week he'd probably be given a new assignment. If he was lucky, the boss might let him have Boxing Day off before calling him in again and giving him another target. It was strange, how you became immersed in a person's world when you were watching them. Jim recognised that he'd come to like Boateng, but he had to keep the bigger picture in mind. Not let personal feelings cloud his judgement. Just be professional about it.

In the rear-view, he watched Boateng get out of the car, pause a moment with his hand on the roof, as if contemplating something. Then Boateng shut the door and locked the vehicle with a click of the remote fob. This was the moment to finish it off.

Jim got out of his car, setting a course to intercept Boateng before the front door, and walked quickly towards him.

There could be no loose ends.

◦

Boateng had spent much of last night thinking about the inquiry. He was still ruminating on it this morning, playing out hypothetical scenarios and repercussions in his mind. That was why it took him slightly longer than normal to register that the shape at the edge of his vision was moving directly at him. He glanced up to see a man, striding across the street, who met his gaze with cold, focused eyes. The guy was average height, medium build, with brown hair that was neither too short nor too long. Boateng guessed he was about forty; not young, not old. He wore a dark jacket, dark trousers and well-worn black shoes. His facial features were even and regular. Not good-looking, but not ugly either. The only distinctive thing about his face was a prominent scar running from nose to mouth – a cleft lip – visible even at this distance. Boateng could see that his left hand hung loosely at his side, while the right was creeping inside his jacket, reaching for something. Two further thoughts occurred to Boateng in that moment. One, this was the man from outside the toy shop two days ago. Two, something bad was about to happen.

Boateng cursed his lack of vigilance. This guy had crept up on him at 10.30 a.m. in a deserted street with no cover, nowhere to hide, no locks or bolts. No time to get to the front door. And no chance of running back to the car. He was in no man's land. Was this how it was going to end?

Hell no.

With a roar, Boateng rushed at the man, who was caught off guard. It was clear from his split-second hesitation that he hadn't encountered much direct action. The freeze before the fight-or-flight response kicked in. But it didn't matter: the distance was too great. By the time Boateng was halfway to him, the man had drawn a pistol and barked 'Stop!' Boateng obeyed, and for the second time in a week, found himself staring down the muzzle of a gun. The man had one eye shut, taking aim. His cleft lip was pursed in concentration.

Boateng held his breath, waited.

Then the guy opened his eye and took his supporting hand off the weapon. He slowly let it fall, the left hand opening out in what Boateng recognised as the 'no harm' stance. The man studied him, his sharp eyes gliding over the details of Boateng's face, hair, wounds, clothing. He holstered the pistol and took out a small black wallet which he flipped open and held up for inspection. But Boateng didn't need to see the details. He recognised the crest, the code, the ID with no name. He'd seen it before, several times in his career, during joint operations.

The British Security Service, better known as MI5.

'Is there somewhere we can talk?' said the guy.

Boateng took a deep breath, wiped sweaty palms on the side of his overcoat, and nodded towards the house.

'So, you're the person who's been following me?' Boateng squeezed the teabag and dropped it in the bin before glancing at his guest. The man, who'd introduced himself only as 'Jim', nodded.

Boateng held his gaze. 'You called the police in Catford?'

Jim nodded again.

Boateng added milk and handed the mug over. He sat down opposite Jim at the kitchen table. 'Thanks. And the ambulance here on Friday night?'

'Yeah.'

'Why were you tailing me?'

'Cleaver Square,' said Jim. 'I'm here to tell you that the IPCC inquiry is going to be shut down. You'll be free to go back to work whenever you want.'

'What?' Boateng thought he must have misheard. 'Why?'

'High-level sensitivities.'

Boateng narrowed his eyes. 'Which are?'

Jim didn't reply. Instead, he reached into his jacket pocket and produced an envelope. He extracted a printed document from it which Boateng also recognised: the Official Secrets Act. Jim smoothed the paper down on the table and placed a pen on top of it.

'Sign this, and I can tell you,' he said. 'Some of it, at least.'

Boateng stared at the paper and pen and thought about it. He knew what this meant: being brought into the circle, at the expense of prison if you talked to anyone about it. There must be a reason why MI5 was doing this. And he had to know it.

He signed.

Jim folded the papers, tucked them into the envelope and returned it to his inside pocket. He took a sip of tea and rested his forearms on the table. 'Do you know who was behind the home invasion burglary at 17 Cleaver Square in May 1998?' he asked.

Boateng frowned. 'A convicted criminal named Arun Gray, smarter than your typical street crook. He got three other guys involved.'

'That's accurate, on the face of it. But it wasn't Arun Gray's idea, bright as he was, up until your mate Troy McEwen shot him.'

Boateng was silent. How did this guy know about Troy?

'Cleaver Square wasn't really a burglary,' continued Jim. 'It was just made to look like one. Most likely, Arun Gray was the only person there who knew its true purpose.'

'Which was?'

'A contract killing.'

'Jesus.' Boateng's mouth opened but no further sound emerged. He composed himself. 'For who?'

Jim cracked his knuckles. 'We believe it was an organised criminal group.'

'What kind of group?'

'High-level stuff. Drug and firearms importation, some people trafficking. Mafia contacts in more than one country.'

'And Arun Gray was in this firm?'

'He did jobs for them, probably arranged via a middleman so they could keep their key players at arm's length from anything that could be traced back to them.'

Boateng frowned. 'I didn't think MI5 worked organised crime.'

'We don't. Not any more. But there was a window of about a decade when we did, starting in the mid nineties.'

'So, how do you guys know about the contract killing?'

'I can't tell you that,' replied Jim.

'Human source?'

Jim blinked.

'Is this gang still operating?' asked Boateng.

'I told you, we don't work on that any more. You'd have to ask the National Crime Agency.'

'Well, I would if I knew the gang's name.'

Jim hesitated. 'The Square Mile Syndicate.'

'OK.' Boateng presumed it was a reference to the City. 'So why did they want to kill Young?'

'He wasn't just a private banker. Young was working for us. A low-level source close to the syndicate told us they were looking for financial services. Large-scale transactions, money laundering, registering front companies, that kind of stuff. So we recruited Young, paid him, and ran him into their group. But one of our officers screwed up; he was inexperienced back then.' Jim paused, appeared to be thinking. 'And Young was discovered. So the firm apparently took the decision to execute him and disguise the murder as a home invasion burglary.'

'We walked right into the middle of it.'

'Yup.' Jim swigged his tea. 'And we'd failed to prevent it. So, we did everything we could to keep it under wraps. You may have noticed the media coverage of it was pretty muted, given what happened.'

Boateng nodded.

'And the internal inquiry passed off quickly.'

'Didn't feel like it at the time,' said Boateng. 'But yeah, see what you mean.'

'It would've been unacceptable if Young's role had been exposed. Public faith in us was already low. After the end of the Cold War, and then the Good Friday Agreement, people questioned why Britain needed an internal security service. Can you imagine the public's reaction if it emerged that one of our officer's mistakes had led to the death of British citizens? Not to mention the damage to our intelligence work. We'd failed to protect our agent. That'd be enough to make half our agents resign and stop dozens more from working for us. Terrorism, counter-espionage, it would've been a disaster for national security.'

'Damn,' exclaimed Boateng quietly. 'So, if it was a contract killing, you're saying Young would've died anyway? Maybe his wife, too?'

'If that makes you feel better, then yeah, most probably.' Jim finished his tea.

'Why are you telling me all this?'

Jim sighed and Boateng detected a twitch in his cleft lip. 'Because the inquiry risked raking it up, making the story very public. People start digging, speculating. We had to get it under control. And you're clearly not the type to let something go. Neither is Tom Summers. Hence the paperwork today, just to make sure you don't talk to anyone else about it.'

'Did Summers know the truth about his father?'

'No, but don't worry. We'll be speaking to him, too.'

'Will you offer him a deal not to pursue his claims?'

'Maybe.'

Boateng felt a flicker of rage kindle inside him, then reminded himself that he had been let off too. 'What about his murder trial?'

'You'll get a guilty verdict, most likely. He'll do his time, maybe with early parole. But don't be surprised if the trial isn't in the news much either.'

'Does DCI Krebs know anything about this?'

'Nope. But her boss's boss does.'

'What do I tell my team?'

'Nothing.' Jim slid the mug towards Boateng. 'Thanks for the tea.'

EPILOGUE

Monday, 25 December 2017

'Is it my turn, Mum?'

Kofi had already selected another present and torn the edge of its wrapping paper, his fingers poised to rip it off. Etta shook her head with a smile, and Zac watched his son turn hopefully to him instead. 'Dad?'

'Don't look at me, mate,' said Zac. 'Let your mum open one. You've done two already.'

The lad groaned but continued to bob with anticipation. They were sitting on the floor beside the tree, with some carols in the background and the fire on. Zac had got the turkey in the oven three hours ago and it would nearly be ready. They'd left the door open and the roast meat aroma was wafting through. People said Christmas was stressful. That depended on what else you'd been dealing with. He glanced around the room, which bore few physical reminders of the carnage that had unfolded here ten days ago. The feeling of contentment he was currently experiencing had kicked in the night before, when Krebs had called to tell him the inquiry was off. She'd spent some time explaining that she wasn't sure why, but she'd try to find out. He kept quiet. That was alright by him. There was a small, gnawing guilt at the feeling that his lies had not been fully admitted, but that was tempered by the new information Jim had given him about Cleaver Square. He took a sip of champagne and winked at Etta.

'Come on, Ko,' said his wife, wide-eyed with mock drama. 'How about I open this one from you?'

'OK,' said Kofi. 'But do I get to go next?'

Zac chuckled. 'Well, since you've got more presents than anyone else, OK.'

The news was greeted with a cheer and double fist pump from his son.

'Remember, Ko,' said Etta, gently. 'Christmas is about being with your family. Grandma and Grandpa are coming over in a bit.'

'Will they be bringing presents too?'

'I give up.' Etta rolled her eyes.

Zac allowed the laughter to come, took another sip of his drink and grinned at her. 'He's got your negotiation skills. Your mum's right, son. It is about family. Not everyone's as lucky as we are.'

Or as unlucky, he thought, glancing up at the photograph of their daughter. Amelia smiled down at him, the little gap between her front teeth frozen in time. The most important thing was family, and theirs still felt incomplete. There was someone out there – going by the name Kaiser – who'd played a role both in Amelia's murder and in stopping her killer from being caught. Boateng glanced from Kofi to Etta and back again as his festive contentment receded and a new thought formed, clearer and stronger than before: he had to find Kaiser.

And that guy Jim was right.

He wasn't the type to let it go.

A LETTER FROM CHRIS

Thank you for reading *Last Witness*, the second Zac Boateng novel.

If you'd like to find out more about the series, please join my mailing list. You can unsubscribe from the updates whenever you like and your email address will never be shared.

www.bookouture.com/chris-merritt/

Nearly a decade ago, I heard about a political assassination in the Middle East. It was said that Israeli agents had injected their target with a paralysing drug, so they could kill him and make the death look natural. To me, it was an inconceivably terrifying thought: two men entering your hotel room, confusion as you see the needle, then a desperate attempt to protect yourself… This seemed a suitably dark method for the serial killer in *Last Witness*, and a suitably complex puzzle for Zac to solve.

I was also keen to explore the topic of police welfare. We take for granted how frequently police and other emergency services personnel see injury and death at its most graphic. Until recently, there was little help available and even some discouragement from voicing any mental health difficulties. Many self-medicated, and I met one ex-copper who shared his story of alcoholism with me. This is changing. But police suicide remains a significant problem. To my knowledge, only one public document has ever been authored on the subject in Britain. We need to do more to help the people who sacrifice a lot to keep us safe.

Real locations are vital to the Boateng stories. If you're a Londoner, you may recognise Nunhead Cemetery, one of the largest graveyards in the capital. Anyone who fancies sparring with Faye Rix should head to the Double Jab boxing club in New Cross, and I can thoroughly recommend the Korean chicken wings Zac scoffs in Brixton market or the Blackheath pubs where he gets the beers in for his team. City-wide, the scrap metal trade is one of the few industries open to those with criminal records, who can be self-employed and start again when they get out. I love discovering these new sides to London and sharing them with readers.

If you liked *Last Witness*, please leave a review of it online. You can also get in touch with me via Twitter or on my website. There, you can find out about my other work in tech psychology research and mental health.

Thanks again for your support, and I hope you continue to enjoy the Zac Boateng series. A third Boateng book is due for release in early 2019… details coming soon!

All best wishes,
Chris

🐦 @DrCJMerritt

🖥 www.cjmerritt.co.uk

ACKNOWLEDGEMENTS

I am hugely grateful to the people who continue to support me in writing the Boateng series, including my family, friends, fellow authors, reviewers and book bloggers. I would especially like to thank my 'team': my fiancée Kate Mason, whose first reading always makes my writing better; my agent Charlie Viney, whose experience and wisdom keep me on track; and those at Bookouture: Lauren Finger, Kim Nash, Noelle Holton, Peta Nightingale and Jennifer Hunt, but most of all my editor Helen Jenner for skilfully guiding *Last Witness* from inception to finished product. It's been wonderful to see this team grow with the arrival of the Boateng audiobooks. Dan Battaglia at Audible HQ has shown a rare combination of enthusiasm and efficiency, while Damian Lynch has brought Zac Boateng (and every other character) to life with seemingly effortless vocal dexterity. Thanks to Eleventh Hour Films for thinking so creatively about adapting the series for screen: Paula Cuddy, Eve Gutierrez, Daniel Gratton and Robert Murphy.

I am indebted to those with experience of the Met Police for educating me on the organisation: Sarah Stephens, Amy Gorman, one serving and two former officers who preferred to stay anonymous. I'd also like to thank Dr Rebecca Dudill and Dr Charlotte Trainer for answering all my strange questions on anaesthetic without batting an eyelid. Nick Kenrick kindly explained the format and vernacular of counselling sessions to me, helping Zac's scenes with Summers sound authentic.

The Reverend Dr Richard Armitage gave his time to discuss the complex topic of police suicide with me. The Watch Repair Centre workshop team in Newcastle upon Tyne expertly determined whether a fire would stop a Rolex. Naana Agyeman and singer-songwriter SiiLHOUETTE continue to teach me about Zac's Ghanaian heritage.

FURTHER READING

For anyone interested in Ghanaian folklore, Bobby Norfolk's *Anansi* storybooks are essential material. *Last Witness* also drew on several scientific publications. Uta Kuepper and her team's pioneering work on detecting sux metabolites in blood is how I imagined King's Forensics unlocking Boateng's case. The research of Rohan Ruwanpura, Chamil Ariyaratne and Tomy Mappalakayil into death by hanging made grim but necessary reading. The same can be said for Melissa Blessing and Peter Lin's paper on shotgun suicides, while Richard Adderley and Peter Musgrove's summary of police IT systems was no less necessary but far easier to stomach. Val McDermid's *Forensics* and the BBC's documentary *The Met: Policing London* were also useful and well worth a look for readers interested in the reality of investigations.

Lightning Source UK Ltd.
Milton Keynes UK
UKHW02f2135100718
325520UK00007B/338/P